HUSHED

JOANNE MACGREGOR

A QUICK NOTE

This book uses UK English spelling, so words like colour, centre, metre, cosy, prise and realise are not spelling mistakes.

For some of the more exotic South African words, there is a glossary at the end of the book.

For all the girls who have been silenced,
and for the girls who speak up.

"But if you take my voice," said the little mermaid, "what will be left to me?"

"Your lovely form," the witch told her, "your gliding movements and your eloquent eyes. With these you can easily enchant a human heart. Well, have you lost your courage? Stick out your little tongue and I shall cut it off. I'll have my price and you shall have the potent draught."

—Hans Christian Andersen, ***The Little Mermaid***

CHAPTER 1
HUNTING

The trick in life, I think, is to figure out what you truly want and then go all out to get it. And what I want, more than anything else, is the Beast.

That's why I'm out here on my surfboard, rising and falling on the gentle ocean swell of the frigid waters of False Bay, just off the southern tip of Africa. I glance around, keeping an eye out for sharks. Surfing at sunset, when great whites make their dinner run, is not wise — but I'm hunting, too.

My prey is on the luxury yacht that lies directly ahead of me, anchored in silhouette against the coral blush of the wide October sky. It's a high-speed, top-of-the-range model, at least twenty metres long, with twin decks, and a jet-ski and inflatable dinghy tethered behind. Two small flags, the South African and the American, hang on a pole projecting out from the back, flapping idly in the light breeze.

It'll be dark in twenty minutes. Back on shore, the sun is setting behind the rugged mountain ridge of the Cape Peninsula, casting the hillside village of Simon's Town into shadow. Out here on the ocean, the last of the day's summer sun shines down through a hole in the clouds, bathing the yacht in rose-gold light. If I squint and crick my head sideways, then the gap in the clouds looks heart shaped. That has to be a good omen for a heartthrob-hunter.

I don't dare approach until night falls — the last thing I need is the Beast's security to spot me. Being an eighteen-year-old girl would make them regard me with more, not less, suspicion. Here, in my black wetsuit, floating among the surface tangle of dark kelp closer to shore, I'm camouflaged. And a little safer from the predators of the deep who might be circling me, even as I hunt *him*.

The sky surrenders its last blush, the clouds smudge charcoal against the deepening wash of indigo, and the first star emerges from its infinity of darkness. On the yacht, the lights come on. A necklace of jewel-coloured lanterns strung around the deck rails, sways gently, while up on the bow of the deck, a string quartet strikes up a theme from one of the soundtracks I know so well. The sounds of music and laughter pulse in disconnected waves across the water.

I paddle nearer, keeping to the shadowed, shoreward side of the yacht. When I'm near enough to hear voices and the clink of glasses, I push myself up and sit astride my board, with my legs dangling in the water. Despite my wetsuit, it's cold. But it'll be worth any discomfort if I just catch a glimpse of *him*.

I lift my binoculars, pop the lens-caps off, and adjust the magnification. The knot in the bow tie around some man's neck comes into sharp focus. Quickly, I tilt the lenses up to check the face.

Not him.

The famous and the fabulous — in a glittering display of sequined gowns, overflowing cleavages, tuxedos, diamonds and painted talons — crowd both the upper and lower levels of the yacht. I admire the balance of the beautiful young women who totter about in stiletto heels on the unsteady surface of the deck. I don't think *I* could stay upright, let alone walk, in such killer heels, even on firm land.

They all look ecstatically happy as they nibble their snacks and sip from their slender flutes of champagne. Their faces are animated, and their laughs free — it's like a sparkly fragment from a different world. What wouldn't I give to be up there, to be a part of all that? To be wearing a designer dress, exotic perfume and gorgeous jewellery, trading funny stories while I waited, like they do, for him?

It's easy to tell the actors from the others. Their bodies are perfectly tanned and toned, their teeth flawlessly white and straight, their hair immaculately coloured and cut. I scan the faces — many of them are familiar to me — but I can't find his.

Is my information wrong?

Zeb, my best friend and fellow final-year student at Table Mountain High School, is usually an excellent and reliable source of gossip. But what he'd told me earlier today when we'd chatted on the phone had seemed too good to be true.

"Did you know that the gods and goddesses are descending tonight?" Zeb had said. "But they won't be mingling with mere mortals, Romy, so don't get your hopes up."

"English, please," I sighed, scowling at the stacks of notes and textbooks piled up on the desk in my bedroom. The last two exams of my finals — biology and chemistry — were creeping closer, and I needed to do some serious studying.

"Well, *you* know what crew is currently in town — making the most of the local currency, filming our magnificent mountain, our rugged coastline, our deadly critters?"

"Zeb! Spit it out." Suddenly I was paying close attention.

"Patience, woman, I'm getting to it. I heard from Lebo, who works down at Luxury Charters, that they've hired a yacht — one of those massive, sleek, pointy-nosed jobs. And they're taking it out tonight, for a party. For *him* — your Beast."

I gasped and clutched the phone tighter.

"Hello? Romy? You still there?"

"I'm here." I swallowed. "You reckon it's true?"

"I trust my sources. Lebo said they were chartering a sunset and evening cruise — for a 'private celebration.'"

That fit. It was the thirty-first of October.

"It's his birthday," I said. "He's turning twenty today. He's a Scorpio."

"Trust you to know that."

"I'm going. I'll tell my parents that I'm at your house, and that we're studying meiosis and mitosis together."

"I don't know what that is, but it sounds disgusting."

"Just cover for me if they call, okay? But I've *got* to go."

"Go? How? They have security to keep people like you away. Are you planning to stow away on board in a crate of champagne?"

"Don't be silly. They probably won't go out far. If they anchor just offshore, then I could swim out —"

"Like *that's* not silly."

"— or go out on my board. Did your source say where they were going?"

"I shouldn't have told you — pretend I didn't! I only mentioned it because I knew you'd be interested. I never thought you'd try to stalk him."

"*Where?*" I demanded.

"No good will come of this. You need to get over this obsession, focus on your exams."

"Don't make me come down there and beat it out of you! Tell me. Now."

"You are such a violent creature, Romy Morgan. Honestly, you scare me sometimes. Off Simon's Town. There, happy now? A party among the penguins, apparently." He gave a bark of laughter. "That would make a good one: *Beast: Black and White.* He could use method acting to master the waddle."

"Thanks, I owe you one. What time is sunset, do you know?"

"Don't you have to study?"

"I need a break."

"Then come over and hang out with me. Or go out and party the night away."

"Yeah, because my social life is that exciting."

"Don't do it, friend. You'll only make yourself feel wretched with what you can't have."

"I just want to look, to see how the other half lives."

"Pfft! What do they have that we don't? I mean," he qualified, "apart from fame and fortune and genetic giftedness?"

"They have a life," I said. "Unlike us, they have a life filled with fun and excitement and travel and magic-making. And freedom!"

Above all, freedom.

"You really think?"

"I really think."

"Well, do what you must then, but don't get arrested for stalking or trespassing. And don't completely lose your head, or your heart. Or," he added thoughtfully, "a chunk of flesh to the sharks."

Easier said than done, I think now, as I bob out on the open ocean, circling the yacht, waiting for *him* to appear.

Someone clinks a glass three times, and the musicians bring their tune to a rapid end.

"Ladies and gentlemen," a voice, strong and female, cuts through the hubbub.

I train my binoculars on the speaker, who stands near the bar on the upper deck. She's older, tall and striking in a flowing black dress. I suspect she's not an actor — her nose is too long and her jaw too firm for Hollywood's idea of female beauty — but I can tell from her aura of power and confidence that she's somebody important. When she turns her head to glance behind her, I see that a bold slash of white streaks her black hair above her right temple.

"Ladies and gentlemen," she repeats over the quieting voices. "I give you — the Beast!"

A loud chorus of cheers and applause greets her announcement, and the musicians strike up the *Beast* theme music. Craning my neck and straining to see the tall figure who's just appeared on deck, I curse the people who crowd around him, greeting and back-slapping and blocking my view. Then the throng parts, and he steps forward. And speaks.

"Please, just call me Logan."

CHAPTER 2
SUN, MOON AND STARS

Logan Rush stands on the upper deck of the yacht, his head crooked under a low-hanging red lantern. A wry smile curves his mouth.

Eager party-goers cluster around him — lesser planets orbiting a dazzling sun — singing "Happy Birthday" and cheering. A series of booms, cracks and whizzes sounds overhead, and every eye looks up at the ruby rocket flares, emerald spirals and cascades of topaz lighting up the night sky. But I keep my binoculars trained on the star below.

One Saturday night four years ago, Logan Rush was discovered playing bass guitar in an unknown band in a grungy nightclub in downtown Atlanta. At the time, the search was on for a teen actor to play the Beast in the film version of the international best-selling books. The rest of the cast, including Britney Vaux who would play the female lead, had already been selected, the locations scouted, and the script written. Thousands of handsome hopefuls auditioned in the countrywide castings that were part talent-search and part publicity stunt, but the lead actor who could bring the beloved character from printed page to silver screen had not yet been found.

And then Logan was spotted and brought in for an audition.

"Instant chemistry!" cooed Britney Vaux on Facebook, Twitter and on E! News.

"He *is* the Beast," enthused Mary E.E. Stephen, author of the bestselling Beast Trilogy of novels.

"Thank God," breathed the relieved producers and the L.A. moneymen.

But the fans of the books had a different opinion.

"No way!" they screeched. "Logan Rush — who's he? He's nothing like we pictured. He's not even handsome!"

One of the rabid objectors, a teen from Ketchum, Idaho, started a blog — NoRush.com — and a petition calling for Logan Rush to be ditched and the lead role to be recast. She got tens of thousands of signatures, too, but then the movie studio craftily released several publicity shots of Logan — all bronze-skinned, tousle-haired, and electric-eyed — and the fans changed their screams.

"Gimme! He's awesome, perfect, epic! Just how we always pictured him, just what we wanted. And he's *so* handsome!"

Fickle.

For the record, I liked him from the get-go. My fourteen-year-old heart knew a good thing when my eyes saw it. And I've remained constant — I still subscribe to seven fan sites and five newsfeeds about him.

In the trilogy of *Beast* books, the hero — a teenage boy called Chase Falconer — takes the natural world for granted, exploiting and polluting until the day he makes the mistake of insulting a shaman, who is a direct descendent of a line of shamans stretching back to the Incas.

The mystical medicine man says, "To learn respect, you must learn compassion. To learn compassion, you must master empathy. To master empathy, you must walk in the feet of the other."

Then he bops the young man on the head with a ceremonial gourd, and from then on, Chase is cursed to wander through nature as a shape-shifter, taking the form of fierce, endangered creatures in the battle against poachers, hunters, land-grabbing industrialists and other greedy humans. Along the way he meets a pretty activist, Fern Lightly, who rescues him from a hunter's trap, and their cross-species love story begins.

It sounds weird, but it's brilliant! And Logan plays the role of Chase Falconer like he was born to do it. Gah! I can't wait for the next movie to come out.

In the movie adaptation of the first book, *Beast: Sun*, which was set in India, Logan's character shape-shifted into the stripes and fangs of a hypnotic-eyed tiger. In the second, *Beast: Moon*, he fursploded into a dagger-toothed wolf in the woodsy, snowy mountains of Alaska. Now he's in my corner of the world, Cape Town, South Africa, filming the last in the trilogy — *Beast: Stars*, in which he morphs into a great white shark, tackling the scourges of long-line fishing and shark-finning under the starlit oceans of the South.

I can hardly believe that he's right here, working the party just in front of me — less than twenty metres away. And more than a million miles out of reach.

He accepts a glass of champagne from a passing waiter, downs it in one, and takes another. Britney Vaux moves in close and chats to him, moving her hands expressively in the air and tossing her blonde hair. She's sheathed in a glittering red dress with a plummeting neckline and a back cut low enough to play peekabooty. I'd be tempted to toss some peanuts down the back of it, if I were up there with them. Which I'm not, of course.

The stripe-haired, tall woman from earlier and a couple of Logan's co-stars join the pair and talk excitedly to Logan. They touch him constantly — squeezing an arm, perhaps to emphasize a point, or patting a shoulder, shaking his hand, or slinging an arm around him while posing for photographs. Britney Vaux picks something off his lapel, then cuddles up close to him to take a selfie on her phone.

I might be imagining it, but to me, Logan looks uncomfortable. His feet move constantly in an odd sort of dance. Every so often, he backs up, stepping away from the people in his space, sometimes under the guise of turning to greet someone else or to accept another glass of bubbly. But they follow him, flowing into the gap left by his retreating feet, always moving in — closer, nearer — every time he buys himself some space. Give the guy some breathing room, people!

I can't hear anything Logan is saying, but I paddle around the yacht, watching his advance-and-retreat two-step. The water around me shimmers with silver light from the half-moon and stars above, and the reflected colours of the hanging lanterns. Shadows of the water rising and falling play tricks on me, taking the shape of rippled wakes and dorsal fins, and when a big swell rolls beneath my board, I panic for a moment then relax as it passes under the yacht. Just a surge — no shark would be able to lift and lower the boat like that.

Some of the partiers squeal as they lose their balance on the rocking yacht. Logan himself topples backwards onto a recessed cushioned bench and then disappears from my line of sight. I should head back to shore — there's no point in staying out here and freezing if I can't see him. Plus, I've been out on the water for over an hour, and my arms are growing tired from paddling and holding up the binoculars to watch the increasingly raucous crowd.

I decide to give it ten more minutes, and if my prey doesn't reappear, I'll call it a night. A wonderful, magical night. A night about as far from my small, boring life in my small, dull world as I could possibly get. I sigh. Tomorrow, it'll be back to books and studying for me.

With my head full of the sights and sounds of the night, I circle the boat one last time, hoping to get a final glimpse before I head home.

And then I see something which changes everything.

CHAPTER 3
OFF AND AWAY

Logan Rush is climbing out of the yacht.

Almost all the partiers are clustered together on the brightly lit upper deck, their attention riveted on Britney Vaux who is stretched out on the bar counter, offering tequila body shots to roars of approval from the crowd. But Logan is on the bottom deck, at the dark and quiet rear of the yacht, where a short steel ladder leads to an inflatable dinghy and a jet-ski on the water below.

He swings one long leg over the side, finds a toehold on the ladder, and then hoists himself over. There's a loud *boing!* and a stifled curse as he bangs his head — hard by the sound of it — on the flagpole jutting out from the back of the boat. My arms stretch up instinctively, as if to catch him, because he's dangling from the ladder by one hand while his feet scrabble to find purchase on the rungs.

Quickly, I paddle closer. At any moment he's sure to lose his hold and plunge into the chilly Atlantic. But he clings on awkwardly, his back to the ladder, heels perched on a rung midway down. One hand covers his mouth, and his head tilts upward as if to check whether anyone might be peering down at him. It seems that all attention is still on Britney, judging by the cheers rising above the loud music on the top deck.

"Shh," I'm close enough to hear Logan say, apparently to himself. "Sh-sh-sh!"

He taps a silencing finger against his lips and then appears to remember something. His hand moves to his jacket pocket into which he's somehow managed to wedge a champagne bottle. Unable to tug it free, he lifts the whole jacket up by the pocket and tips some of the liquid down his throat. As his head tilts back, he sways, and for a few seconds it looks like he'll lose his balance again, but then he moves with careful, deliberate steps down the remaining rungs of the ladder until he gets to the last one. Blinking hard as if trying to focus his gaze, he stares at the dinghy floating on the water in front of him and shakes his head several times. It must hurt, because he clutches his forehead again and groans before turning to face the jet-ski.

With a decisive nod, he leaps onto it, clambering like a drunken monkey over the handlebars and dropping heavily onto the seat, facing the rear of the jet-ski. After a moment, an expression of deep puzzlement steals over his features.

"Hey!" he protests loudly. Immediately his eyes widen, and he puts his forefinger back onto his lips. "Sh-sh-shhh!"

I giggle, but I don't think he hears me because although he looks up, it's to check over his shoulder, back at the yacht.

"There 'tis," he exclaims, spotting the handlebars and dashboard behind him.

While he struggles to coordinate his limbs into turning

around on the seat, I paddle around to the side so that I can see his face. He looks very pleased with himself — until his hand goes to the ignition slot and gropes the space where the key should be, but isn't. He pats the jet-ski all over its dash and sides and seats, and then checks his own pockets — where he rediscovers the champagne and consoles himself with another slug.

"Gone!" he says forlornly, slumping in the seat. But his face lights up when he catches sight of the dinghy again, and at once he swings both legs over the side of the jet-ski.

Uh-oh.

When he stands up, the jet-ski lurches sideways, pitching him head-first into the dinghy, legs and feet splashing into the water.

With much cursing and shushing, he pulls himself into the inflatable and plonks down on one of its bench seats. He spends the next several minutes taking off his shoes, rolling off his wet socks and tucking them neatly inside the shoes, muttering incoherently the whole time. I watch, but my fascination turns into concern when he loosens the rope tying the dinghy to the yacht and it begins drifting away from the larger craft.

I don't know what to do. He doesn't look sober enough to manage the dinghy — he's still clutching his shoes and socks to his chest, for crying out loud! Should I alert someone on the yacht? The same people he seems so intent on escaping, the same people who're now chanting, "Take it off! Take it off!"

Maybe I should paddle over and offer to help him? I could — I know how to handle an inflatable. I pretend to weigh the options, even as I begin closing the distance between us.

"Aha," Logan crows from his unsteady perch.

He leans over and pulls the starter cord. The outboard engine snarls into life and the dinghy shoots forward, toppling him backwards.

"Oh, crap!" This time, the curse is mine.

Clearly, the last fool to use the boat left the motor in gear when he turned it off, and now the dinghy is headed straight out to sea, with Logan Rush lying in the bottom of it. It's moving slowly — thank God he hasn't discovered the throttle, yet — but still, there's no way I can swim or paddle fast enough to catch it.

I'm about to return to the yacht to get help, when I glimpse Logan's head rising above the edge of the inflatable. He must be on his hands and knees, crawling towards the motor.

"The kill switch!" I yell. "Pull the kill switch!"

But either he can't hear me, or he doesn't know what I mean because instead of stopping, the boat begins turning in tight circles, throwing up arcs of water as it pushes against its own wake. He must have pushed the rudder.

I stand up on my surfboard, shouting and waving to get his attention. In the dinghy, Logan rises unsteadily to his feet.

"No! Stay down!" I yell.

He teeters for a few seconds, then as the boat hits a big swell, he tips sideways, pitches over the side furthest from me, and disappears into the black water.

Frozen in horror, I stand and stare at the still-turning dinghy, looking for some sign of Logan, expecting his head to bob up out of the sea at any moment. But I see only churned-up water rippling outward from the craft. I tear the Velcro cuff off my ankle, freeing myself from my surfboard, and dive into the cold water. I'm only about fifty metres from the dinghy, and with panic spurring me forward, it doesn't take me long to close the gap. As I swim, I look up and glimpse a flash of white in the darkness. It's Logan's face. As I get closer I see that one of his hands is twisted in the inflatable's side ropes, and he's being towed around in circles by it.

I time my final few strokes carefully to avoid the blades of the motor's propeller. With a hard push out of the water, I haul myself into the boat, lunge at the engine, and put it in neutral. The dinghy slows to an idle on the choppy water.

I peer over the side of the boat — straight down into the surprised face of Logan Rush.

"Oh," he says, with a spluttering cough. "Hiya."

"Um, hi," is all I can think to say in this most amazing, most bizarre moment of my life.

"What just happened?"

"You fell out of the boat. We need to get you back in."

"I'm stuck," he says, looking at his right hand which is still caught in the ropes.

"Here, let me."

Half of my brain is focused on untangling his hand, the other half is freaking out that *I* am actually touching *Logan Rush*. For a brief moment, we're even holding hands — kind of.

"Tha's better," he says, rubbing his wrist in relief.

"Not really, no," I mutter, because now that he's no longer snarled in the ropes, Logan is sinking down into the water.

CHAPTER 4
LOSING SHOES

I make a grab for Logan's disappearing form and manage to snag a handful of hair — this is not how I fantasized about touching those luscious locks — and tug him back up to the surface.

"Ow," he says, hiccupping and looking at me with a wounded expression. "Hurts. S'not a wig, y'know."

"Sorry," I say, placing his hand back on the side of the boat and curling his fingers around the rope handle. "But you were sinking into the sea. And you weren't trying to swim."

"No," he replies, frowning. "Is the shark."

"Where?" I scan the ocean for the dark crescent of a dorsal fin.

"Not here. On the green screen. Is the shark that does the swimming. Not me," he says in the tones of someone making a sad confession.

"Are you trying to tell me you can't swim?"

"Uh-huh."

"Not even a little?"

"Huh-uh." He waggles his head from side to side as if considering a tricky question. "Maybe just a little … Not very much," he says, then adds, "Hardly a'tall."

"So you set off for shore when you can't swim or handle a boat?"

"S'many things can't I do." He hiccups again. "Pardon me."

"Let's get you in the boat."

I hold out my hand and he grasps it. Trying not to get distracted by the thought that I'm holding Logan Rush's freezing hand, I pull hard and yank him into the dinghy. I straddle the seat nearest the outboard motor while he lies on the bottom of the boat, barefooted and bow tie askew, shivering and panting.

Pushing his hair out of his eyes, he spies his shoes and socks.

"There you are!" he says, snatching them up and placing them neatly side by side on top of the dinghy's inflated side — all the better, apparently, to admire them.

"These shoes anner socks are mine," he says proudly.

"They're very nice," I reply, and he smiles.

Whoa, that smile!

"Uh …" It takes me a long moment to pull myself together. "Look, we need to get you back to your party."

At that moment, loud cheers and applause erupt from the yacht.

"No!" He shakes his head mutinously, then groans. "You hurt my head, pulling my hair like that."

"*I* didn't hurt your head. That was *you* — you bumped it on the flagpole when you were climbing down the ladder." I point toward the yacht.

"Did I?"

"Yes you did. What were you trying to do, anyway?"

He considers this for a few seconds before answering, "'Scape!"

"Escape?"

"Not going back," he says, nodding gingerly. "Say, why's everything moving up and down?"

"Because we're in a boat in the middle of the freaking ocean."

"Right. Okay. Well, we could have a drink, though. I have a bottle right here."

He pulls and tugs at the bottle wedged into his jacket pocket until he frees it, and lifts it to his lips, before seeming to recall his manners and offering it to me.

"No thanks." Though it pains me to turn down the chance of putting my lips where his have been, I figure the bottle contains more salt water than bubbly by now. "I don't think you should drink that either."

He waves my caution away with an airy hand, and tips the bottle to his lips. A moment later he sputters and coughs.

"Tastes terrible! S'awful. Did y'all spike it?"

"No, you did! You fell in the ocean, and the seawater —" I begin, but there's no point in trying to explain.

Logan Rush, teen heartthrob and action-hero extraordinaire, is well and truly pickled.

"Can't drink that stuff." Logan sets the bottle aside with a disgusted sniff, then eyes me hopefully. "Say, you don't happen to have a bottle, do you?"

"Not me, but they've got lots on the yacht. Should I take you back there?"

"No." He folds his arms across his chest. "I won't go. An' you can't make me."

"But they'll be worried — they might alert the NSRI to search for you."

"Who's Enniserai?"

"Sea Rescue. Let's go back, okay?" I put a hand on the tiller.

"No. I only jus' got away! Told them I had a headache and needed some time in my cabin. An' I left a note there — *Taking a break, see ya in Cape Town!* I'm very responissable."

"But —"

"If you try an' take me back to the piranhas, I'll throw myself in the sea!"

"Well, we can't just stay here all night."

"Why not? S'nice being with a beautiful lady — if you don' mind me saying that. S'nice and cosy."

Logan Rush just called me beautiful. I'm tempted to squee but force myself to sound business-like.

"Cosy? It's not cosy. It's cold and wet. We can't stay here." Inspiration strikes. "You know where we could get more champagne, though?"

"The good stuff? Not the salty one?"

"Yep, the good stuff — the best."

"Where?"

"There." I point to the shore where the distant lights of Simon's Town harbour form a bright beacon.

"S'go!"

"Alright then."

Gently twisting the throttle, I put the motor into gear and steer the boat back to where my surfboard floats. I drag it on board and wedge it tightly under the benched seats.

"Just promise me this — if I get arrested for kidnapping, you'll get me out of jail," I say.

"S'not kidnap," he says, looking offended. "I'm not taking you anywhere. S'you driving the boat."

"Damn straight, it is."

I turn us in the direction of the small harbour and increase the speed. Two light splashes signal that Logan's shoes have declined to make the trip to land, but I say nothing. He seems awfully fond of those shoes, and no way am I going back to search for them.

The trip to Simon's Town harbour will be quick — the dinghy has a powerful engine and we aren't that far out. For most of our full-throttled, bouncing charge for shore, my passenger sits on the seat opposite me, smiling and humming what sounds like *Row, row, row your boat.* When we hit one particularly big swell, he falls off his seat but manages to stay in the boat.

"But where are my shoes?" he shouts over the racket of the motor, staring at his bare feet in bewilderment.

I point to the noisy engine and my ears, and shake my head, playing deaf.

The wind is cool on my face, and I'm high on the boat's speed and the thrill of Logan's presence. The dark water is limned silver by starlight and phosphorescence. It should be romantic — I am, after all, alone with arguably the most handsome and desirable man in Hollywood's galaxy of stars — but Logan Rush is not behaving like a romantic lead.

He alternates between complaining about his cold feet and hunting for his shoes — rummaging around on the floor of the boat and peering under my surfboard. He bends double to search under the bench seats and emerges clutching a black package from which he extracts a white, waterproof poncho — the sort kept under the seat for passengers on the boat. When he shakes it out, the wind rips it from his hands, and it flaps backwards into the night like a giant, spooky bat.

Immediately, I throttle back and turn the boat around. Shoes will probably just sink to the bottom of the ocean where they'll slowly disintegrate, except for the soles, but plastic is a different thing entirely.

I spot the poncho floating in pale folds on the dark water.

"Grab it, will you?" I say to Logan as we pull alongside. "And don't fall in again."

"Why are we saving the … this thing?" he asks, dragging the wet, dripping mass on board.

"We're not. We're saving fish and turtles and sea birds."

Logan frowns, clearly puzzled.

"Sea creatures eat plastic — they mistake it for jellyfish — and then they choke, or clog up their insides and die. The ocean," I explain, "does not need more plastic pollution."

"No." He nods slowly. "But you know what I need?"

"Let me guess — more champagne?"

"Yes!" The wide smile is back. "And also, shoes."

We draw close to the shore, and by the bright lights of the small harbour, I see something that makes me think our landing won't be simple or unobtrusive.

"I think you'd better put on a poncho — see if you can find a dry one," I tell him.

"Why?"

"Because you're cold. Plus, you might want to stay hidden."

Logan glances to the shore, and his gaze fixes on the small crowd of girls and women, noisy even from this distance, who're thronging the main pier that stretches out from the waterfront restaurants into the small harbour. Apparently, I'm not the only fan who found out about tonight's party. They've probably been tweeting about it all evening, putting out the word on the *#RushTo* hashtag, sharing in WhatsApp groups, pulling in fellow fans from across the Cape Peninsula.

A hunted look comes over Logan's face.

"I'm guessing you want to avoid that lot?" I check.

He nods.

"Okay, then. Find another poncho and put it on. Pull the hood up to cover your face. I'll try to land us around the other side."

Obediently he reaches under the seat, extracts another of the coverings, and wrangles its flapping shape over his head. I slow the boat down and steer us away from the pier and concrete slipway, and around the back of the marina's jetties where dozens of yachts and motor boats are moored.

At the far side, a small stretch of sand forms a natural inlet between scrubby overgrown bushes and small trees. Locals know the spot and often use it to launch their canoes, but tonight it's dark and secluded, and the gaggle of girls probably wouldn't know of its existence. It's also right below the place where I've parked my car, so it's ideal for a quick getaway.

"Hold on tight," I say and give the dinghy a last burst of speed.

CHAPTER 5
CHASED

I cut the dinghy's outboard engine and then flip it up as we speed onto the small beach and lurch to a stop. Together we drag the inflatable as high onto the sand as we can, and I tie it to the base of one of the stunted trees growing on the shore.

"Look — penguins!"

Logan is crouched down on his haunches, pointing at two African penguins nesting in a hollow under a low bush. One of them — more curious, or perhaps more eager than its mate to defend their spot — steps out and shakes its head fiercely at us.

I love these knee-high birds which nest all over Simon's Town, sometimes even in people's gardens. With their white chests, sharp black beaks, and white-rimmed eyes, they're the most dapper of the sea creatures I treasure, so I can understand Logan's fascination at seeing one up-close for the first time. But they're not pets, so when he reaches out as if to pat it, I quickly push his hand away.

"Don't touch! They're cute, but they're wild. And they draw blood when they peck."

As if on cue, the penguin flaps its wings, stretches its throat, opens its beak wide, and lets out a series of loud braying calls, sending Logan toppling back onto his rump in surprise.

He laughs, and his laugh is as wonderful as his smile.

"It sounds like a donkey!" he says.

"That's why they're sometimes called jackass penguins. Come on, this way." I tug him in the direction of the small rise beyond the line of bushes, aware that I keep finding excuses to touch his hand.

"But what about my shoes?"

"What is it with you and those damned shoes? Forget about them! They are gone. They are no more. They have ceased to exist."

I lead us towards the spot where my car is parked. Logan trails behind, emitting little hisses of pain every time he steps on a sharp stone or twig. Truly, he must be a very good actor, because in real life — from what I've seen so far — he's nothing at all like the brave macho man he portrays on-screen.

When we reach my small hatchback, I hoist my surfboard onto the roof rack.

"There's a towel in the boot," I tell Logan, tossing him the car keys and turning back to strap the board securely in position.

"What boot?"

He's turning around in a circle, peering intently at the ground, searching for footwear. Again.

"The trunk — of the car," I translate.

"Ah."

While he dries his face, I reach behind my back for the zipper of my wetsuit. No doubt a million girls have fantasized about taking off their clothes in the presence of Logan Rush, but I feel self-conscious rather than excited. If I'd had the choice of what I *could've* looked like when I met him, I would have chosen to look a little bit more like those goddesses on the yacht — elegantly dressed, my shoulder-length, chestnut-brown hair bouncing in sleek, shiny curls, my oval face subtly but expertly made up to maximise my lips, which I know are nicely full, and to emphasize my eyes, which are a pretty enough shade of golden brown.

Instead, here I stand in the unflattering wetsuit, my wet hair hanging like dripping rats' tails and my face bare of even a swipe of mascara. At least the light in the parking lot is dim, hiding the details of my appearance.

In his bare feet, wet tuxedo, and the limp plastic poncho, Logan looks goofy. Goofy and adorable.

When I start peeling off my wetsuit, he gives me a wary look.

"Um …" He rubs at his hair with the towel, letting its ends drop over his face.

I realise he might think I'm stripping. I've read reports of girls, naked as jaybirds, waylaying him in the men's restrooms of restaurants and hotels, or lifting their shirts for him to sign their bare chests as he walks the red carpet. Perhaps he thinks I'm planning to get nude and then jump his bones.

"It's okay, I've got a bikini on underneath, see?" I reassure him, freeing myself from the clinging black wetsuit.

"I do."

He gives a slow, appreciative smile at the sight of me. Hoping the dim light of the parking lot hides the blush I can feel warming my cheeks, I turn to retrieve my clothes from my bag in the car.

"You planning on keeping that poncho on?" I ask him, tying my hair up into a rough bun.

"Oh!" He seems surprised to find he's still wearing it.

By the time he's wrestled his way out of its damp folds, I've pulled my jeans on over my bikini bottoms and slipped into a T-shirt.

"Sharks do it with their fins," he reads the logo on the front of it

"We should go now."

"You like sharks?"

"I do."

"*I'm* a shark — in my movie."

"I know you are. And we need to get you back to your hotel, so that tomorrow you can carry on making your movie." I crouch down to fasten my sneakers.

"You have shoes," he says in a piteous tone.

"So where is it?"

The Cape Peninsula is stuffed to the gills with the sort of luxurious hotels stars like Logan Rush would stay in.

"I don't know. I don't know *where* they are. One minute they were there, the next — gone! Vanished."

"Who were?" I ask, completely confused.

"My shoes."

"Oh for the love of fudge! Get in the car," I order, but he's leaning back against it for support with one foot raised in the air, and seems set to argue.

"What about my —"

A high-pitched screaming noise pierces the stillness of the night. The hairs on my arms stand up at the other-worldly sound, and Logan freezes, foot up, like some Kung Fu master poised to deal a killer kick.

The sound grows louder. Closer.

"*Help*." Logan's voice is a soft, pleading moan. He stares, eyes round with horror, at something over my shoulder.

I glance back. The pack of girls is running through the parking lot, straight towards us. Their faces are contorted in feral glee. Their wordless shrieks are the battle cry of an advancing army of crazed marauders. In less than a minute, Logan will be surrounded.

"Help me, please," he whimpers. "They'll tear me to pieces."

"Get inside!"

I slam the boot shut, run around the car, and slide into the driver's seat. As soon as Logan's inside, I lock the doors. Just in time. The wave of fans surges up against the car, swirling around and drowning us in a sea of writhing, squealing Rushers.

They press their phones and cameras up against the windows, and blind me with flashes of bright, white light. Someone tries to open the door on Logan's side. Tears stream down the cheeks of a middle-aged woman who has her face jammed up against his window. Around her, and on my side of the car, too, girls — and a couple of guys, too, I now see —jostle for a glimpse of him. Some hold out paper or photographs with marker pens.

Even though Logan has thrown the towel over his head and can't see a thing, several fans hold up signs for him to read.

I ♥ U, Chase!

Be my Beast!

*I'm a Chaser **and** a Rusher*

Bite me — I know it hurts!

One girl in shorts and a skimpy pink top, and carrying a handwritten sign, climbs onto the front of my car.

"Hey!" I shout, pressing hard on the hooter and waving a finger at her.

But she has eyes only for Logan. She leopard-crawls up the hood in front of him and swings her leg around in front of her. Clamped on her foot are the sharp teeth of a very realistic-looking replica of an animal trap. At least, I *assume* it's a replica — and that the blood oozing from her ankle is fake. She slams her sign against the glass in front of Logan.

I jump at the bang and he looks up. The towel slips behind his head, exposing his face, and the screams kick up to fever pitch. His lips move silently as he reads the sign.

I want your cubs!!!

The girl points dramatically at the sign, then at her foot, and then at Logan.

He swears violently and puts his hands over his face.

"Let's go — now! Please!" he begs.

I fumble in a compartment of the dashboard to grab the glasses I need to wear for driving and slip them on. My hands are shaking. It takes another few moments to get the key into the ignition, and the fans start rocking the car in time to chants of "Lo-gan, Lo-gan, Lo-gan."

I start the engine and begin inching forward as slowly and carefully as I can. It'll be a miracle if we get out of this without squishing a few of them. The girl on the hood stretches out her arms, trying to hang on to the car as we start moving. I turn on the windscreen wipers to move the sign off the glass, hoot again, and roll forward a bit more. The Rushers sense our imminent escape, and the hysterical squealing reaches an ear-splitting crescendo.

Some fans peel away from the car and sprint off in different directions across the parking lot, no doubt headed for their own cars. As we turn into the road, the girl on the car finally slides off, landing in a pile of litter on the pavement. I glance back in my rear-view mirror as we pull away to see her standing, holding the chain of her trap out after Logan in a melodramatic, supplicating gesture.

"Right," I say when we hit the main road heading out of Simon's Town. "Where are you staying?"

"Hotel," he replies, yawning widely.

"Yeah, I guessed that much. Which one?"

He shrugs. "Dunno what it's called. They drop me there every night and collect me every morning."

"Do you know where it is?"

"Cape Town."

"That narrows it down." To a few hundred.

I head for Cape Town, taking the back road which cuts through the Cape Point nature reserve. I usually steer clear of this route after dark — the winding roads which hug the precipitous cliffs jutting out over the ocean offer spectacular views in the daytime, but at night they can be treacherous, especially if baboons come scampering into the road.

I hope the drive will dissuade the fans because, as expected, a long crocodile of cars follows us in hot pursuit. We lose a few as we pass the last of the houses and resorts built on the coastline, but seven or eight persistent Rushers keep tailing us. Worse, unless Logan also has a niche fan-following of middle-aged men with expensive-looking photographic equipment, I fear the car directly behind us belongs not to fans, but to paparazzi.

"This is like a car chase," I say. "Only, it's kind of slow. And no one's shooting, or crashing."

"Yet," Logan says ominously.

He burrows down in the seat to get more comfortable, using the bundled towel as a makeshift pillow behind his head, and yawns widely.

"Hang on, you can't fall asleep," I protest, lowering Logan's window to give him a blast of the cool, fresh evening air, pungent with the astringent, herby scent of mountain *fynbos*. "I don't know which hotel to take you to. Can't you describe it for me?"

"Very nice rooms. Big."

"Nice and big? That's as specific as you can get?"

"The bathroom has a massive shower and neat little bottles of shampoo and gel made from diffren' kinds of wine. Like Chianti conditioner and Burgundy body wash," he says, apparently trying to be helpful. "Great minibar in the room, too … It has British candy." His eyes close and he speaks softly and slowly. "You eat British chocolate over here?"

I sigh in frustration. I wonder if he's still buzzed. I hope he is, because otherwise he's dead stupid, and that'll kill my crush.

"Logan, I don't know what the inside of luxury suites in five-star hotels look like. Can you describe the outside of the hotel, or the lobby, or something I might ever have seen?"

No reply.

"Logan?" I glance across and see that he's fast asleep. Oh, that's just perfect.

I drive on into the darkness, the lead car in a procession of vehicles all headed in the same direction, with one of the most famous men in the world sitting next to me — all long limbs, tousled hair, and soft snores in the passenger seat.

CHAPTER 6
HOT PURSUIT

I have no idea where I should take my comatose passenger.

It's about half an hour since we left the marina — surely by now the partying celebs will have discovered that their guest of honour has gone AWOL? I hope like heck they also discovered his note and haven't initiated an official search and rescue for him. If they check on shore, they'll surely hear all about the commotion of fans and how Logan Rush was driven off by a young woman. Will they think I've kidnapped him?

Trying to get away from the cars following us, I take a series of turns and wind up in an unfamiliar and derelict industrial area on the outskirts of Cape Town. The one-way road is three lanes wide, lit by the sulphurous yellow of streetlights, and mostly deserted. Two homeless men argue drunkenly at an intersection, and I hurry on. In a quiz with the question "By whom would you prefer to be accosted, late at night, on a deserted street? (a) Two intoxicated hobos, (b) An armed car hijacker, or (c) A pack of rabid Rushers," I would choose (d) None of the above.

I've got to find a safe place to park until Logan wakes up and is sober enough to give me a clue as to where I should take him. Plus, I need to shake off our tail of fans and paparazzi before we pick up even more in the city. A glance in the rear-view mirror confirms that another couple of cars have already joined the procession.

One of Zeb's favourite sayings is, "We only chase the ones that run."

Are the fans and photogs only following because we're trying to escape? If I give them a proper chance to see Logan and calmly take pictures of him, maybe they'll behave politely and then go on their way and leave us be.

Yeah, and maybe pigs will grow wings and fly.

The traffic lights ahead turn amber. I'll have to stop. Is there any way I can turn the tables on my pursuers?

I speed up to the lights, now red, and wrench the wheel around to park us sideways across the road's three lanes with my door facing our oncoming entourage. I yank up the handbrake and, with the engine still running, get out of the car to face them, closing the door behind me and raising my hands in a *stop* gesture. The other cars pull up to a halt, and expectant faces stick out of windows.

"Come see," I call loudly, beckoning them closer.

One photographer and a couple of fans climb out of their cars.

"Come on, quick! He's asleep in the car. You can take some pictures."

As soon as the first few race over towards us, phones and cameras held at the ready, the rest scramble out of their cars to follow suit. Just as I hoped, now that they've been given permission to intrude, they drop all the hysterics and walk over quietly to stand clustered at my side of the car. The lead girl bends down to peep in through the window of my closed door and asks politely, "May we? May we take pictures?"

"Yes, of course. Can everyone see? Is everyone close enough?"

They're all out of their cars now, clustered close by and chattering excitedly.

"He's there — in the car!"

"It's really him!"

"She's going to let us take pics."

"Aww, my battery's flat!"

The traffic lights change to green. A bald, gum-chewing paparazzo with a narrow, ferret face steps right up to me.

"We can't see through metal, lady. Or through you."

"Of course," I say with what I hope is a disarming smile. "I'm sorry. Here, let me get the door for you."

I turn to open the car door and, in the same movement, fling myself into my seat, release the brake, and screech off down the intersecting road.

"Go, go, go!" I yell at my car, slamming my foot down flat on the accelerator.

The engine whines a loud protest, but the crowd isn't on my tail. Yet. The red light probably won't stop them, but they'll still have to run back to their cars, get inside, and start their engines. If I can just find a good side road, somewhere … somewhere — there!

I careen into a dark street which curves out of sight of the main road, and turn up the first open driveway I see, speeding past gates dangling off broken hinges and down the dark driveway beyond. The ghostly white of my headlights illuminates tall Cypress trees growing on either side. Fifty metres in, I cut the engine, switch off the lights, slide down in my seat and sit still, panting as hard as though I've just outrun a chainsaw-wielding maniac.

Beside me, Logan still sleeps as deeply as a dead man. My crazy stunt-woman driving must have flung him around some, but it hasn't woken him. He looks so peaceful that I poke him in the ribs to check he's still alive, and relax when he grunts then hiccups. I feast my eyes on his face. No two ways about it, the boy is a looker — despite the purple lump now visible on the top of his forehead.

Incredibly, impossibly, he's even more attractive in person than on the screen. He's the real-life embodiment of everything I've ever learned about him. And I have learned pretty much all there is to know about him.

Logan Rush. Age: 20. Nationality: American. Height: 6 ft. 1 inch (which my online converter tells me is 1,85 metres). Foot size: 10. Hair: black. Eyes: blue.

The websites don't give details of the exact shade of his eyes — plain old 'blue' is good enough for them. But not for me. Zeb can call me obsessive all he wants, but when it comes to Logan Rush, I believe accuracy is important. I've studied the movies and photographs, and I think his eyes are a deep cobalt blue. Deep enough to hold secrets. Deep enough to fall into.

The last time I watched *Beast: Sun*, forcing Zeb to watch with me, I'd pressed freeze-frame on a close-up of those eyes and saw that the blue of his irises was rimmed with a darker outline. I sighed and stared, batting away Zeb's hands as he scrabbled for the remote control.

"He has beautiful eyes, admit it," I insisted.

"They probably exaggerate them using CGI."

"What?"

"Computer graphics imagery. His six-pack is probably CG-enhanced, too."

"It is *not*."

I forwarded the movie to the point where Logan peeled off his shirt, about to transform into a tiger, and studied his form.

Phwaor! (I may or may not have said that aloud.)

"Yup, photoshopped. Definitely," said Zeb. "Or maybe it's body paint."

"Cynical much?" I said. "You just don't want to admit that you think he's hot, too."

"Do not."

"Do too."

"I prefer the other one — with the blonde hair and dimples. Is he in the next scene?" Zeb said. He snatched the remote, and then we were looking at the fair-haired villain.

"I love Logan Rush." I said it every time I watched one of his movies, and I meant it.

"You don't love him — you don't even know him!" Zeb objected.

"I do," I said stubbornly. "I know he has a younger sister who lives with their mother in Atlanta, Georgia, in the States, and that when he was just seven years old, his father died in a car crash and they were left penniless. Poor little thing. His first acting role was as Peter Pan in a sixth-grade school production."

I knew everything there was to know about his rags-to-riches story. I even knew he had a crooked baby toe on his right foot from when he'd pulled a sewing machine onto himself at the tender age of eight. (Where was his mother — the negligent woman? He might have killed himself!)

"You know what his publicity department puts out — that's not the same thing as knowing *him*. He could be gay for all you know. He probably is."

"Wouldn't change how I feel about him," I say loftily. "And, for your information, we have loads in common."

Zeb laughed out loud at that. "Like what? You're eighteen — just — and he's what? Twenty-five?"

"He's not even twenty! That's a difference of less than two measly years."

"Both your parents are still alive, you live in South Africa while he lives in the USA, plus there's that little fact of him being a massive movie star and you're Miss Nobody just finishing high school!" He batted away the popcorn I threw at him. "To me, it seems like you have *nothing* in common."

"Well, that goes to show how little *you* know."

Like Logan, I also had a sister. Four of them, actually. I was also passionate about ecology — I figured he must be, given the subjects of his movies. I had a dog and so did Logan. Mine was a mongrel called Lobster. His was a beagle called Toffee that he'd adopted as a puppy from an animal shelter four years ago. Awww!

"A dozen magazines have crowned him the 'Sexiest Man Alive,'" I told Zeb. "He's also ranked #1 on Movie Newz's 'Hottest actors under 25' and been Teen Screen's 'Hottest Heartthrob' for the last three years in a row. They call him the Prince of Hollywood."

"Romy," cried Zeb. "I'll admit he's the hottest star in the freaking Milky Way if you just stop talking about him. Please!"

Zeb looked to be near breaking point, so I'd eased up on the public raving about Logan. But I didn't stop dreaming about him in private.

It feels like I'm *still* dreaming now as I sit beside him, watching him sleep. I study him in the faint light, feature by 3D feature. His hands have long fingers and surprisingly slender wrists. His jaw, shadowed with slight stubble, is squarer than it looks on-screen, and his face leaner. His slanted brows are the same pitch-black as his hair, which he wears just a touch too long, and his eyelashes are impossibly long. Lashes like that are totally wasted on guys.

I wish I could pry open an eyelid and check the precise colour of his irises. But mostly what my hands long to do is to touch him. Gently. To smooth back the thick lock of hair that flops over his forehead when he shifts in his seat, to trace the line of his cheekbones, to test the pressure of his lips.

My hand is halfway to his face when I check myself. It's not okay to caress people when they're practically unconscious. I remember his attempts to evade all the touching and invasion of his personal space on the yacht. Poor guy, people are probably always trying to get a hold of him — mere mortals wanting to touch a god. I've read accounts of fans snatching at his clothes and even yanking hairs out of his head. No, it wouldn't be right to touch, no matter how seriously tempted I am. And I *am* seriously tempted.

I tuck my hands under my arms and force myself to look away. Tilting the rear-view mirror, I check behind us and see the lights of a car slowly cruising past along the road, but no one has followed us up the driveway. I reckon I've shaken our tail. Still, it's probably a good idea to hide out here for a little longer. Then it occurs to me that I have no idea where 'here' is.

From my position sunk down low in the seat, all I can see out of the window are the low-hanging, shadowy-leafed branches of a tree. I raise my head just a few inches and peep out.

In the dim light, I see an angel, pure white and draped in robes, with wings outstretched towards me.

I jerk bolt upright and stare around, my eyes taking in the shadowy details — the angel mounted on a massive stone plinth; the rows of marble headstones and stone crosses; the badly mown grass, plastic floral arrangements, and in a grassy patch just next to where we're parked, the deep rectangular hole with a mound of loose earth alongside.

I've driven us straight into the dead centre of town.

CHAPTER 7
ANGELS AND DEMONS

Sitting in the dark graveyard, I half expect to see a zombie rise out of the open grave, eyes staring blindly, flesh rotting, mouth dripping blood and pus. I'm being ridiculous, I know, but when I laugh at myself, the chuckle sounds forced.

Zombies aside, this probably isn't the safest place to allow Logan Rush to catch some z's. There's a real risk of meeting vandals and modern-day grave-robbers here to prise brass plaques off gravestones and memorials to sell for scrap, or to source free flowers for their girlfriends. They might decide that I'm richer prey and turn their attention and screwdrivers on me. Plus, if one of the paparazzi or fan cars spots us from the road and drives up behind, we'll be trapped. It's time to move.

The lane is narrow, bordered on either side by raised brick edging, and obviously intended for one-way traffic only. With my luck, if I try to reverse my way out or turn around, I'll steer us straight into an open grave. So I start the car and drive forwards, looking for an exit sign or a spot to turn.

The place is as creepy as a crypt, and pitch-dark apart from our headlights. Eerie, distorted shadows shift around us. I wish Logan would wake up — I could use some company. Deliberately, I go too fast over a speed bump, but though the car bucks and bounces, Logan's head just lolls onto his other shoulder. Honestly, if people knew how much of a heroine-protecting action-man he *isn't* …

Well, they'd probably *still* love him.

The lane curves in a loop — surely it'll spit us out at an exit soon? The headlights illuminate the cold ashes and bits of wood from an old fire built in the hollow of a tree trunk. What if those are the remains of an evil circle of devil worshippers, gathered around a pentagram drawn in blood over a grave, sacrificing a cat? Or a monkey. Or a cat-monkey mutant. I shiver, then I spy gates ahead. The exit!

But the gates are bound shut with a thick chain and sturdy padlock. Crap. We'll have to go back the way we came, after all. Muttering under my breath, I shift gears and begin the toing and froing and wheel-turning of a three-point turn. Or a twenty-three-point turn, to be more accurate — the lane is extremely narrow.

The difficult manoeuvring distracts me, for a brief minute, from things that creep and pounce and ooze, but once my clammy hands are steering us back to the other gate, my feverish mind shifts to local legends — the restless ghosts of the slaves once housed in wet, slimy tunnels beneath the old parts of the city, and the hairy, evil dwarf *Tokoloshe* that comes in the night to bewitch, and eat toes, and cart off the unwary. Silly!

When we finally reach the entrance, I see that one side of the gates has swung — or been pushed? — closed. To escape this place, I'll need to get out of the car and push the gate back open.

Unnerving images flash through my mind — the plot of every horror movie I'd ever seen, the gruesome details of every graveyard urban legend I'd ever heard. There's that one about a couple making out in their car. They hear a strange noise, and the man gets out to investigate but doesn't return, and the woman grows frantic with worry. Then she hears a dripping on the car roof. She thinks it's rain, but it's really the blood of her boyfriend's slit-throated corpse, dangling from a tree limb above the vehicle.

I do not want to set foot outside of this car. I cast a hopeful glance at my companion.

"Logan? Logan?"

No response. Unchivalrous git.

I take a good look around for any men or monsters before I unlock the door and climb out, ducking to avoid braining myself on the low-hanging branches of a cedar tree. The angel's wings now seem more imploring and less protective. And is it my imagination or does the mound of earth beside the empty grave look like it's grown? I scurry towards the gate, hyper-aware of mysterious rustlings, the sighing of the wind in the trees, and the weird whistling hoots which I hope like heck are just the calls of night birds and not the secret signals of gang members.

I swing the gate back open, jam it in place with a loose brick, and dash back to the car. Once the door is closed and locked, I sigh with relief and laugh a little at my foolishness. Which is when it happens — a long, screeching scrape of sharp claws on the metal roof of the car — and I scream.

It's a terrific scream, too. Short and sharp, but glass-shatteringly loud and high. It comes from deep inside of me, powered by all the tension and frustrations of the day. Maybe even of the year.

Logan levitates. I swear he lifts at least a hand's height out of his seat. He might not have the Beast's superpowers, but the boy can fly. Also, he can yell — lower than me, but maybe even louder. His eyes start open and his hair seems to stand on end, although that may be because it's dried in that position, mashed up against the crumpled towel.

"*Wasser?*" he yelps.

I'm already feeling much better. The venting, cathartic scream helped, plus I've realised that the screechy scrape was probably just a tree branch. Right now, I feel a lot calmer than Logan looks.

"Anything the matter?" I ask, aiming for cool and collected.

Logan looks over at me with wild eyes and recoils in fear. From me! I've saved his ass not once, but three times already — more if you count the fact that I've protected him from potential robbers, serial killers and the *Tokoloshe* — and now he stares at me with deep suspicion and a wariness verging on panic.

"Who are you? Where am I?" He peers out of the windows, spots the tombstones, celestial beings and open graves, and glares back at me, clearly horrified. "Where have you brought me? And why?"

"Relax, Braveheart. We're just in a cemetery."

"You won't get away with it!"

"With what?"

"With whatever you're planning to do to me." He fiddles with the door, trying to find the lock.

"So this is the thanks I get?" I push my glasses up on my nose, start the car, and drive back out into the road. "You're welcome, I'm sure."

"And what have you done with my shoes?" Logan demands, staring down at his bare feet.

"Not that again! Jeez, you're obsessed with your shoes — you know that?"

A moment later, we're back on the main road in the deserted industrial area, and this time, undistracted by pursuing cars, I clearly see a road sign ahead pointing the way to the central part of the city.

"Where are you taking me?"

"You tell me — last time we spoke you couldn't remember the name of your hotel. Any luck now?"

He frowns. Hiccups. "No."

"Remember what it looks like at all?"

"It's very big —"

I roll my eyes at him.

"And there's a silver dolphin in the lobby, if that helps. And —"

"Say no more, it's the Cape Majesty."

I navigate a route towards the V&A Waterfront, where the super-exclusive hotel is located. Logan sits quietly for a few minutes, hiccupping every now and then.

When he speaks, he sounds embarrassed. "Um … I'm sorry, I may have been a bit rude back there. I was unnerved — with the graveyard and all. I'm Logan Rush."

"I know," I say, smiling at him.

"Yes, but … um?" His eyes look a question.

"Oh, yes, sorry. I'm Rosemary Morgan."

"Right, right … And, um, why am I in your car?"

"You don't remember what happened?"

He frowns, narrows his eyes, and cocks his head. Which, for the record, makes him look super cute.

"I remember the party and then … did I go swimming?"

"You could say that."

"And there were screaming girls —"

"Yup."

"And a penguin!"

"It's all coming back to you now."

"And my sho —"

"Logan," I interrupt. "I swear, if you mention the sh-word again, I will personally feed you to the lions."

"What lions?"

"You're in Africa. Lions are never far away," I threaten, completely untruthfully. Still, it distracts him from his preoccupation with his missing footwear.

He shakes his head as if trying to clear it, then winces and lifts a hand to his forehead.

"You've got a nice egg forming there," I tell him.

He quickly flips down the visor, lifts his hair off his forehead, and peers worriedly into the small mirror on the back.

"Damn!" He examines the lumpy bruise from different angles and then tries to hide it under a thick lock of hair.

"Yeah, your looks are totally gone," I say, amused. No other guy I know is this vain. Zeb will laugh his head off when I tell him the story.

"They're going to kill me." Logan flips the visor back up and slumps back in his seat.

"Who?" I ask as we drive through the entrance to the massive waterfront tourist complex where trendy restaurants, exclusive hotels, hot nightclubs and high-end stores almost entirely disguise the working docks of Cape Town around which they're built.

"Make-up, lighting, continuity. Cilla." He groans the last word. "Cilla?"

"My nemesis and slave driver. The queen of the underworld. If they have to reshoot, she'll skin me alive!"

"Who *is* this woman?"

"My director." He suddenly sits bolt upright and swears, then casts me a contrite glance. "I apologise. Bad language is one of my vices."

In person, his accent is more lilting and Southern than it is on-screen, and perfectly charming, though his words are a little blurred around the edges. He's obviously still slightly buzzed.

"I should let her know that I'm okay. She'll be really worried." He pats his pockets. "Well, not *worried* so much as enraged and on the warpath."

"You said you left them a note."

"I did?" He sounds impressed at his own foresight.

"And I think you'll find that your phone —"

"— doesn't work, yeah." He holds up the sleek, black cell phone. A bead of water oozes out of its bottom seam and drips off. "What the hell did I do tonight? Go swimming in my tuxedo?"

"Pretty much. You know, they say memory blackouts are a sign of drinking too much."

"I don't do it often," he says defensively.

"Here we are — the Cape Majesty," I announce as we pull up to the impressive high-columned entrance of the swanky hotel, where a horde of tourists is disembarking from a luxury coach.

I've already turned into the short approach leading to the

guest drop-off point, where a pair of doormen in top hats and gold livery wait, when I see *them*. I reach out my left hand and shove Logan's head down.

"Get down. Rushers!"

Logan bends over double in the passenger seat of my car, but to be extra sure he isn't visible to the rabid fans outside, I pull the towel over his back and head. I whizz straight past the surprised hotel doorman, who's already stepping forward to greet us, squeeze around the luxury bus, and keep going. As one, the waiting girls scan my car quickly, find it lacking in the hot heartthrob department, and return to watching the incoming road.

I've got to figure out a way to get Logan inside his hotel without alerting the pack of Rushers.

"Now what?" Logan's voice is muffled under the towel.

I rack my brain for a few moments. I'm quite enjoying this — today is the most exciting day I've had since, well, ever really.

"I have a plan," I say, zipping into an entrance to the multi-storey, under-cover parking garage that adjoins the back of the Majesty hotel. "You can sit up now."

"I'm sorry to keep repeating myself, but where *are* we now?"

"There's a direct entrance through the mall into the hotel," I say, driving up the ramp that leads to the upper parking level. "It should be mostly empty at this time of night, provided it's still open."

It is. Once I've parked the car in a bay right outside the entrance, we get out and I run an appraising eye over Logan. He looks dishevelled in his damp and wrinkled tux. His bow tie is askew, his hair sticks up messily, and his feet, of course, are bare.

Unfortunately, he still looks unmistakably like his very famous self.

"Here," I say, fishing a pair of sunglasses out of my handbag. "Put these on."

"And? How do I look?" He holds his hands up in a *voila!* gesture as if presenting me with an excellent disguise.

"You look a little less like Logan Rush."

Maybe one half of one percent less.

"What about your disguise?" he asks.

"I don't need a disguise — I'm not famous."

"I don't want to be the only one who looks dumb — wearing sunglasses at night."

"Fine." I snag a faded baseball cap from my tog bag in the car and pull it on. "Happy now?"

He turns the cap sideways and nods. I have never in my life worn a cap sideways, like some lame wannabee rapper. But we need to get him inside quickly, so I don't waste time arguing.

"Come on, this way. Once you're in the hotel, you should be safe."

"Let's hold hands," Logan suggests. "We can pretend to be a honeymoonin' couple. Or" — he taps the dark glasses — "I could be a blind man, and you my Seeing Eye … guide."

I sneak a suspicious glance at him and see one end of his mouth is hitched in a grin. Even though he's treating this as a joke, I don't object. In another few minutes, we'll go our separate ways and I'll never see him again, except at the movies. Future me will cherish the memory that Logan Rush once asked to hold my hand.

"Okay." I put my hand in his — so big and warm — and my heart gives a fidgety sort of hiccup. "Here we go."

CHAPTER 8
HOGS AND BUNNIES

We head straight through the entrance to the mall, past a lone smoker getting his nicotine fix, and walk along the short row of stores — closed at this hour — that lead to the hotel's other entrance. We pass a few people, but perhaps the cemetery angel is protecting us, because none of them is a female under thirty and the only glances Logan attracts are disapproving ones directed at his unkempt appearance and bare feet.

A minute later we reach the glass doors of the hotel, but here the doorman steps forward to block our way.

"He's a guest, okay? He got mugged, and I'm taking him back to his room," I say quickly, before the doorman can point to the *right of admission reserved* sign on the wall behind him, or mention dress codes.

I probably didn't meet their standards either, in my scruffy jeans and T-shirt, my old sneakers, and the tatty cap perched on top of my messy bun. No one would buy me as the date of the hot guy by my side — better to pretend to be his Seeing Eye dog.

"Plus, he's blind, and he needs me to guide him," I say, but the doorman still looks unconvinced.

Logan sticks out his hands, lays them on the man's shoulders, pats them up to his surprised face, and begins feeling his features.

"Is it my father, Miss Morgan? Is it my long-lost father?" he says, in a piteous tone.

"No, Mr Falconer, it's not. It's a hotel employee who is discriminating against a disabled man — a blind, handicapped guest of the hotel. What is your name?" I demand of the doorman.

He looks from me to Logan and back again, then shrugs and steps aside.

"This way, Mr Falconer, this way." Holding Logan by both hand and elbow, I escort him into the hotel.

I want to giggle and so, judging from his shaking shoulders, does Logan. But we sober up immediately because the lobby just ahead of us is filled with more than the silver, water-spouting dolphin. The crowd of tourists from the bus outside the main entrance now throngs the reception area, cell phones out and cameras slung around their necks. It's too much to hope that Logan could walk unnoticed through the midst of them.

I look around wildly. Ahead of us are the tourists, behind us is the doubting doorman, to our left is a massive ficus plant which maybe has some potential as a temporary hiding place, and to our right is the hotel's all-night coffee shop.

"Right — change of plan," I announce.

I tug Logan into the café and steer him to one of the private booths with high banquette seats. As soon as we're seated — me facing the door and him with his back to it — a waitress ambles over and hands us two oversized menus.

"Here." I hand Logan my cell phone. "You'd better call your

director and let her know where you are. And please tell me you know her number, because I don't think you're going to be able to get it off your phone."

"No, I don't. But" — he holds up a finger and retrieves his wallet out from an inner pocket in his jacket — "I do have this." He carefully extracts a sodden business card. "It's from the first audition. I hang on to it for luck."

"Good thing. I'm going to order something to eat — I'm ravenous. Do you want something?"

"Sure, whatever looks good."

"You're not a vegetarian or a vegan or something equally … Hollywoodish, are you?"

"Me? I'm from Alabama. We're not scared of meat. We eat hogs whole there."

Logan squints at the card, trying to decipher the smudged ink of the number scrawled on the back, and taps numbers on my phone's touchpad.

"Hi, Cilla, it's Logan … Hello? Is that Cilla?" He pulls a mystified face and hands the phone over to me.

I listen for a moment then say, "*Jammer, verkeerde nommer,*" into the mouthpiece. "You dialled the wrong number," I say.

"What was that she was speaking?"

"Afrikaans."

"Sounds like gargling."

He tries again, being careful to enter the right codes, and this time he gets through to his director. While he speaks, I pretend to read the menu, but my ears are 'flapping'— as Zeb would say.

"Cilla? Yeah, it's me … I know, I know — I'm sorry. I just had to get away, y'know … No, I'm fine … Yes, but I *didn't* die. I got rescued by a sea siren." He grins at me and my stomach flips over. "A girl, okay? A very lovely local lady … What?" He looks at me again, this time a little warily. "No, no, I'm sure she's legit … Wait, I'll ask her." Then to me, he says, "You're not a reporter, are you?"

"No!" I say, as though offended. Secretly I'm flattered he thinks I might be old enough.

"She says no … Well, I guess so … What's that? I have no recollection, but y'all hold on, I'll ask her — she knows everything." He looks at me and says, "The captain of the yacht wants to know where we left the dinghy."

"On the sandy inlet, to the south of the main causeway, in Simon's Town."

He repeats my directions word for word and then listens for a while before answering. "I am so sorry, Cilla. I wouldn't have put you out for the world, you know that. We're hiding out in the coffee shop at the hotel … No, I'll sit tight, promise … Okay, see you soon."

He hangs up and hands me back my phone.

"Well?" I ask.

"She's already on her way over." He doesn't sound too thrilled about this. "She's in full damage-control mode because she thinks you're a tabloid journo in disguise."

"Really?"

"Say, what colour are your eyes?" he says, leaning forward and staring into them.

I find just enough breath to reply, "Uh, brown?"

I seize the moment to look deeply into his gaze, and examine his irises. They're the cobalt blue of the eye of a peacock feather, and they *are* edged by a purplish-black rim. Sucks to Zeb and his

CGI theory.

"Ready to order?" The waitress has returned and is tapping her pen on her notepad.

I look down at the menu, but everything's blurry — I'm still wearing my driving glasses. I perch them on top of the baseball cap and try again.

"Since you should never mix your drinks," Logan says, "we'll have a bottle of —"

"A pot of strong coffee, please," I say sternly. "And a large bottle of mineral water."

"You're so bossy," he grumbles.

"And two lamb bunny-chows," I tell the waitress. "Make one hot and one," — I eye Logan speculatively — "medium."

"We're going to eat rabbits?" he asks as the waitress leaves.

"It's a local delicacy. Besides, I thought you were from Alabama, and not scared of meat?"

"Yeah, but … *bunnies?*"

"Phff! It's made from lamb, and it's the best thing for hangovers."

"I'm not hungover."

"Not yet, but sure as they eat hogs in Alabama, you will be."

"Did I drink a lot?" Logan asks wryly, toying with a few paper tubes of sugar from the dispenser on the table. He has what my Nana calls 'piano hands,' with long, slender fingers.

"You did."

"Did I do anything stupid?"

"You did." I give a sad nod.

"Did I do anything … offensive?" He looks a little worried now.

"You mean, like, did you rip open my shirt, throw me onto

the beach, and grope me?"

He stares at me, horrified. "Did I? I didn't! I wouldn't! Would I?"

"No." I laugh at his expression, and he pelts me with sugar tubes.

The waitress brings our coffee, gazes impassively at the sugar tubes for a moment, then walks off again. I pour the coffee. He takes a few sips, sighs appreciatively, and gives me a long look before speaking again.

"But I did do something really stupid?"

"Logan, you set out to sea without knowing how to sail. Or swim."

"I told you that?"

"And lots more," I tease.

Something like real concern crosses his features.

"Relax! Nothing incriminating," I add, letting him off the hook. "Here, be kind to your liver — drink some water."

He chugs down half the glass I pour for him.

"I guess I should have stayed on the yacht — it was my party and all. I just needed a break, you know? I needed ..."

"To get away. Yeah, I know. I saw."

"But that's the part I don't understand," he says, pouncing on my words. "How did you see? Where were you? Where did you come from at night on the ocean? Were you —"

"Hey, our food has arrived." Saved by the bunny. "This, Logan," I say, pointing at the hollowed-out, half-loaf of crusty bread filled with steaming-hot, fragrant lamb curry, "is a bunny chow."

"It looks real good, but how ..."

"It's okay to use your fingers. This," I say, picking up the small dome of bread which acts as the lid, "is the virgin. And you dip it into the gravy, like so, and then you eat it." I pop the delicious morsel into my mouth.

He looks me straight in the eye and gives a slow, sexy grin. "Hmm, so I start with eating a saucy virgin, and then move on to the hotter stuff?"

My face flames, and I'm glad my mouth is full, because I have no idea what to say. I take a sip of cool water, swallow hard, then show him how to eat the bunny, tearing off chunks of bread and using them to scoop up the spicy filling.

Logan follows my lead and eats with relish, his awkward questions about what I was doing out near the yacht apparently forgotten. We're just finishing our meal, with me urging Logan to drink more water, when I hear a strident, nasal voice, with a distinct American accent, coming from the doorway.

I recognise the woman from the yacht — the tall one with the long nose and the streak of white in her bob of black hair. This must be Cilla. The waitress she's interrogating points in our direction, and the director stalks over.

"Logan! Oh, Logan — look at you!" she says, as soon as she gets to our table. "I was so worried. You might have died! How did you get away from your security detail? Their asses are so fired! Budge up there," she orders, sliding into the seat beside him. Then she turns her attention to me.

"What have you done to him?" she asks fiercely.

"Nothing!"

"She made me drink water! Nearly drowned me in the stuff." Logan's voice is accusing, but his eyes are laughing.

"I *saved* him from drowning."

"Oh, wait — I remember now — she did! But she pulled my hair, and ruined my champagne. And she took my shoes and hid them — or worse."

"I did not! I saved him from a horde of screaming girls and the paparazzi. You ought to be grateful, you rat," I tell him severely. He winks back. My stomach gives a little whirl.

"Who have you told about this?" Cilla demands, all business.

"No one."

"Then you won't mind me checking your phone, and your purse for a camera."

"Knock yourself out," I say, handing my bag over. She rummages through it thoroughly, emerges with my iPhone in her red-taloned hands, and proceeds to check my call list, photographs, tweets, texts, emails, and Facebook posts.

"Satisfied?" I ask.

"Hmm." Cilla studies me critically. "A young lady who can hold her tongue. That's a first."

Logan, who's been quiet for a few minutes, now starts telling tales again. "And she drove me to a graveyard, where she scared the shit out of me!"

"Logan, what have I told you about swearing in public? Remember your image — sizzling hot but squeaky clean!" Cilla reprimands him.

His face immediately falls into a chastened expression, but the foot nudging mine under the table tells me it's an act.

"Why'd you take him to a graveyard?" Cilla asks, pinning me with her sharp gaze.

I tell her how I shook our pursuers by ducking into the cemetery. It comes out sounding like an ingenious and well-thought-out plan, rather than the desperate move it was.

"And how did you get him in here without triggering the fans? They were swarming outside when I came in."

I explain about avoiding the main door and coming in via the quieter mall entrance.

"She made me pretend to be a blind man," Logan says.

"Excuse me, but that was *your* idea!"

"And she threatened to report the doorman for discriminating against a handicapped man. She was scary."

"I didn't really threaten him, I just implied —"

"I'm impressed," Cilla interrupts, still staring at me in a speculative way.

"And then she made me eat a bunny!"

"Oh, cork it, you," I say, throwing my napkin at him. I give Cilla a shrug. "It was a busy night."

"And what do you want for your services tonight?"

"What do I want?" I repeat, confused.

"A reward, I suppose." She takes a fat wad of bills out of her purse and starts counting.

"I don't want your money." I'm insulted by the offer.

Her eyes narrow in suspicion. "You must want something."

"We-ell," I say slowly.

"Let's hear it," she says, her expression one of *I-knew-it* smugness.

"A 'thank you' would be nice."

Ha! That takes her aback.

"Well, young lady —"

"My name's Rosemary Morgan."

"Well, Miss Morgan, you have my sincere thanks, and my

admiration. Keeping this one on track" — she jerks her chin at Logan — "is like herding cats." She writes her cell number on the back of her business card and hands it to me. "Call me if you need a job, Miss Morgan. I could use someone with street smarts and local knowledge, especially one who can keep her mouth shut, and whose brain doesn't go weak in the presence of beauty."

She stands up and tosses cash onto the table — more than enough to cover the bill.

"Speaking of beauty, come on, Logan, let's get you upstairs. My God, you *are* barefoot!"

"I told you she took my shoes," Logan says, grinning broadly at me.

"Goodbye, Logan Rush, it was nice meeting you," I say, stretching out my hand to shake his. Any excuse for a last touch.

"Goodbye." He encloses my hand in both of his and squeezes gently. "And thank you for saving me. I enjoyed it enormously. Except for the screaming in the cemetery — that freaked me out majorly."

Cilla spins on her heel and marches out. Logan follows, but not before adding, "And except for spiking my champagne."

I laugh. He's incorrigible.

"And pulling my hair," he says over his shoulder as he reaches the door. "That hurt."

"Wuss!" I call after him.

He turns, waves, and gets in the last word. "And drowning my shoes!"

Then he walks out the door behind Cilla, and I can't see him anymore.

CHAPTER 9
WISH I COULD BE

One week and two exams later, a faint watermark where Logan sat in his wet tuxedo on my passenger seat is the only reminder of everything that happened on that crazy night.

That and the business card with Cilla Swytch's number on it.

I toy with the card now, turning it over and over in my fingers, reading and rereading it. I must've done this a hundred times in the last seven days — holding it in my hands like some magic talisman, while dreaming, wondering, fantasizing, and dismissing. I almost tear it to shreds, but instead I slip it back into my wallet.

Lobster sits beside me on the bed, watching me pack my small black handbag with lip gloss, a tiny hairbrush and my cell phone. And the wallet containing the business card of a big-time Hollywood movie director.

My parents have arranged a special dinner for me tonight, to celebrate the end of my final matric exams — the end of my schooling really — and my entry into what my father calls "the next phase of my life."

My mom will wish I'd chosen a smarter outfit, but the simple black sundress suits me just fine. She'd also prefer me to wear high heels, but I hate heels, and the strappy, flat sandals look good enough. I'd be way happier in shorts, a T-shirt and bare feet, having a sunset *braai* on the beach with a couple of my best friends from school. But Dad insisted on throwing this party, and what the head of Poseidon Industries wants, he generally gets.

Most of my friends will be raging hard this December — hooking up and partying non-stop on a group vacation in Plettenberg Bay or flying out to start their gap years in London or Sydney. But my parents insist that I spend the next three months — before university starts — working. Mom says I'll be "clarifying my future." Dad says I'll be "demonstrating my work ethic." I call it what it is: slave labour.

I brush my hair and teeth, sticky-roller Lobster's dog hair off my dress, and check my phone for messages. While I wait for everyone else to get ready, I tidy my room. At least that will please my parents.

I like my bedroom. The bleached white wooden bed and desk, the Oregon pine strip floors and the pale aquamarine walls give it the feel of the beach — like foam and sand and water. It would probably look better without the posters that cover most of the walls. A calendar with pictures of breaching whales and schools of dolphins is stuck up beside protest posters condemning shark-finning and the destructive long-lining, drift-netting, and bottom-trawling practices of commercial fishing. Directly opposite my bed, I've hung an enormous picture of the *Syrenka*, a former Russian icebreaker now converted into an environmental warrior ship.

For as long as I can remember, I've dreamed of joining an expedition down to the Southern Ocean to disrupt Japanese whaling operations there. I even sent in a crew application back in March when I turned eighteen, but when the reply email came, it was to inform me that although I'd made the shortlist, I hadn't been chosen for the December trip this year. But I'll go and see the ship when she docks to refuel and stock up in Cape Town before making her way south into Antarctic waters. Maybe I'll be able to meet the captain and persuade him to take me next December, during the university end-of-year break.

At least half of my room is dedicated to my other passion. Posters and collages of Logan Rush adorn my wardrobe doors, inside and out. A little figurine of him, tied to a red velvet ribbon, dangles from the handle of my underwear drawer. I stuck a life-size poster of him as Chase Falconer on the wall alongside my full-length mirror so that when I stand in front of the mirror staring at my image, and his, it's kind of like we're standing next to each other.

He looks so real in that picture, so lifelike, that the photographic version of him seems more real to me than what actually happened last Saturday. That was more like a dream now, a hallucination.

I plant a kiss on his lips, and I'm applying lip gloss to my own when a voice sounds from the door.

"Knock, knock."

My mother, wearing a flowy salmon-pink dress, a necklace made of coral, and delicate high heels, looks more like an elegant royal than the hard-working university lecturer in marine biology that she is. But I have not inherited her talent for immaculate grooming, so her quick inspection of me ends in a wince.

"Not dressed yet?" she says hopefully.

"I am dressed, Mom, this is what I'm wearing."

"Not the blue silk I bought you?"

"No, I'm comfortable in this."

"But you'll be putting on some make-up, yes?" She picks up my brush from the dressing table and brushes my long hair with firm strokes.

"Mo-om, I've put on mascara *and* lip-gloss."

"I consider myself honoured." She smiles gently at me. "Just a heads-up, Romy, your dad's on his way. He's looking for a conclusion to his speech tonight."

I don't respond, except to take the brush out of her hand and return it to the dressing table.

"Still not decided?" she asks.

Mom is kind and gentle, but pressure is pressure. I shake my head.

"Ah, well, either one would be good experience for you, but," she leans down and kisses me on the cheek, "I hope you'll choose me. You're my favourite, you know."

"Mom, you say that to each of us."

"Because it's true!"

The doorbell peals. Barking furiously, Lobster leaps off my bed and hurtles for the front door downstairs.

"That'll be Meriel, come to collect Nana." Mom pauses at the door to offer more advice: "A little blusher wouldn't kill you, Romy, you're as pale as a *Parapeneus Margaritatus*."

"Go on — say it. You know you want to."

"A Pearly Goatfish."

"Charming." My mother has a habit of comparing things, including her family, to ocean dwellers, but 'Pearly Goatfish' is a new low. "Very flattering," I call after her departing form. "And highly maternal!"

I'm still muttering when the youngest of my four older sisters bounces into my room, and — as she always does when she visits — raps my *Syrenka* poster three time with her knuckles for luck, saying, "One day, Romy, it'll happen one day."

Meriel's my favourite sister, and the only one in my family who encourages my eco-activism dreams. She's a meteorologist who specializes in studying marine weather patterns and, like me, she loves the ocean and its creatures.

"Are you catching a ride with Nana and me, or with the folks?" she asks.

"With you guys. I'm trying to avoid Dad."

"Did I hear my name?" my father says, coming into my room.

"I'll go make sure Nana's ready," Meriel says, abandoning me without a moment's hesitation.

"Thanks for that, Meriel," I say sarcastically.

"Anytime," she calls back.

My father, solidly-built, with sleek grey hair and an air of self-importance, wears a dark suit and a red tie imprinted with a diagonal pattern of tiny black tridents — the corporate symbol of Poseidon Industries. Whereas Mom was disappointed by the way *I* look, my father is more disapproving of my *room's* appearance. He knows that the protest posters are a dig at the environmentally unfriendly methods used by some of the fishing operations supplying Poseidon Industries.

He averts his eyes from the posters, clears his throat, and addresses me.

"Rosemary."

"You look smart, Dad."

"Well, now, Rosemary, you look very nice, too."

"Tell that to Mom."

"What I'd *like* to be able to tell your mother — what I'd like to be able to tell all our family and friends at tonight's celebration — is what you have decided to do with your life. And, more immediately, where you plan to work during your vacation: in your mom's department at the university, or with me at the office?"

"I haven't decided yet, Dad. But you'll be the first to know when I do, promise."

I grab my bag and head for the door, hoping he'll take the hint. But subtlety is wasted on my father.

"It depends, naturally, on what you intend to study next year," he continues. "Will you follow in your mother's footsteps and study the denizens of the deep? Or will you register for a business degree in preparation for one day taking up a position at Poseidon — I would so love to keep the business in the family."

"You've got Cordelia for that."

My second-eldest sister, Cordelia works in Dad's business. More than once, she's tried explaining to me what exactly she does there, but terms like "strategic planning" and "enterprise architecture" make my eyes glaze over in boredom.

"The point is, would you prefer to study science or commerce, Rosemary?" Dad asks, leading the way downstairs.

"Are those my only two options? Study either one thing or another in the family line, then settle down and have babies?"

He stops beside the tropical fish tank on the landing and gazes up at me in genuine puzzlement.

"What more are you hoping for?"

"I just …" I blow out a frustrated breath. "Sometimes I just wish I could be out *there*." I fling my arms out, gesturing to some far horizon.

"Out where?"

Anywhere but here — that's the honest answer. But saying it out loud would only hurt him and Mom.

"I think it's time for me to stand on my own two feet, Dad, to find my way in the world." I don't expect him to understand what I mean, and he doesn't.

"I agree completely. Now you're talking more sensibly. So, would you prefer to spend the next few months in preparation for your career with your mother or with me?"

"I'm still not sure."

That's a lie. I am sure. I don't want to do either.

Part of me is tempted to take up the position at Poseidon — I could try to make the people who work there see how commercial fishing harms endangered species, try to change their attitudes and procedures. But who would listen to me? Certainly not my father — he never did. Besides, how much could one person accomplish? How likely would a student intern be to change the ways of a long-established business?

Following in my mother's academic footsteps is hardly more appealing. I love the ocean, but I want to be out there actively *doing* something to fight for its protection and survival, not sitting in a laboratory, studying the minute differences between sea slugs, sea squirts and sea cucumbers. Everyone just assumes I'll follow either my mother's or my father's path, but both only fill me with strong feelings of *meh*.

"I'll think about it, Dad, okay? I'll let you know as soon as I've decided."

"We tried to give you everything you could possibly need, but you always were an unusual child, Rosemary." He sighs.

"Comes from being a Pisces, they always want to swim against the stream," comes my grandmother's voice from downstairs.

Today Nana looks as if she's costumed for the theatrical role of an eccentric great-aunt, even though it's been more than twenty years since she was last on a stage. She's a vision in purple satin and exotic feathers, her cheeks are rouged a lurid pink, and thick black eyeliner sweeps up dramatically at the edges of her eyes. Still barking frantically, Lobster leaps up against her, eager to get his bared teeth on the hideous and slightly mangy fox fur slung around her neck.

"Mother," Dad says.

He's always wary of Nana. It's like he lives in constant fear that she'll do something crazy — strip naked and run through the streets, perhaps — for the sole purpose of embarrassing her son. Actually, I wouldn't put it past the old devil.

"Rex, you look admirably conventional."

"Lobster, sit! Nana, you can't wear that." I point to the mangy circle of fur which ends in a sharp-nosed face, complete with beady, black glass eyes and eternally pricked ears.

"And why not, young lady? If you can wear those," she arches a disparaging eyebrow at my flats, "then I hardly think you are qualified to give me fashion advice."

"Furs are disgusting; no one wears them anymore. And yours looks diseased. Besides, it's summer, Nana."

She merely clutches the fur tighter around her throat with pale, veined hands heavy with enormous rings — intricately designed twists of gold inlaid with brightly-coloured stones.

"Rhea, it makes you look old," my mother says simply.

At once, Nana removes the fur and flings it onto a nearby sofa.

"Begone, accursed thing," she says in throbbing tones.

"Right, who's going in which car?" Mom asks.

"I'll take Nana, and we'll collect Genna on the way," Meriel says.

"And I'll go with them, too," I say.

Dad seems ready to protest — no doubt eager for an opportunity to lecture me further — but Mom, perhaps sensing that I've had enough nagging for one day, intervenes.

"Good, that means we can go straight to the restaurant, Rex, and check that everything's organised and on track before the guests arrive. See you there, girls."

"Give me a moment to perfect my appearance, *mes petites filles*, and then we'll be off. Romy, I have a surprise for you. Hound, release my fox!" Nana commands imperiously, wrestling Lobster for possession of the fur.

CHAPTER 10
SURFACE AND SETTLE

On the way to collect Genna, Nana insists on sitting in the back seat with me. She's replaced the fox fur with a long feather boa, and now the white feathers float around us in the strong air-conditioning of the car.

"I feel like a taxi driver up here alone," Meriel complains.

"I have something I want to give Romy," Nana says, opening her enormous red crocodile-skin handbag. "I gave each of you a gift when you came out, and now it's Romy's turn."

"I don't think girls have 'come out' since the Victorian era," Meriel says.

"Here!" Nana hands me a large, purple velvet box and claps her hands in excitement as I open it.

Inside, clipped to a bed of white satin, is a pair of beautiful earrings. In each, a fat pearl of palest blue nestles in a curved petal-shaped wrap of glistening mother-of-pearl. They look like arum lilies.

"Oh, Nana — thank you!"

"They're antique and awfully valuable, my dear. They were a

gift from a dashing Yugoslavian nobleman — Prince Alexander Petrovich — who was on the run from the Bolsheviks. I was only a little older than you are now when he saw my Lady of Shalott on the West End, and was utterly captivated by my charms. *Ravishing*, he called me! He said I made *these* beauties look dull by comparison."

I'm never sure how much of Nana's tall tales to believe, but it makes her happy to tell them, and I enjoy listening. Now that all four of my sisters have homes of their own, Nana's reminiscences add variety and spice to the usual talk of university politics and fishing quotas that tend to dominate our dinner table.

Nana clips the antique earrings onto my earlobes. They're very tight.

"There! And with a little colour" — she pinches the apples of my cheeks — "lovely! Now *you* look fit for a prince. And, if I may say so, it's about time you started looking for one, dear. Youth, sadly, fades."

"They pinch a little," I say, pulling off the earrings and rubbing my already-tender earlobes.

"Uh-uh-uh," she chastens, and fastens them back on again. "A woman must be prepared to suffer for her beauty."

"Says who? Why are women even expected to be beautiful?" I say.

"Darling child, don't be tiresome. I do believe you rival your father in obstinacy."

"Speaking of Dad, have you decided about your vac job yet?" Meriel asks.

"No."

"And your career?"

I shake my head.

"Career!" Nana says dismissively. "Careers are for stout little typists with crooked teeth and bad skin who cannot net a man without being *efficient*." She shudders in delicate distaste, despite the fact she herself pursued a lifelong career.

"Perhaps you should run away and join the circus, Romy." Meriel's smiling eyes meet mine in the rear-view mirror.

"Don't tempt me," I mutter.

"I once met an acrobat from the circus. He could tumble the length of a cricket pitch and drink vodka while standing on his head. And he could bend in the most extraordinary ways when we … but, ah, here is Genna, waiting for us. *Sensibly* clad, as usual." Nana eyes Genna's beige slacks suit and comfortable shoes with deep disapproval.

Genna runs a home for orphaned and abandoned babies in the impoverished Cape Flats just outside of Cape Town. It's selfless, noble work, and I admire her for doing it even though I cannot comprehend why anyone would choose to spend their days wiping snotty noses and poopy bums. But then, all my sisters — except for Meriel — baffle me.

Half an hour later, while we're all tucking into our dinner at the restaurant, I try to explain it to Zeb.

"One way or another, all four of them have settled for suburbia and a little patch of land. It's like they stuck their heads above water, had a quick look around, and then sank back again to settle down. Their lives are all so … tame."

Together with a couple of our school friends, we're seated at a table as far from my parents as possible — I had to bribe a waiter to rearrange the name-cards to wangle it.

"Case in point: Marina," I say, pointing at my eldest sister with an asparagus spear.

Zeb glances over to where she sits with her husband and their three sulky children at the table next to my parents. Marina's a qualified marine biologist, but she stopped working when the first baby arrived, and never went back.

"I don't know," Zeb says. "She looks content. All your sisters do."

"*Content?* They used to be kickass."

My older sisters had seemed so exciting to me when I was a little kid — watching as they dressed up to go out nightclubbing, or snuck out of a window to date a boy Dad had forbidden. I had believed they could do anything, be anything. They'd seemed so vital and free, and now they just seemed stuck in dull, domestic lives.

"I want something different, something more," I say, breaking a stalactite of wax off the candle on the table and feeding it to the flame.

"Have you told that to your dad?" Zeb nods over to where my father stands behind a microphone at the front of the room, shuffling speech cards.

I groan.

My father taps the mike a few times to get everyone's attention and begins.

"Ladies and gentlemen, dear friends and family, Sally and I would like to welcome you here to celebrate the conclusion of our youngest daughter's schooling. When one door closes, as they say, another opens, and so it is time for Rosemary to venture out into the wide world."

"He says that, but he doesn't mean it," I whisper to Zeb. My chest is tight. There's no fresh air in this place.

"… to find her own path through the confusing highways and interchanges across the open vistas of life …"

Yeah right. My future is more like a narrowing tunnel than an open vista.

"… and her mother and I are confident that she will choose wisely …"

"Translation: we pray daily that she won't scare us stupid by trying anything new or different." I cross my arms and glare at the hollandaise sauce congealing on my plate.

"… pressed her for an answer, but Rosemary delights in surprises, so we don't yet know if she will opt for (a), a sensible business degree leading to a rewarding and satisfying career at that most impressive of corporations, Poseidon." He pauses here for laughter and applause. "Or, (b), a stimulating study of the ins and outs of marine creepy-crawlies." More polite laughter.

"I choose (c), none of the above," I mutter.

"Either way, my dear, we wish you all the best and congratulate you for the exemplary matric results which we are sure are headed your way. Ladies and gentlemen, please raise your glasses in a toast to Rosemary."

"To Romy!" everyone echoes. Except my father, who says, "To Rosemary!"

"Speech, speech, speech!" the general cry goes up and all faces turn expectantly to me.

I stand up but stay next to my seat. No way am I making a long speech at the microphone.

"Thank you all for coming and for your kind wishes. And

thanks to my parents for all their support during my years of educational imprisonment." Zeb snorts his drink out of his nose at that. "Today, my father recommended — again — the rewards of business and study, and my mother reminded me of the pleasure of working with family. Meriel, however, suggested I run away and join the circus."

"I was only joking!" Meriel shouts over the laughter.

"Nana, meanwhile, urged me to find a passionate prince before my hair turns grey."

"*I* was being perfectly serious," Nana retorts, and polishes off her glass of wine.

"I think … Well, I'm pretty sure, actually," I begin, and my father sits up straight, looking at me eagerly, "that I will only find my path by walking it myself." My father slumps back in disappointment. "So here's to legs!" I say, raising my glass of Coke.

Everyone around me cheers, and I sit down.

"Short and sweet," Zeb says.

"Just like you."

He taps his nose with his middle finger while giving me an evil look. The music starts up and people trickle onto the dance floor.

"Ah, never mind Romy, you'll figure it out sometime. Right now, though, it looks like your gran wants a word. See you later."

Zeb nags and drags the rest of our group onto the dance floor, and they begin moving self-consciously to the hits of the seventies — my parents' choice of music.

Nana, carrying two glasses of wine and shedding white feathers, walks over to me. Although her balance is unsteady, her gaze is as keen and perceptive as ever.

"Here, have a drink." Nana plants herself in Zeb's vacated chair and slides one of the glasses of wine over to me. "You're too young to be so sad, and I am too old to waste time in sobriety. Let us be gay!"

I laugh as she clinks glasses with me. "Nana, you know what that word means now?"

"I do, and I lament the loss of a wonderfully twinkly word. Drink up and tell me, what's the matter, my dear?"

"Nothing really. I mean," I puff out an irritated sigh, "somewhere kids are starving to death and villages are being bombed and sharks are having their fins cut off — so really, I'm fine. I have nothing to complain about. I'm probably just being a spoilt brat. I've got a good life, my parents haven't beat me, or starved me, or sent me to work in a sweatshop. They love me — I know that — they want what's best for me. But ..."

"But?" Nana leans over and studies me intently.

"But I feel trapped, locked in ... I want to live my life, Nana, not theirs! Is that so strange?"

"Ah."

"I mean, look at them." I gesture to where Marina, Cordelia, Genna, and Meriel sit chatting to my parents. "I'm young — I'm not ready to be an old woman yet."

"You feel restless," Nana says.

"I do. That's exactly what I feel."

"You crave adventure."

"Yes."

"And excitement."

"*Yes.*"

"And fun and drrrammah!"

"Well, not drama so much. But fun, yes. Definitely fun."

"And, love!"

"What?"

"I smell romance in your restlessness. A grand affair looms on your horizon!"

"Hardly," I reply, a little sourly.

"But there is a man, yes?"

"Well …" I dip my thumb into the hot melted wax of the candle, and peel off the milky fingerprint. "Sort of."

"*Sort of?* What a lukewarm, lily-livered response! You must reach out and snatch at love when it comes your way, sweet child. Grab it and hold on tight. It comes around so seldom!"

"Nana, you've been married five times," I point out.

"And I regret none of them. I loved them all. Such marvellous, handsome, dashing men. Though, perhaps, Arnold was not quite as appealing once he lost his hair, or Thomas his money, but there, one can't have everything. The point is, we all need love. And *you*, it seems, have a chance at it."

"I doubt he even remembers me — we only met once, and he was pretty pickled at the time."

"You could reintroduce yourself."

"I probably couldn't get close enough to talk to him." Even as I say the words, the thought of that business card in my wallet flashes through my mind.

"There is more than one way to talk, Romy. You have a lovely figure, a beautiful face, and eyes which are positively eloquent! You'll capture his attention, I guarantee it. Never," she clicks her fingers at a passing waiter for another glass of wine, "underestimate the power of body language, my dear."

Despite myself, I giggle.

"There — a smile — that's better. Now, about your future." She rubs her hands together like a mob boss planning a jewellery heist. "Nobody is holding a gun to your head. If you choose neither of the paths your parents have planned, they will be disappointed, yes, but —"

"That's putting it mildly."

"But one does not die from disappointment, Romy. Nor" — she fixes me with a knowing look — "from disapproval. The same cannot be said for boredom, however. Decide what *you* want to do, and do it."

"What about Dad?"

"Leave him to me. Rex has had his own way for too long. Let him be thwarted for once — it's character-building."

I look back at my family, sitting and talking contentedly together. Why isn't that enough for me? Why do I feel so different to them? I wipe a quick hand over my eyes.

"Romy, Romy, listen to me." Nana places her arthritic hands over mine and clasps them tightly. "Life goes by so quickly. Too quickly. Make sure you've lived a little before you die. Trust me, you get years and years to spend with your memories — it's a good idea to spend your youth creating some moments worth remembering."

"But what if —"

"If you fail, you fail. At least you will have lived! A life without risk is a life without passion and love. And a life without those, is a life without soul."

"Thank you, Nana." I lean over to hug her tightly, and kiss her soft, wrinkled peach of a cheek.

"Dry your tears, love. No one's appearance is improved by blotchiness. There. Now hear my last word on the subject. Laurence Olivier, who was a great actor, though a sadly disappointing lover, once told me: 'If you can dream it, you can become it,' but that was always a bit airy-fairy for me. I have always believed: if you can dream it, you can *begin* it. So that is my advice. Take the first step."

I give her hand a squeeze, grab my phone, and leave the stifling heat of the noisy restaurant. Outside the air is cool and tangy with the ocean smell of ozone. I thumb my phone on and enter the number imprinted onto my memory.

"Yeah?"

"This is Romy Morgan. Last week you offered me a job. If the offer's still open, I'd like to take you up on it."

CHAPTER II
THERE BE DRAGONS

I climb the few steps and knock tentatively on the door labelled *Star Room 1A, Cilla Swytch — Director*. The next door along is labelled *Star Room 1B, Britney Vaux*. Both rooms, along with a few offices, are located on the outside of one of three massive warehouses which dominate the film studio lot. The lot itself is an enormous operation located out on the flatlands near Cape Town International Airport.

No answer. I knock again, harder.

"Yeah?" barks a voice from inside.

"It's Romy Morgan, Miss —" Miss, Mrs, Ms? "Ms Swytch. You said I should come speak to you today?"

"Who?"

The door is flung open. I take in many things at once — the white stripe in Cilla Swytch's black hair, how much taller than me she is, the vivid red of her lipstick, and the large lizards perched on her shoulders. The one on her left shoulder fixes its beady eyes on me, opens its mouth wide, puffs up a spiky collar of spines, and hisses.

"Crap!" I take an automatic step backwards and tumble down to the ground. Embarrassed, I scramble to my feet, dusting the seat of my jeans.

"And who are you, now?"

"I'm Romy Morgan — here about the job?"

"Oh," she says, looking me up one side and down the other, "it's you. I hardly recognised you. Hang on, I'll just put my baby away. She bites."

She disappears back into the room, and peeking into it after her, I see her carefully lower the prehistoric-looking creature into a giant glass tank with a floor of coloured sand, and a bright light stuck on the side.

"There, my little chickabiddy," Cilla croons, replacing the screen lid on the tank and returning to me.

Warily, I eye the other creature still attached to her right shoulder.

"Relax, the male of the species is always less deadly. And he's a sweetie, aren't you?" She tickles the beard-like spines under his chin. "Here, give him a stroke."

I don't much feel like touching the thing — I'm quite attached to my fingers — but perhaps this is a test. I'd better not act like a wimp if I want her to give me a job.

"Nice lizard. Er, good boy," I say, stroking one finger down his rough back, towards his tail and away from his mouth.

"He's a bearded dragon, not a lizard. Oh look, he likes you."

The reptile raises a front hand — paw? — into the air and waves it in circles at me.

"Right, let's get to it, uh, what's your name again?" she asks.

"Romy Mor —"

"Right, Romy. We're due to start filming when the breakfast break ends — in precisely fourteen minutes. We can talk on our way to the sound stage."

"Yes, Ms —"

"Call me Cilla. I'm the director, not a school teacher."

She locks the door of the room behind her and marches off across the gravel at a rapid pace. I run to catch up, looking all around, hoping to catch a glimpse of Logan.

"What you see all around you is our lot. The fence keeps out press and other strays."

She points in the direction of the high perimeter fence topped with electrified wires. It's still early, not yet seven o'clock, but people swarm in all directions, carrying clipboards, megaphones, lights, cameras, and what look like sections of narrow railway tracks.

"Those are for the dolly, but you don't need to worry about the gadgets and gizmos, you're not going to be doing anything technical. You'll be a personal assistant."

We stride across the lot towards the other two warehouses which are labelled with giant signs — *Stage 2, Stage 3* — and have small golf carts and big trucks parked outside. People disappear into and emerge out of the warehouses' enormous sliding doors like bees at the opening of a hive.

I'm just about to ask who I'll be assisting, and how, when we come around the corner of the first warehouse, and I walk straight into a gigantic shark's head. The enormous jaws, at least a metre in diameter, are wide open, and the serried rows of sharp and bloody teeth are right in my face. I just manage to stifle my instinctual shriek. The muted whimper which escapes is drowned by Cilla's loud laugh.

"Fabulous, it's fabulous! Has it got horizontal motion?"

Now I see that the shark's head is on a high trolley, and that the back end of it is a mass of wires, switches and levers. A young man with a shaved head and tattooed arms stands beside it, holding a set of controls that resemble a video-game console. He wiggles a lever on the console and the shark thrashes its head from side to side.

"Fabulous!" Cilla repeats, stroking the head of the bearded dragon on her shoulder. Its eyes close in apparent bliss. "But you know what I'm going to say?"

"More blood?"

"More blood!"

She yanks me away from my fascinated inspection of the model.

"Amazing, isn't it? Kyle's a genius. Sad that animatronics is a dying field — so last century. We do almost everything with computer-generated graphics these days, but the actors find it useful to have something to act against."

"It's fantastic, and so lifelike!"

"We make magic here, Romy. Watch it, don't trip on those," she warns as we step over a tangle of electricity cables. I'm touched by her concern, but then she adds, "They're connected to my lights, and lights are expensive."

"Assistants come cheaper, I guess."

She frowns at me. "And they're easier to replace, so don't you forget it."

We step from the early morning sunshine into the cool gloom of one of the sound stages, and I stop in shock. The warehouse is gigantic — bigger than several aircraft hangars combined. A catwalk of complicated metal platforms and gangways runs overhead, mounted between massed banks of powerful lights and fat aluminium air-conditioning tubes. An orange crane, with arm extended to the domed ceiling, lifts a man on a platform up to the lights. Trolleys, tripods, rigging and cabling litter the floor, but what snags my gaze is an enormous, full-sized fishing trawler "parked" on the concrete floor of the warehouse in front of a vast lime-green wall. The sides of the trawler are encrusted with rust and printed with faded lettering. It looks amazingly realistic.

"Wow," I say, taking in the scene.

We walk up to the enormous boat, and Cilla leans forwards to inspect the decorative workmanship. A woman in paint-spattered overalls, who's sticking fake barnacles onto the trawler's sides, gives me a friendly, "Hiya."

"This is Romy, she's the new gofer," Cilla says.

"Hi," I say.

I make to shake hands, but the artist shows me that hers are covered in glue and paint. Then she reaches out and sticks a fake barnacle onto the back of my right hand before turning back to her work with a friendly, "Good luck!"

"Add a few mussels, and that rust needs more brown and less orange," Cilla says, and then she's on the move again. I sneak out a hand and tap the prow of the boat. It sounds oddly light and hollow.

"Moulded fiberglass," Cilla explains, indicating that I should follow her to a refreshment station at the far end of the warehouse.

On top of a trestle table is a hot-water urn, two coffee machines, rows of cardboard cups, a wide basket of muffins and donuts, a fruit and nut platter, packets of chips and sweets, and a few dozen bottles of mineral water. Plucking a small grape from a bunch in the fruit bowl, Cilla peels it and holds it up to the dragon's mouth between two of her blood-red nails.

"Here my little chickabiddy," she says in a sing-song voice.

The reptile snatches it up between his jaws and swallows it in a series of gulps which make his throat bulge unpleasantly.

I peel the barnacle off my hand and surreptitiously stick it on the underside of the table.

Cilla picks up the only porcelain coffee mug on the table — a green one as big as a cauldron and emblazoned with the words *She Who Must Be Obeyed* — fills it with coffee, and takes a large swallow of the steaming brew.

"What's a gofer?" I ask, rubbing at the residue of glue on my hand.

"You go for this and you go for that. Gofer." Cilla's sharp gaze scans the warehouse and fastens on a small mound of rocks covered in brilliantly coloured sea urchins and starfish. "Jake!" she barks. "I see you hiding there. Where are my storyboards?"

A man rises sheepishly from behind the rocky outcrop and calls back, "Coming right up, Cilla."

"I'm going to do some raking over the coals today — I can see it coming," Cilla says darkly. "If I don't check up on everything, things get out of control." To the man, she yells, "Well? What are you waiting for?"

The man runs off, stumbling against a large boulder and sending it rolling right at me. I leap aside before it can wedge me against the table, but Cilla stops it with the toe of her high-heeled shoe.

"Put it back where it belongs," she tells me. "And don't put out your back. Bend from the knees."

I grab hold of the huge rock and heave — but it's as light as a beach ball. I give a surprised laugh and turn to look at Cilla in wonder.

"It's all an illusion, Romy. But what an illusion it is!" She laughs loudly, a startlingly deep, throaty kind of cackle. "You realise that working here, seeing the magic, is going to spoil you for the real world? There's no going back once you've caught the fever of movies."

CHAPTER 12
ZIP YOUR LIP

"So what exactly will I be doing?" I ask Cilla Swytch.

Her eyes continue to rove over the organised chaos of the film set, on the lookout for any flaws, while she speaks.

"Right, let me spell it out for you, Romy. You are going to be his runner, fixer, local guide, his handler and wrangler, his general dogsbody and assistant. He wants mineral water from a secret spring in Switzerland, you find it for him. He wants a pillow stuffed with the feathers of a hundred baby eiders, you get it for him. He has an early call, you make sure he's woken up and on set in time. He needs sleep, you make sure he gets it. He needs new script pages, you fetch 'em. If he can't work his phone, make his coffee or wipe his ass, you do it for him. Understand?"

"I have to wipe his, uh, bum?"

"Not literally!" she eyes me like I'm nuts. "I mean, he's a handful, but he's not … mentally deficient. Is that the politically correct term for it these days? You've got to be so careful. Can't even call a moron a cretin anymore. They're all just ready to pounce on you."

"Who is?"

"The press, the public, all the little bottom-feeding, web-crawling trolls and self-appointed guardians of public morality who have nothing better to do! And that reminds me — don't let him tweet or post on Facebook unless it's been checked before he submits. And don't you post anything, either!" She glares down at me suddenly, as if I've just threatened to tell all. "Everything gets run by publicity first, *capiche*? Even better, let them write the posts for him. And when he goes out, he must have his bodyguards with him. But make sure they keep their distance when photos are being taken — those hulks beside him all the time make him look like a nervous mobster."

She pours the rest of her coffee down her gullet and thumps the empty mug back down on the refreshments table. "Bottom line, anything you can do to make his life easier, you do it. Because what makes his life easier, makes my life easier. Get the idea?"

I nod.

"Any questions?" she asks as we set off again.

"Uh, one or two." *Hundred.* But only one that I really care about. "Who is 'he' — the one whose assistant I'll be?"

I know who I hope it is, who I desperately *want* it to be, but she hasn't actually said his name yet.

"Who the hell have we been talking about all morning? Logan Rush, of course."

Yes! I want to punch the air, but I make myself give a cool nod.

"The last PA didn't last five days. He sure does go through them. Well, I guess he can't help how he looks. That's why I'm pinning my hopes on you, Missy. You seemed sensible and not too much affected by him last week. Able to think on your feet and keep your mouth shut. That's why I'm hiring you. But you are not to go falling in love with him, you hear me?"

"Sure."

She gives me a sharp, suspicious look.

"Of course not," I say, trying to cram conviction into my voice.

She still looks unconvinced.

"It would be impossible for me to fall in love with him." Because I already am.

"Are you gay?"

"No."

"Pity, pity. Well, watch yourself, because if I catch you going all weak at the knees for him, you're out. Though I strongly suspect that I'm wasting my breath — they all go weak at the knees *and* soft in the head around him," Cilla says sourly. "But I tell you this, he will not fall for you. So don't go breaking your heart or mooning after him. And — hear me on this one, Romy — if I catch you in his bed, you'll be out on your skinny ass faster than you can say chickabiddy."

She peels the skin off another grape with her sharp talons and feeds it to her scaly pet monster.

"Is *he* gay?" I can't resist asking, though I'd be willing to bet my legs against it.

"No he is not, young lady. Not that it's any business of yours."

Ha! Another of Zeb's ridiculous theories bites the dust.

Cilla narrows her eyes at me in disapproval. "Do you always speak this bluntly?"

"I guess I do."

"Well cut it out. I don't like it. *No one* likes a smart-mouthed assistant. Good PAs are seen and not heard."

I nod mutely.

"Just keep your eyes open and your mouth shut, and you'll find your feet soon enough." When we emerge back into the bright sunshine of the back lot, she tells me, "You'll have to smarten yourself up. You're not crew, so don't model your appearance on these clowns."

She rolls her eyes at two workers passing by. One carries a realistic-looking bundle of seaweed and the other a huge ship's steering wheel; both of them wear stained jeans and T-shirts. I run my hands over my own jeans, wondering if they're still dusty.

"Your jeans aren't smart enough, and those shoes will definitely have to go. Fugly doesn't begin to describe them. You can't be seen in public, near Logan Rush, looking like that. In fact, you can't be on my set looking like that."

"Like what?"

"Looking like a mundane, a rube, like one of those poor souls out there!" She flings an arm wide to gesture to the real world of ordinary people beyond the fence. "What are you aiming for — *au natural?* This is showbiz kid — glamour and glitz. We can't let the ugly show."

"I'm not ugly. And I like looking natural."

"Uh-uh!" She wags an admonishing finger at me. "Seen and not heard, remember? You're with the beautiful people now. People who," she casts a disparaging gaze at my face, "wear lipstick and pluck their eyebrows. If God wanted women to look natural, She wouldn't have invented tweezers and silicone and mineralizing powder. Looks matter — sad, but true."

"But, I'm not the one being filmed," I protest. "What difference does it make what *I* look like?"

"There'll be photos taken of him, and you may be in some of them. You reflect on this production. Besides, if I say it makes a difference, it makes a difference. Because what I say goes, *comprende*? Now will you do a makeover?"

"I don't really want to." Though I did really want a chance to be with Logan again.

"Life's full of tough choices."

"Okay, fine," I agree. "But I still don't see —"

"*Hush!*" she hisses at me so loudly that the bearded dragon flinches and starts bobbing his head in agitation. "What did I tell you about talking back? Just shut up and learn. And here's lesson one: anyone who argues with me is out! Understand?"

I bite my tongue to keep from giving her a piece of my mind as we crunch over the gravel back towards her room.

"Right, so we have a deal. What day is it today?"

"Friday."

"You spend today getting a makeover and you can start tomorrow, providing you clear the security check they'll run on you. Be here at six a.m. This Sunday is a break day. Stop by security before you leave today to get your photo taken, and go see Bob in payroll." She points to one of the office doors. "He'll sort out your paperwork and ID. Remind him to give you a key for Logan's room here on the lot."

She pauses to rifle in her handbag and withdraws a white badge with the word *ASSISTANT* printed on it.

"You can use this temporary ID until your personal one is ready. Here, put it on."

As I struggle with the catch on the back of the badge, the pin springs free of its clasp and stabs me in the thumb. A fat drop of blood wells up.

"And lose those effing hideous shoes. Get yourself some heels."

"Okay."

"No, I mean take them off. Now."

Reluctantly, I crouch down and remove my sneakers and socks. As I straighten up, Cilla snatches them out of my hands and tosses them to a passing lackey with the instruction to get rid of them.

I gasp in outrage. But when Cilla glares at me with a raised eyebrow, I mime zipping my lip, turning a key, and flinging it away. An evil smile twists Cilla's own lips, and she nods approvingly.

"You might just make it, kid," she says, spinning around and heading to the next warehouse.

I follow, stepping gingerly on the gravel surface of the lot. She cackles again. *Witch!* I think loudly as I hobble along silently in her wake of orders and warnings.

"If you piss him off, you're out. If you let the papz or the Rushers get him, you're out. If you let your brows grow back after you've plucked them, you are so out. If you let him eat or drink too much, you're out — we haven't shot all the shirtless scenes yet, and I need those abs cut and ripped."

CHAPTER 13
BLOODY HEELS

The white-coated, latex-gloved beautician arches an eyebrow at me and warns, "If madam is unable to stop screaming, we will have to ask madam to leave — the other clients in the salon are being disturbed."

"It hurts!" I yelp.

Ignoring this, she spreads another spatula of hot wax onto the tender flesh of my legs. I try to be brave, but when she rips the wax off, I can't suppress a squeal of pain — it feels like she's torn a strip of skin off with it. Amnesty and the United Nations should be notified of this kind of torture, because it must be in violation of international human rights.

"A woman must be prepared to suffer for her beauty." I repeat Nana's words silently to myself, hoping the mantra will get me through this makeover day or, as I've begun to think of it, Armageddon Friday.

"If madam would refrain from wincing and blinking when I pluck, then we can shape these eyebrows much quicker. There is a lot of growth to, er, prune." This time, the beautician's implement of torture is a pair of tweezers.

By the time she finishes scraping the skin all over my body with what she calls "a gentle and fragrant body exfoliation" and I call "a rough sanding down with vanilla-scented grit and gravel," I've surrendered — resistance is futile. I'm reduced to a whimpering, quivering mess. But I *am* a smooth and mostly hairless mess, and my eyebrows arch perfectly over my streaming eyes, so I figure Cilla would approve.

Next up is the full valet. I sometimes take my car through the automatic car wash in town, and this is a lot like that process. Showers of water hose me down from eight different angles — first screamingly cold, then blisteringly hot, then mind-numbingly cold again.

"Stop, please, I'll tell you what you want to know. Mercy. I surrender!" I cry uselessly against the cold white tiles.

Then like a car continuing its journey to sparkling completion, I'm buffed (dried), waxed (moisturised), and spray-painted (with instant tan), before I get the customized detailing — foundation, powder, eyeshadow, eyeliner, eyelash extensions, lipstick, and lip-liner in a long round of brushes, pencils, and confusing instructions.

I'll never get this right on my own.

The production line spits me out back in the salon's reception, where I'm relieved of a hefty chunk of my savings — being beautiful apparently doesn't come cheap — before being delivered into the hands of Zeb, who's promised to be my wingman through my right royal makeover. He compliments me so lavishly on my "improvement" that I wonder how long he's been holding himself back from commenting on my bushy brows and substandard grooming.

Zeb escorts me to my hairdresser then plants himself at a table in the coffee shop just outside — probably to make sure I don't make a dash for freedom — and enjoys a relaxing few hours eating cake, drinking *rooibos* chai, and surfing the Net while I'm subjected to more beauty treatments. Guys know nothing of suffering. Sitting with strands of my hair smothered in chemicals and wrapped in squares of tinfoil, I have a moment where I wonder what on earth I'm doing. And why. But then I find a magazine with a feature entitled *Log On to Logan*, accompanied by several pics of him that I've never seen before, and I'm happily distracted from the torments of my transformation.

After an age, the hairdresser declares me ravishing — I'll have to tell Nana that — and Zeb seems dead impressed, but I'm not at all sure I like the feathery style and blonde highlights. Or the heavier make-up, though I have to admit that my new brows are an improvement.

"I don't look like me," I complain.

"I think that's the point," Zeb replies.

"Can I have some ice for that burn?"

Next up is clothes shopping. Zeb keeps urging me try on and buy elegant, dressy clothes that I don't like and have never dreamt of wearing.

"They're not my style," I protest.

I no longer look like me, and I'm beginning not to feel like me either. Who is that young woman in the red dress I see reflected in the mirror?

"There's no point in merely buying more jeans and T-shirts," Zeb says, thrusting a silky, spaghetti-strap top through the cubicle curtains for me to try on. "She wants you to look different. Smarter, more stylish."

The lowlight of the day comes when we shop for shoes. Again, Zeb directs the operation, explaining, "Reluctant as I am to be a cliché, there is no doubt that I have better taste."

I merely nod, conceding the point. But, oh sweet mother of mercy, those shoes! Red as blood, sharp as knives, black as my language when I squish my feet into pair after pair of pointy-toed, killer-heeled torture devices.

"I can't walk in these — I can't even stand in them!"

This is literally true — every so often my ankles give in and I fall off the heels. All around me, women strut their stuff confidently, trying on heels as high as mine, or even higher, but I can only manage a wobbly shuffle.

"It just takes some practice," Zeb says.

He says it with such confidence that I cast him a suspicious look.

"How do you know? What makes you the expert?" I challenge.

"I'm not a cross-dresser, Romy!" he says, throwing a silky stocking at me.

It's enough to make me flounder and lose my balance.

When I've bought almost more than we can carry, Zeb finally calls time.

I groan in relief and slip my sneakers back on. On the drive back to my place, I dream of putting up my sore feet and sipping on something long and cool. No such luck — Nana meets us at the front door, gives Zeb an exaggerated wink, and leads me to the long passage that runs almost the full length of our house.

"Time to learn how to walk. Shoes on, please," she says.

"My shoes are on."

"Those" — she points at my comfy sneakers — "are not shoes. They are athletic equipment. Put on the heels, please."

Grumbling, I put on a pair of the dagger heels. Nana instructs Zeb to put a book on my head. He has to do it again at least fifty-seven more times in the next hour as Nana makes me walk up and down the passage, and sit and rise from a chair, all while balancing the wretched thing on my head.

"It helps your posture," Nana says. "Head up, chin back, bust out, tummy in, buttocks tucked under."

Occasionally she gives my shoulders or my butt a sharp rap with her pearl-handled walking stick. I'm grateful that she only has the stick to whack me with, and not a walker.

"Don't shuffle, Romy, float. Glide like a swan. I said *swan*, not duck!"

Eventually they're satisfied, or perhaps they just know a lost cause when they see it, but they leave me with my tower of parcels and my new face. I close the front door behind Zeb and kick the stilettos off my aching feet, grumbling to myself that high-heeled shoes are like a modern version of Chinese foot-binding. Then I remember what I'll be doing tomorrow, who I'll be seeing. If crushed and blistered feet are the price, I'll pay it. And perhaps I'd better work on suppressing my winces and whines, because tomorrow I'm due on set at sparrow's fart, and there'll be no complaining allowed then, no voicing of my own opinions. Cilla Swytch spelled that out clearly enough.

I limp back to the living room and collapse into the nearest chair. It's a good one, too — my father's enormous recliner, complete with headrest, extending foot rest, and built-in back massager. I fiddle with the controls and sigh in deep pleasure as the chair lifts and lengthens and cradles my battered body and blistered feet.

I've been waxed, buffed, plucked, dyed, tanned, highlighted, cut, curled, mani'd, pedi'd, steamed, exfoliated, masked, and moisturized. I can now stand, and even walk, in ridiculously high-heeled shoes. I'm smoother, browner, blonder, and softer. And I'm exhausted. Right now, I plan to do nothing more than binge-watch reruns of *Glee* on Netflix.

But the sound of keys in the front door ends that plan. Dad's home.

As soon as he enters the room, he notices my transformed appearance.

"Rosemary? What have you done to yourself?"

"It's called a makeover." Aah, what the hell, I may as well break the news now. "It's for my vac job. I'm starting tomorrow on the film set of *Beast: Stars*," I say.

And he explodes.

"What do you mean you're starting on a film set?"

"I've got a job, Dad, on the set of a movie."

"You've already got a job — with your mother or with me!"

"Yes, but this is a job I actually want." More than anything.

I need to get out of the chair — I don't like being at such a height disadvantage — but the controls aren't doing what I want them to do. I struggle with the lever that's supposed to drop the foot rest, but instead of putting my feet on the ground, it lifts them higher into the air and drops the headrest further down. I'm practically upside down.

"What job?" His eyes narrow to slits as he looms over me. "As an actress?"

I snort. "Hardly." Giving up with the controls, I clamber out over the side of the recliner. "I'll be a runner — a general assistant to … one of the cast."

"You're going to run around, assisting, in those?" He points at the high-heeled shoes lying on the carpet.

He has a point, but I ignore it.

"It will be a great work experience, Dad. I'll learn all sorts of new skills, get to know a really interesting industry, make some good money —"

"I'll pay you twice what they're offering," he says quickly.

"Dad, it's not about the money. It's a once-in-a-lifetime opportunity!"

Even though I speak loudly, I can tell my words aren't getting through. His jaw is set, and his bottom lip protrudes as it does whenever he's opposed.

"I forbid it!"

"You're kidding, right? You're going to do … what? Lock me in my room? I'm eighteen, not eight. I start early tomorrow."

"Who starts work on a Saturday?"

"Time is money — isn't that what you always say?" I retort. "See? I'm already learning about the world of work."

"Beast … Beast …" He looks suddenly suspicious. "Aren't those the movies with that fellow in them, the actor you fancy?"

Careful now. "I had a schoolgirl crush on him, yes," I say, thankful that on the rare occasions my father comes into my room, his attention is always so captured by the provocative protest posters that he never much notices the Logan Rush wardrobe shrine. "But I don't even know the guy, or him me. We move in different planetary systems." I make independent orbiting motions with my hands.

Dad glowers at me, planning his next move. I know, from years of experience, my father's five-step process for conquering rebellion and resistance. He's already zoomed through shock, denial, angry outrage and bargaining. Next will be emotional manipulation.

His face takes on a benevolent expression as he sits down on a sofa and pats the seat next to him

"Rosemary, my love, come sit here with your father."

"S'okay, thanks, I can hear you from here."

A spasm of irritation crosses his face before he gets his expression under control again.

"You know your mother and I love you dearly, and we want only the best for you," he says, the epitome of gentle reason and loving kindness.

"I know that, Dad, but we disagree on exactly what that is."

"Family and tradition, that's what we hold dear. And in this family, our tradition *is* family."

"Huh?"

"We're sea folk, Rosemary. Your mother and Meriel study it, Cordelia and I buy and sell it, Marina volunteers at the Penguin Rescue Centre. We've all made the sea our lives — we may as well have fish tails."

"What about Genna? She works at an orphanage."

"The *Little Fishes* orphanage."

I give a disgusted snort. "You're reaching, Dad."

"The point is, they've all stayed close to home."

"The point is, I'm not them. I'm different. I need to get out and see the world."

"Haven't we given you enough right here? Do you dislike us so much that you can't stand to be with us? Don't you love us, Rosemary?"

Uh-uh, no way is he going to manipulate me into the usual outcome of our arguments: guilty capitulation rewarded by gracious fatherly forgiveness.

"Dad, I love you, but you're being a bit silly now. I'm not leaving home. I'm just going to work on a film set. And who knows? You may be right — I may be nuts. Maybe it'll be a lot of hard, boring work, and I'll get it out of my system and settle down into the family way next year."

"The 'family way,'" he repeats, sounding horrified.

"I'm not going to get pregnant, Dad!" I snap. "I mean the family business."

"But, the *movies*, Rosemary. Honestly!"

"I don't see how a world that makes such amazing magic can be all bad."

I kiss him on the forehead, pick up my shoes and packages, and walk towards the door. But Dad is still stuck on step five.

"I'm disappointed in you, Rosemary."

"I'm sorry you feel that way," I say.

I'm not, though.

I'm nervous, excited, scared, and only the teensiest bit guilty. But not sorry at all. There's a looseness in my shoulders that feels like relief, and a lightness in my chest that whispers of freedom and fun ahead.

CHAPTER 14
FLOUNDERING

The next morning, just as dawn breaks over the flat silhouette of Table Mountain, I present myself at the main entrance to the film studios. A guard at the security checkpoint takes my name, verifies it with someone on his walkie-talkie, then opens the gate and shows me where to park.

"Someone is coming to fetch you," he says.

I wait, wondering what the day will hold. I have almost no idea what my duties will be, but I've armed myself with my new face and hair and clothes, a clipboard, three pens, a multi-tool, a fully-charged phone and backup battery pack, and a small cosmetics purse filled with my newly purchased lipstick, blusher and mini-brush. And a roll of breath mints — just in case.

A red-haired young woman, perhaps in her mid-twenties, beetles over to me in a golf cart.

"Are you Romy? Mr Rush's new personal assistant?" she says in an American accent.

"Yes, hi."

"I'm Becka." She shakes my hand and indicates for me to take the seat next to her. "Polyp sent me."

"Who?" I ask, as we set off with a lurch down the road that leads to the warehouses.

"Cilla's PA His name is Phillip, but we call him Polyp."

"Why?"

"You'll understand when you see him. Here's your ID."

She hands me a new photo-identification badge which I pin to my shirt.

"Hey, when I say we call him Polyp, I don't mean to his face. So don't make that mistake!"

"Noted."

"I guess Polyp's too important to give you the grand tour himself. He told me to show you the ropes, but I'm sorry, it'll have to be really quick. Britney's in make-up now, but as soon as she's out, she'll have me hopping."

"Britney? Britney Vaux?"

At that precise moment, it strikes me — I'm really here, on the set of the latest *Beast* movie. I'm going to meet megastar Britney Vaux. I'm going to see a bunch of other famous actors in action. And I'm going to be spending my days with Logan Rush. *The* Logan Rush.

"The one and only." There's something sour in Becka's tone as she says this.

"Are you her —"

"Yup, I'm her chore-whore."

Torn between a gasp and a giggle, I say nothing. Cilla would approve.

"Here we are." Becka parks the buggy and climbs out. "Come, this way."

She sets a cracking pace across the lot, pointing out the various departments I'll need to know. She's tall and rangy, and I have to hustle to keep up with her, particularly as I'm wearing heels. So is she. I'm pretty sure this can't be industry practice — there must be a reason PAs are called *runners*, after all. The heels must be one of Cilla's cruel idiosyncrasies. I fervently hope she doesn't have any more.

"These" — Becka points at the three massive warehouses — "are our sound stages. Most of the shooting takes place in them, except when we're on location. Pay office," she says, gesturing to the room where I filled out half-a-dozen forms yesterday. "That's where you submit your time sheets, and they'll explain about expenses and reimbursement. The canteen is that way. They make fantastic choc-chip cookies, but their coffee's poison. Rather get your caffeine fix from the machines on the catering tables inside the sound stages. Officially, breakfast is between five and seven, and lunch between noon and one-thirty. But be prepared to grab something when you can and eat on the run, because they keep us hopping in this job. Well, Logan's not as bad as Britney. I mean," she adds in an afterthought, "who is?"

"Is she difficult to work for?"

I don't care, truth be told. I'm much more interested in Logan, but don't know how to ask about him without sounding like I'm already everything Cilla warned me against becoming — infatuated, obsessed, besotted.

"Oh, she's a real princess, alright. Here we are — first stop: *Hair and Make-up*."

She yanks open the door of another of the rooms at the back of the sound stage, and we walk into the air-conditioned coolness. Large mirrors, each bordered with rows of blue light bulbs as well as fluorescent lights, hang at regular intervals along the length of two of the walls. Black, barbershop-style chairs are set in front of the mirrors, and against the far wall are two chairs backed by hairdressing basins.

The huge fishing tackle boxes which perch on counters below the mirrors, overflow with cotton-wool and cotton-buds; bottles, tubs, tubes and colourful palettes; make-up brushes as big as feather-dusters, as small as toothpicks, and every size in between. Baskets filled with combs, hairbrushes, tongs, dryers and flat-irons are wedged into the corners. And a tall rack of shelves is crammed with wigs, false eyelashes, silicone nails, flesh-coloured bits of "skin," a few bulbous false noses, and silicone bags that could only be for padding bras.

A handwritten sign stuck on the wall between two mirrors reads:

The impossible we do at once. Miracles may take a little longer!

"Let me introduce you to the miracle workers — Lindy, Mindy, and Ed," Becka says.

I greet the man and two women who're all working on the face, hair and nails of a blonde woman reclining in one of the chairs. The man positions a tool resembling a medieval torture device on her lashes, and clamps down hard.

"Becka? Is that you?" the woman says.

"Yes, Miss Vaux. Something I can get for you?"

"A skinny soy latte. And did you find the wheatgrass, Becka?"

"On it, Miss Vaux."

"This year, Becka?"

"Yes, Miss Vaux." To me, Becka says, "We need to keep

moving. But remember where this room is — you'll have to take and fetch Logan every day."

"Can't he find the way himself?"

"Honey, sometimes I don't know how the stars find their own noses to blow. But, no, it's more to make sure he gets there and back on time. This way, I'll take you to his room."

I swallow. This is actually happening.

"For some reason, he wanted the one farthest away. Likes his privacy, I guess. Britney's room is next to Cilla's. They all overnight at the hotel — the Cape Majesty for stars and PAs, though not you because you're local — and then get transported by courtesy bus to and from the set every day. But they like to have a place to crash between scenes. Around there, at the back of Stage 2, is the viewing room. That's where they watch the rushes — the day's filming," she clarifies, catching my puzzled expression. "Hey, you don't happen to know where I can get fresh wheatgrass, do you, for smoothies?"

"There's a health bar on the Waterfront. I'm pretty sure they could help you."

"Excellent! Her highness has been kvetching about that grass for days now. I know twenty-two places I could source it in L.A., but I don't know this town."

"I hope Mr Rush doesn't ask for too many odd things."

"Ah, he's a sweetie, not too demanding, just kinda helpless, you know? And he needs to be hustled along, because he dawdles, and that drives Cilla crazy. Be thankful you're not *her* PA. She's a total control freak. Now Britney positively enjoys being demanding and difficult. I've got to do *everything* for her — well, except going through her lines. She's got some freakish kind of memory thing going on there. Only needs to read or even hear a line once and it's memorized. But she makes me do everything else, including forging her autograph on stacks of photos for fans. Do you know — oh, special effects and animatronics are that way, beyond the pay office — that in June, when her dog got cancer, I had to take him to the vet to get him put down, then find a place that would cremate him and turn the ashes into a diamond?"

"You're kidding me?"

"I am not. Some days she wears him in a ring on her little finger, and acts like a deeply grieving dog widow. As if! She hardly knew that dog. A little Chihuahua called Bugeye. I had to walk him and play with him. Once she called me at two in the morning to come clean up where he'd been sick on the stairs of her house. This here is Stage 3. But she loved having her picture taken with it. Good for her image — the public are such saps for dogs. When it died, I had to hunt around for another dog that looked just like it."

"Logan also has a dog," I say, pleased that I know something about my star, too. "It's a beagle called Toffee."

"Oh? Never seen it — wonder where he keeps it? Right, here we are."

She thumps on a door at the back of the third warehouse labelled *Star Room 3A*. The nameplate beside the door states: *The Beast*.

There's no reply.

"Why is his different? I mean, everyone else has their name, but he has the movie title."

Becka shrugs and knocks again. "It's like he *is* the Beast, isn't he?"

"Well, no. I mean, he's Logan Rush — the actor who *plays* the Beast."

"Same diffs. Either way he's supposed to be in hair already. You better go on in and bring him out."

"Me?"

"*You're* his PA, not me. Go on," she says, giving my back a little push, "you got this."

CHAPTER 15
RUSH HOUR

I knock again on Logan's door and, when there's no answer, open it and step inside.

"Mr Rush?"

At once, I glimpse him at the back of the room. Sticking my head back outside, I tell Becka, "He's asleep. Now what?"

"Now you wake him up — stat! His call time is eight a.m. He must have crashed after they dropped him off this morning. Here are his call sheets for today and tomorrow. Good Luck! You can expect to feel like a fish out of water for a few days, but if you're seriously not dealing, give me a shout. My best advice: just think on your feet and figure it out as you go along, but always, *always*, act like you know exactly what you're doing. And remember, when it comes to the stars and Cilla, there's no such thing as 'no.'"

She shoves some papers into my hand and strides off, already talking into her cell phone.

Back in Logan's room, I take a moment to look around as my eyes adjust to the dim interior light. To my left is a compact kitchenette complete with fridge, microwave, minibar and cupboards. A set of blue dumbbells and a Pilates stretch-band sit on top of a round dining table ringed by four matching chairs. I walk silently over the Persian carpet to the middle of the room, where a long leather couch and paper-strewn coffee table face a huge, flat-screen television, with a DVD-player, iPod docking station, hi-fi with Bose speakers, and a PlayStation nestling in the shelves beneath.

The bedroom area is at the far end of the space — complete with four-poster bed, a narrow desk with leather office chair, and a free-standing wardrobe flanking the doorway to a bathroom. I peek inside. Black tiles, white porcelain, fluffy towels and a fair-sized shower.

Wow. I could *live* in a room like this.

As if they've saved the best for last, my feet carry me over to the bed. It's huge, with creamy drapes twined around the posts, and a mosquito net knotted above. And in the centre of this princely bed, sleeps Logan Rush.

He's curled into a C on his side, his face smooshed into a hand tucked under his head, and his other arm flung back behind him. He's wearing jeans and a white T-shirt, and his hair is tousled and slightly damp, as if from a recent shower. I must *not* think about Logan Rush in the shower.

"Um, Mr Rush? Logan?"

He mumbles something but doesn't move. I lean over and give him a gentle shake. His shoulder is hard beneath my fingers.

"Mr Rush? You need to wake up. You're supposed to be having your hair and make-up done already."

He opens one eye and peers sleepily at me.

"What's that?"

"You need to wake up. Quickly. We" — ooh, I like the sound of that word — "we need to get you to hair and make-up."

"Right. Yeah. Sorry, must have drifted off."

He rubs a hand over his eyes and yawns widely, then looks up at me with more focused eyes. Blue eyes. With a dark rim.

"Do I know you?" He frowns.

"I'm Romy."

"Romy. Romy," he tests the name, looking confused. "No, doesn't ring a bell. But there's something about you. Hmm … Did we … Are we …?"

"No! I'm just your new PA."

"Oh, that's a relief."

I don't know whether to be amused or offended. I opt for feeling flattered instead. He clearly doesn't recognise me at all after my makeover. Obviously, I look nothing like that bare-faced, wet-haired, bespectacled girl from a week ago.

Or maybe he doesn't remember much from that alcohol-fuelled night, period. Should I help him connect the dots? Rather not — there's no real reason to mention it, plus he might be embarrassed to learn that his new PA has witnessed him blind drunk, scared stupid, and bizarrely obsessed with shoes.

"Gimme a moment, will you?" Logan yawns again, stretches, and rakes a hand through his hair. One stubborn black lock immediately flops back across his forehead.

"Okay, but … um … you're already running late. And Cilla —"

"Sure, sure."

When he swings his long legs over the side of the bed and makes for the loo, I scurry outside, where I frown at the *Beast* nameplate until he emerges a few minutes later, wiping his dripping face on his arms. I set out at a brisk pace, but I'm soon walking alone — Logan's top speed seems to be a leisurely amble. I pause and try to make sense of the call sheet now clamped to my clipboard while I wait for him to catch up.

We set off again — together this time and more slowly — towards the make-up department. I'm hyper-aware of him next to me. Six foot one is taller than I imagined.

"So," he asks, "What happened to the other girl? Cayleigh? Caitlin?"

"I don't know. Cilla hired me yesterday."

"Ah, Cilla," he says, as if this explains everything. He stretches his arms behind his back, and cracks his neck. "And you're Romy?"

He still seems a little puzzled. Maybe a memory of me is tugging at the back of his mind.

"I am. Here we are."

I open the door to the hair and make-up room, and Logan trudges inside.

"Logan!" Britney Vaux says brightly, flashing a smile of teeth so white they're almost blue. "Here you are!"

"Here I am."

"Finally," Ed mutters, "the star of the show arrives."

"*One* of the stars." Britney's smile turns tight and brittle.

"Have you been sleeping on your face, again?" Ed asks Logan. "You're going to need the Extreme Makeover edition today. Look at those bags under your eyes! Where's my haemorrhoid cream?"

Haemorrhoid cream? Precisely what part of Logan do they intend filming?

Ed catches my expression and explains, "It's an old trick of the trade. Tightens the skin under the eyes."

"If you say so."

Logan sinks into a chair in front of one of the brightly lit mirrors, closes his eyes, and leans back to receive Ed's ministrations.

"What time should I collect him? He's due to film at" — I consult the call sheet — "eight a.m."

"We'll be done in an hour," Ed says.

"Can I get you some tea or coffee, Mr Rush?" I ask.

"Please, call me Logan. Everyone does."

Logan grins at me in the mirror, and for a few moments I stand like an idiot staring back at him, struck dumb and immobile by the wonder and wattage of that smile. Sweet mother of all things beautiful, but he's hot.

Ed clears his throat loudly. Jerked out of my daze, I see that Lindy and Mindy are watching me with knowing, pitying smiles.

I run to the sound stage refreshment station, but I'm brought up short by the bewildering array of options on the hi-tech coffee machine. Filter coffee? Espresso? Cappuccino? Americano, Turkish, Viennese, Jamaican — it's like a United Nations of coffee beans. Maybe one of the reasons movie stars are so pernickety is that they're given way too many choices.

I settle for a double shot of espresso and a separate cup of filter coffee. I'll finish off whichever one he doesn't want — I could use a charge of caffeine. I know from our meal in the hotel coffee shop that he takes his coffee black, but I toss some packets of sugar and artificial sweetener in a paper bag to be safe. Maybe he'll want a snack, too? I add a giant blueberry muffin and a glazed donut to the bag and then, Cilla's strictures about shirtless scenes ringing in my head, chuck in a low-calorie protein bar for good measure.

Back inside the hair and make-up room, Mindy — or perhaps it's Lindy — is slathering Logan's hair with styling mousse and pulling it into a high, emo-vampire style at the front.

I catch Logan's eye in the mirror and hold up first one and then the other cup. "Espresso or filter?"

"Espresso. Tell me it's a double."

"It's a double." I hand him the cup and fish the paper packets out of the bag. "Sugar or white death?"

"Neither, just as it comes."

"Delicious pastries or chemicals not worth eating?" Again, I weigh the two offerings in my hands.

Pulling a face, he reaches for the protein bar. He downs the espresso in two gulps, shudders, and sighs. "Ah, you're an angel, thank you, Romy."

I can feel a blush rising. Not wanting him, or either of the two sharp-eyed make-up ladies, to notice, I quickly exit the room with a casual, "See you in thirty minutes," and set off to sort out the one item I've already written on my to-do list.

CHAPTER 16
UP AND RUNNING

Half an hour later, I've completed my errand and I return to collect Logan. I'm not generally into guys wearing make-up, but he looks fabulous — the subtle make-up enhances his eyes like nobody's business. If Zeb was here, he'd change his crush, no question. With my inexpertly applied eyeshadow and blusher, I feel like a clown beside Logan. Maybe I can get the miracle workers to give me a few lessons sometime?

My star's next stop is the wardrobe department. Hanging on the rail marked with his name are five of every single item of clothing — duplicates, in case the costumes get damaged while filming, I guess.

After his fitting, I try to hurry Logan to the sound stage, but he never moves faster than an unhurried stroll. All his movements — and I *am* very aware of all his movements — are leisurely, almost lazy, yet somehow we make it to the set with thirty seconds to spare before his official call time. Britney's already waiting with Becka beside her.

Cilla, who's inspecting the fake boat, checks her watch as Logan and I arrive, and nods at me. Logan grabs a canvas chair and drops his long frame into it. It's eight o'clock — any second now they'll start filming his scene and I'll finally get to see Logan in action. I stand a little behind his chair, fidgety with anticipation.

For the next forty-five minutes, nothing happens.

I mean, Cilla barks orders at her minions: the cameramen fiddle with different positions and angles; lighting specialists adjust the illumination of the body doubles who stand on set in place of Logan and Britney; sound technicians rig up a microphone on a boom; and the set artist makes touch-ups to the boat. But not a frame is filmed.

Trying to make good use of the down time, I perch on a stool next to Logan, run through a list of questions to check all his preferences, and ask whether he has any special requests.

"Just some chipotle-smoked barbeque ribs, a little N'Orleans jazz for my iPod, a Dr Pepper and a couple of Moon Pies, the Atlanta Daily Mail every morning, and a big tub of Ben and Jerry's Caramel Walnut Fudge — but you'll need to remove the bits of nut. I like the taste they give the ice cream, but not the feel of them in my mouth. You can just pick 'em out by hand."

I can feel my eyes growing wide — I have no idea what half those things are, let alone where to get them.

Then Logan winks at me, slowly and deliberately. "Only kidding. Though I wouldn't say no to a bottle of water."

It takes me only half an hour to realise that I've landed on easy street. Apart from the joy to be had from simply staring at Logan — how his lips move when he says "Dr Pepper" and "bottle," the way his fingers run through his raven hair and his eyes crinkle at the corners when he laughs — I also discover he's friendly, polite, and completely reasonable in his requests.

Cilla, on the other hand, keeps her assistant, Phillip, hopping. As soon as I see him, I understand why the crew calls him Polyp — he's short and slight, peculiarly colourless, and has an elongated, stalk-like neck above which his pale face seems to float. He scampers about fetching and carrying for Cilla, screening phone calls, and plying her with vitamins. At least, I *think* they're vitamins.

While Cilla and the chief cameraman debate whether to use a pan or a tilt in the opening shot, Polyp sidles up to me so silently that I jump when he speaks into my ear.

"You're the local girl?" he whispers, standing too close.

"Yes."

"Do you know where I can source baby crickets?"

"I beg your pardon?"

"Or fly larvae, or butter-worms?" His breath is unpleasantly hot in my ear.

I only hope my face shows confusion rather than revulsion. "I'm sorry, I don't ..."

"For the chickabiddies. They need protein!"

"Ohhh. No, I'm sorry, I've never needed to buy *goggas*."

Now he's confused.

"Sorry, *goggas* are insects. Perhaps you could try a pet shop in town?"

When he creeps away, I resist the urge to wipe my ear on my shoulder.

Poor Becka doesn't have a moment's peace from Britney.

"Becka, where's my Chinese weight-loss antioxidant herbal green tea?"

"Becka, Charlie hasn't called yet. Make it happen, will ya?"

"Becka, fetch someone from wardrobe. They've taped my boobs up too tight again."

They tape up boobs?

"Becka, fetch my bag from my star room, will you?"

"No, I meant the other bag."

There's an awkward moment before filming starts when Britney tries to rope *me* into running errands for her, too.

"Ronnie," she says, looking at me, "just run along to the writing department and get my new pages for tomorrow, will you? Becka's gone AWOL again. I swear I don't know how I put up with her!"

"Um …"

I don't know what to say. I have a feeling that if I do this one thing, it'll be the start of me running for her, too. But Becka's instructions had been clear: no saying 'no.' And Cilla had told me to keep my mouth shut and not talk back. I'm about to cave when Logan rescues me.

"'Fraid I can't let you have my PA, Britney. I need her by my side all the time."

My heart goes warm and fuzzy at this, but then he adds, "For my exclusive use, at my beck and call, twenty-four seven."

I open my mouth to protest — though, to be honest, being at Logan's side 24/7 sounds like something I'd like. A lot. But Logan tips his head back at me and, with the eye that Britney can't see, winks again.

This time, I wink back. I do. I wink at Logan Rush! I want to run around giggling and squeeing, but I play it cool. Perhaps there might be a future for me in acting after all.

"Right, clear the doubles. Places, please," somebody calls.

The technicians and operators take up positions behind their equipment, Lindy gives Logan's face a final dusting of powder, and Mindy reapplies Britney's lipstick. Cilla settles herself in a chair behind a small video monitor streaming the feed from the cameras.

Logan and Britney walk to the trawler and stand on the small crosses of masking tape stuck to its deck. The lights dim, and suddenly it's as if the two are standing on a real boat in the middle of a moonlit ocean. Apart from the bright green screen behind them, that is.

"Picture up!" the assistant director yells.

Logan cricks his neck one last time, and Britney practises pouting and smiling.

"Quiet, please!"

It's as though a spell is cast over everyone. Front of camera or behind, cast or crew, everyone goes still and silent. A thrill of excitement ripples through me. In this dark space of make-believe, anything is possible. Anything could happen. In the next moment, a story will be brought to life, something enchanting will be crafted — not analysed or researched, or bought or sold — but *created*. I lean forward, holding my breath

The roll call of mysterious signals sounds across the stage.

"Roll sound!"

"… sound speed."

"Roll camera!"

"… speed."

An assistant holds an electronic clapper board with *Scene 27, Take 1* on its red display in front of Logan and Britney. She snaps the clapper shut and ducks out of the shot.

"Action — background!"

A few extras, playing sailors on the boat, start moving about, silently pulling in a net and cranking a winch handle. The boat rocks gently. Looking down, I see that the hull is cradled in a complicated piece of machinery designed to simulate wave action. A gentle breeze from the wind machine ruffles the actors' hair. Britney adjusts herself so that her hair blows back from her face, rather than onto her lipstick.

"And … action!" Cilla calls.

And it begins.

Logan's unhurried chill has totally evaporated — he's now the tense, terse, primed-for-action man that is Chase Falconer. He grabs Britney by the arm and says urgently, "We *have* to do it, you know that. We can't let them get away!" There's no trace of his Southern accent in his voice.

"But, Chase, you could be killed!" Britney's face is softer, kinder, more animated than it is in real life, and her voice is huskier.

"That's a risk I'll have to take. If I don't stop them, it'll be a massacre."

"Oh, Chase, don't go!"

Britney throws herself into his arms and hugs him tightly.

It's magical. I forget that I'm in a largely empty warehouse; that the boat, the wind, and the moonlight are all fake; that the two people in front of me are actors rather than lovers in mortal peril. It's gripping and intense — more vital, in some crazy way, than my real life back at home. I'm utterly absorbed and enthralled.

"Cut!" Cilla yells harshly, breaking the spell.

Logan (all at once Logan again), and Britney ("Becka, water!") turn expectantly towards her.

"Not bad, let's do it again. But on the embrace, push your hips together for more intimacy," Cilla says, smacking her hands together and pressing hard to demonstrate the intense level of pelvic smooshiness required.

"Places, please," the assistant director yells, and the whole process starts over.

They film several takes of the scene. Each time I learn a little more of the craft and science behind the illusion. And each time it's a little less captivating for me. I have no idea how the actors can say the same lines over and over again and still keep it fresh, but they do. Even Britney — credit where it's due — never sounds rehearsed or forced or bored.

After the twelfth take, Cilla calls a break. I'm sure they've finally captured the scene, but it's only to reset the lights, and change the camera and mike setups. Logan dozes in his chair, and Britney orders Becka to give her a neck massage while they wait. And then they film the scene all over again, first from over Logan's shoulder, with the camera focused in close-up on Britney, and then the other way around. It takes over three hours to shoot a scene which lasts, in real time, maybe two minutes.

"Well, now that you've seen your first scene, what do you think of moviemaking?" Logan asks me when they finish.

"I think it's one-part action and three-quarters hurry-up-and-wait."

CHAPTER 17

RULES OF THE GAME

Finally, the assistant director calls the lunch break, and most of the cast and crew troop off in the direction of the canteen.

"Do you mind bringing my lunch to my room? I've got some calls I need to make," Logan asks me.

"Sure. What would you like?"

"Anything, as long as it's high in protein, and low in carbs. If there's steak, I take it medium rare."

Less than fifteen minutes later, I'm back at Logan's room, food in hand. He's on his bed, surrounded by papers, talking on the phone.

"Will they consider me at least?" Logan asks whoever's on the other end of the line.

I search the cupboards in the kitchenette for a table setting, transfer the steak and salad from their polystyrene container to the plate, place the sachet of low-fat salad dressing and a pair of salt and pepper shakers beside it, and pour mineral water into the glass.

"I'm 'too commercial'? How is that possible? What does it even mean?"

I wave to get Logan's attention and show him the food. Then I tap my watch, mouthing, "Two o'clock," point a thumb back in the direction of the sound stage, and make to leave. But Logan holds up a hand to stall me.

"Ah, for Pete's sake! Work on them, Nick, wear them down. I want this one. I'm right for it, I can do it … Yeah, sure … Chat later. Bye."

He tosses the phone onto the bed and strolls over to the table. "Looks great. Thanks."

"Sure. I'll come fetch you just before two, okay?"

"Wait." He takes my arm. His fingers are hot where they touch me, and when his hand falls away, my skin tingles a protest at the absence.

"I noticed my nameplate — the one outside — has been changed to *Logan Rush*. Was that your doing?"

"Uh-huh." I wonder if I've made a mistake.

"Thank you," he says, tilting his head a little. "That was real thoughtful."

"Sure, uh, no problem." The words stumble on their way out my mouth. "It's just a little reminder — people seem to get confused between you and the character you play."

"Sometimes I do, too."

"Right."

"Join me for lunch?"

"No. I mean, thanks, but I don't think I'm supposed to fraternize with the cast. I've got …" I lift the bacon and brie baguette I got from the canteen for myself.

"Come on, sit yourself down. We'll share. If y'all don't tell Cilla about me having some bread, I won't tell her about your … fraternizing, did you call it?" He grins.

That grin — it's wicked. It does things to the core of me. Melty, liquid things.

Mentally shaking myself, I fetch another setting and sit down at the table. Hey, no "no," right?

Logan slices his steak and slides one half onto my plate; I cut my bread roll in two and put one chunk on his. He takes a big bite and moans in pleasure.

"Ah, this is so good. I'm more tired than I can tell you of broiled steak and broiled fish and broiled skinless chicken."

"Hey, happy is a five-letter word. So is cheese, and so is bacon. Coincidence? I don't think so."

He laughs but adds, "Just do *not* tell Cilla you fed me fried bacon, bread and full-fat cheese."

"Is she really that strict about what you eat?"

"I can't really blame her. She just wants what's best for the movie. It's the role. I don't know if you've ever seen one of the movies?"

I give a non-committal shrug.

"I'm supposed to be this cut and ripped beast, so I can't be carrying any spare flesh. Plus, the camera always puts on five pounds."

"I've heard that."

"It's true. Tomorrow I'll be on protein only and reduced liquids, because Monday we're shooting transforming scenes and I'll be half naked."

I'll make sure I'm on hand for the filming of that scene — purely in case Logan needs anything, of course.

"What's on my schedule this afternoon?"

I check the call sheets. "Pickups for scene fifty-one, on sound stage two. Then a gym session with your trainer. You're free after seven-thirty."

"Don't believe it — we always run over."

I want to ask why. I want to ask a hundred questions. Why did he become an actor? Does he like playing the role of the *Beast*? Does he ever miss playing in a band? Who was he talking to on the phone earlier, and about what? Does he have a girlfriend, how did he get that small, silver scar on the back of his hand, who babysits Toffee while he's on location, and what will he be doing tonight after filming wraps for the day?

But I think about how he's been ordered around all morning — how people have powdered his nose, tugged at his hair, physically shifted him into position, demanded he play the scene louder, softer, gentler, crazier — and I swallow my questions.

We eat in comfortable silence, with me sneaking covert glances at his wrists, his eyes, the place where the muscle begins its curved bulge under the sleeve of his T-shirt. When I give him some more of my baguette, he looks pathetically grateful. He pushes some more salad onto my plate and squirts dressing onto it. When he licks his fingers, my mouth drops open — literally — but I cover the moment by popping a chunk of carrot into it.

When we're done, I put the plates in the sink and hunt for dishwashing liquid. Logan flops onto the bed and picks up the paperback I noticed him reading earlier, between takes on set: *Method Acting — Lee Strasberg and the Actors Studio.*

It feels curiously domestic — me at the sink washing dishes, him half-reading, half-dozing on the bed nearby. If I'm not careful, this might begin to seem real. I could easily lose my head, and my heart, entirely. I remind myself that while I might be playing house with Logan, in reality I'm no more a part of his world than I was two days ago. He's like royalty, and I'm like the hired help. Scratch "like." I *am* the hired help.

Still, a cat may look at a king, and look at him I do — peeping out from under my lashes at his hands holding the book, at the rise and fall of his chest as he slips into sleep, at the thickness of his hair on the pillow.

Damn. I might be completely new to this world, but already I'm falling for him, hook, line and sinker. It's only day one, and I've already broken Cilla's most important rule.

I need to set some rules for myself to keep my feet firmly on the ground. As I dry and pack away the dishes, I make a mental list.

Rule 1: Thou shalt not fall in love with Logan Rush.

I draw a mental line through the rule. Too late for that commandment.

Take two.

Rule 1: Thou shalt never expect Logan Rush to fall in love with thee.

Rule 2: Thou shalt not forget that thee and he are from different worlds.

Rule 3: Thou shalt not be dazzled, nor confuse fantasy and reality.

Rule 4: Thou shall enjoy it while it lasts.

Rule 5: Thou job may not be brain surgery, but thou shalt try to do it well anyway.

A knock sounds at the door. Logan lifts his head groggily, but I motion for him to relax.

"I'll get it, you rest. I'll be back for you at two."

It's Polyp, with revised script pages for Monday's shoot.

"Thanks, I'll make sure he gets them," I say.

When Polyp slinks off, I sit down on the sun-warmed stairs outside Logan's room, guarding his sleep.

I spend the second half of the afternoon running interference for Logan, liaising with the wardrobe mistress, reassuring the A.D. that I'll ensure his star memorises the lines for Monday's scenes, and shuttling Logan from his room to make-up to the sound stage, and then to the makeshift gym set up in a hot, almost airless office behind Stage 3.

Logan has to stoop to get into this room — with his high-rise hero hairdo, he's too tall for the doorway. I go through his lines with him as the trainer puts him through his paces — cardio on a rowing machine, weights on the bench, and painful-looking Pilates stretches, twists and lifts for his abs. It's wrong to sexually objectify people, I know that, so I try not to ogle his body. His beautiful, sweat-sheened, hard-muscled, breath-snatching body. I fail.

The piece we rehearse is not a romantic scene — bummer — so I force the breathy desire out of my voice and attempt an American accent when I read the lines of Chase Falconer's arch-nemesis. I waggle my eyebrows and twirl an imaginary villainous moustache to get a laugh out of Logan, because I adore it when laughs. It makes his face look more open and free, somehow. I also seriously like it when the trainer makes him lie back and bench-press eighty-kilogram weights, because then I can gaze freely at the ab and arm porn without fear of him catching me at it.

When the trainer calls it quits, I lead Logan to the minibus that ferries the cast to and from their hotel. Britney Vaux is already inside, and as soon as she spots Logan, she straightens her spine, thrusting her improbably large and perky breasts out, and pats the seat beside her.

"How about a swim at the hotel, Logan? The water will be lovely, and I bought a new teeny-weeny bikini! It's adorbs — I know you'll love it!"

I slide the door shut before I can hear his response. *Rule 2: Different worlds.* It's time for me to return to mine.

I slip off my heels and walk to the parking lot. I'm dead tired, my feet ache like I've been walking on daggers all day, I long for a shower, and I'm due back on set at four a.m. on Monday.

I'm also happier than I can ever remember feeling.

CHAPTER 18
SPEECHLESS

On Sunday, I sleep in late, dreaming of lizards eating eel-sized worms.

At lunch, I keep up a steady stream of chatter about my job on the movie set. Nana loves hearing the details, but my parents? Not so much. I studiously avoid my father's pointed looks and gobble down my food so I can excuse myself as soon as possible.

"Goodness, Romy. What's the rush? It's like watching a school of migrating sardines being swallowed up by a *Delphinus capensis*," my mother says.

"I know what that one is," I say as I take my plate to the kitchen. "It's a dolphin."

"It's a *common* dolphin, dear," she calls after me.

In the afternoon, Zeb comes over to use my PC to submit his final application for university. He has no internet because scrap metal thieves have stolen the phone lines in his neighbourhood again. Zeb knows what he wants to study — business economics. It makes me edgy seeing him taking step after certain step towards his future when I'm still clueless about my own, so I distract myself by treating him to a blow-by-blow account of life in the celebrity lane.

"It doesn't sound too glamorous, actually," he says.

"I'll admit it's a lot of hard work, but it's never boring. And besides, there are perks."

"Yeah, the Beast."

"Don't call him that — he's much more than just the one role."

"Oh yeah? Like what?"

"Well, for one thing, I think he's a lot more serious about acting than people know. He doesn't have to do too much in these movies, but I think he could do something more demanding and challenging. I bet he'd be fabulous. Plus, he's really funny — he teases and strings people along all the time."

Zeb hits the final enter key and spins around to face me. "Just make sure he doesn't string you along."

"He's not like that — he hasn't put a finger out of place." More's the pity. But it has only been one day. I'm not ready to give up hope yet. "I just mean that, well, take Britney for example. Half the time she can't tell when he's being serious or feeding her a line."

"She sounds like a piece of work."

"No kidding. She chucked a donut at the key grip's head yesterday, and Becka says Britney once threw a stapler at her!"

"Yet on-screen, she looks like butter wouldn't melt in her mouth. Just shows to go ya — you can't always believe that what you see is what you'll get in real life."

"Are you warning me, Zeb?"

"You only *truly* need to worry if he begins saying 'trust me.'"

"My eyes are wide open, and my feet are firmly on the ground," I assure him.

My eyes, like most of the crews', are only half-open when I drag myself onto the lot at four a.m. on Monday. I had to set my alarm for three in the morning — my new hair and make-up routine is a major time suck.

The day is unseasonably cold and breezy. I figure the wind will probably be howling on the beach where we'll be doing our location shoot, so I make quick pit stops at Logan's room and the wardrobe department to grab a padded jacket and a blanket before boarding the bus designated for crew.

The VIP cast will leave a precious half-hour later and travel in a smaller, much more luxurious bus along with a bodyguard or two. I slide into the seat across the aisle from Becka, bundling the coat behind my head and snuggling under the blanket. With a smoky belch from its exhaust, the bus sets off on the highway headed north, followed by several trucks loaded with equipment.

"Where is this place — Paternoster?" Becka asks me.

"It's a tiny fishing village about 150 kilometres up the West Coast. It should take us about an hour and a half to get there — long enough for a nice nap."

"Not likely. The chances of Britney leaving me in peace long enough to catch a nap are about on par with Cilla allowing Logan to write his own lines."

"Logan wants to write his own lines?"

"He keeps nagging Cilla to allow him to try his hand at

writing a scene. But she says she hired him for his pretty face, not for what's inside his head."

"She actually said that to him?" I ask, appalled.

"Not directly to him, no. I heard her saying it to Polyp. She likes to keep the talent sweet until the shoot's wrapped, so she hasn't given him an outright no. Yet."

"That's not right."

"I wouldn't advise you telling her that."

"No. She told me to keep my mouth shut and my eyes open."

"That's our beloved director for you. She cans anyone who speaks up against her. Even Britney makes an effort to watch her mouth around Cilla, which causes her real strain, though you couldn't tell it from her face — Botoxed up the ying-yang!" Becka whispers the last phrase.

"Really?" I give up trying to sleep, eager to hear the down and dirty on the high and mighty.

"Oh yeah, every eight weeks. She had another boob job last year, and the nose was done before she ever even started in the business, back when she was a beauty pageant queen. She denies it publicly, of course — likes her image as a natural-born beauty." Becka snorts in disgust. "As if!"

"Well, she is beautiful," I concede. "But she already uses Botox? Really? It's not like she even has any wrinkles yet — she can't be older than twenty-two."

"Twenty-four," Becka mouths. "But don't tell anyone. Anyhoo, she has the injections to prevent wrinkles in the future. There's a short shelf life in this job. On the dark side of thirty your ingénue and romcom options start fading."

"Wow."

I consider that for a while, staring out into the dark beyond the window. To be over the hill at thirty is pretty bad. And sad.

"What did I tell you?" Becka says a little while later when her phone buzzes an incoming text message. "Let the bitch-bossing commence."

"Britney?" I ask.

"Where am I supposed to get a skinny soy chai out here?" She indicates the open spaces on either side of the road. "Do you think there'll be somewhere at the village I can get it?"

"I sincerely doubt it."

"She is such a PITA!"

"A what?"

"A pain in the ass."

I laugh. "I definitely got lucky with Logan."

Becka sits bolt upright and goggles at me, a wide grin splitting her face. "You did?"

"No. *No*. I don't mean that. No way!"

She makes a sound like a disappointed kitten and slumps back in her seat.

"I just meant I'm lucky to be assisting him, rather than someone like her. He's really easy." I realise what I've just said. "And by that I don't mean he's —"

"Yeah, I know what you mean. Logan's a sweetie, we all love him. Especially Britney. She's got her claws out to catch him."

"She likes him?"

Becka shrugs. "Who knows? But she *wants* him. It would be a great career move for her — for both of them. Imagine the huge celebrity wedding, babies, maybe a reality show along the way."

I shudder. "And … is he, you know, into *her*?" I try to keep my voice casual.

"The official rumour mill has it that they're a couple off-screen as well as on-screen."

"There's an *official* rumour mill?"

"Oh yeah, Cilla 'leaks' news all the time. She often gets me to feed juicy tips to reporters. She says it's good publicity for the movies if people think Logan and Britney are an item."

I've read about the Rush-Vaux romance rumours in the fandom and on the celebrity news sites, of course, but I always just assumed it was wishful thinking. There have never been any photos of Logan and Britney actually holding hands or kissing — except as their on-screen characters.

Have they or haven't they hooked up? Are they or aren't they a couple? It's a game of hide and tease played with their fans across the world.

"So are they?" I must know.

"Who knows? Even if they are, like, together, Cilla wouldn't allow them to make it official. She likes to keep the public guessing. The anticipation goes out of it when it's confirmed one way or the other. And then what if they broke up before the release of the movie? PR Disaster of Brangelina proportions. We probably won't know either way for sure until a good six months after this movie's released." Becka highlights an item on her list and returns to sending emails on her phone.

I nestle back into my seat, thinking about what I've learned, and I must drift off to sleep, because when next I peer out of the window, we're driving down the main street of Paternoster, headed towards the beach.

The small village is still shut up tight in the predawn darkness — and although there are signs for art galleries, pottery sheds and several restaurants, there's no hint of the sort of speciality shop that would dispense a skinny soy chai.

Even in the pale-yellow glow of the few street lights, the village is picturesque enough to inspire the location scout and the second unit cinematographer to start identifying possible establishing shots.

Becka's delighted by the simple, white-washed thatched cottages; the reed-roofed verandas decorated with strings of shells, cork buoys and old fishing nets; and the stony front gardens dominated by old rowing boats filled with earth to make quaint flower gardens or veggie patches. Lights shine from inside a few of the small cottages — the fisherman are already awake, getting ready to go out in their colourful boats to bring in the morning haul of snoek or crayfish.

"This place is too cute!" Becka says.

"Maybe you'll get a chance to come explore later."

"Yeah, right."

The bus driver deposits us all in a road near the beach. Becka and I grab our bags and troop through the chilly darkness towards the shore, while the technicians unpack equipment from the trucks. The cinematographer is delighted with the foul weather. The clouds and the ghostly mist blowing in from the sea will, he says, "add texture to the dawn," and the wind will give "a sense of drama."

A thin line of gold on the horizon is just beginning to lighten the sky when the minibus with Logan, Britney, Polyp, and Cilla arrives.

Cilla — minus her pet dragons today — is no sooner out of the vehicle than she starts yelling instructions through a megaphone.

"Everyone — hurry up and haul ass before we lose the light!"

I reach the catering table before they've finished setting up, and cadge a double-espresso for Logan. I find him, on his own, shivering in the dark on the leeward side of an equipment truck. He's wearing only a pair of low-hanging, cut-off denim shorts, and rubbing an oily Vaseline mixture onto himself — all over his bare arms, his smooth chest and his knotted abs.

Sweet mother-of-pearl.

I stare, wide-eyed. Speechless at last — although for a reason that would not please Cilla. When Logan notices me standing there, I stick out an arm and hand him the small cardboard cup of espresso.

He downs it in one go. "Th-thanks."

His teeth are chattering. And are his lips tinged blue? I'm tempted to kiss some pink back into them.

I shake myself mentally. Perhaps I shake myself physically, too, because Logan gives me a puzzled look. Then I reach into my giant tote bag and pull out his jacket and the blanket.

"Ta-da! I come prepared," I say, consoling myself that his body will only be hidden until they start filming which, judging from the commands being shouted all around us, should be any minute now.

"I love you!" he says dramatically.

"I bet you say that to all your assistants." I'm grateful for the dark which hides the evidence of my heated cheeks.

"Only the ones who come bearing gifts."

He takes the coat, but drops it on a nearby equipment box, and instead holds the jar of cream out to me.

"Can you help? I can't reach my back, and without a mirror, I'm not sure I've got it everywhere on my front. They want me to have a sweat sheen — which isn't g-going to happen in this weather — so I need to oil up."

"You want me to … rub this on your back? And chest?"

Not only am I having trouble talking now, I'm having trouble breathing. And I'm suddenly very hot in my own jacket.

"Yeah," he says. When I don't move, he adds, "Do you mind?"

"No! Um, no — not at all."

He turns around, and there's his back — all smooth skin and curved muscle — mine for the looking. *And* the touching.

I scoop up a big glob of the cream from the jar, warm it between my hands, and smooth it onto his shoulders. As if in a dream, I massage it around the curve of his neck, then back and forth over the corded ridges of his shoulder muscles, and down the length of his spine and the tight lines of his waist to where the base of his back disappears below the denim of his shorts.

Logan sighs in pleasure when I rub against the tension in his neck and shoulders, but as I continue, he grows still and quiet. My hand stops moving but lingers against his skin. As Logan turns — very slowly — to face me, my fingers trail above the denim waistband, across the hollow of his back, around his hip, over his taut abdomen, and come to rest just below his navel. In the pit of my belly, something tightens then melts. Perhaps my ovaries are exploding.

Logan looks down into my eyes. His are the endless reflecting blue of the darkest sapphire. The wayward lock of black hair falls to rest over one eye. We're alone in a bubble of heat and awareness. The noise, the wind, the cold — all have vanished. Sucked out from the air around us, like oxygen feeding a flash fire. My heart hammers me closer to him. A pulse beats in his throat. His head dips towards mine. His lips move.

"Logan? Logan!" Cilla's harsh voice ruptures the moment. She lets rip with a stream of curses, demanding to know where her leading man is hiding.

I draw in a ragged breath, look away, clear my throat. Logan hasn't moved a muscle.

"Now this spot right here doesn't have enough glisten," I say, striving for a light tone as I smear a dab of cream on his collarbone.

He passes me the now-crumpled little cardboard cup. As I take it, our hands touch, and though I can't be sure, it seems like his fingers linger, slow to pull away. I glance up from our hands to his face, but he's already turning around.

And then he's gone, and I'm alone behind the truck, holding the cup and the cream in my trembling hands.

CHAPTER 19
STEEL CAGE

The beach is a long white expanse of wind-rippled sand. It stretches endlessly in both directions, bounded on one side by scrubby *fynbos* dunes and on the other by the cold Atlantic. Massive boulders huddle shoulder-to-shoulder in the grey water, and long strands of slimy kelp lie marooned on the sand. The rising sun dissolves the mist and glistens on the inky-green seaweed but then slips back behind threatening clouds.

While seagulls, cormorants and gannets squabble noisily in the distance, Logan Rush runs the length of the beach, past the ranks of cameras and crew. Then runs it again. And again. Over and over he sprints one way, turns around, strolls back to his starting spot, and repeats the performance — first through the mist, then through the wind and a steady, fine rain. Between takes, I wordlessly hand him the coat and blanket, and Cilla, drinking endless cups of coffee from a thermos mug, stalks over to give him more instructions.

A small gaggle of curious onlookers has collected on the road above the beach. It won't be long before the Rushers find out exactly who's here, but Logan's bodyguard — a mountain of a man called Thabo — has cordoned off the site with tape and barricades to make sure no one bothers the stars. I check with catering to find out what will be available for Logan's lunch. Steak or grilled fish. Again. Surely I can find something better for him in town?

"I need to get something in the village — want to come with?" I ask Becka.

"Nah, can't," she says, rolling her eyes towards the VIP cast bus where Britney sits out of the cold and wind, waiting for her scenes to be called.

"Anything I can get for you?"

"Some gum — sugar-free and berry, cherry or strawberry flavour — and butt-glue if you can find it."

"Come again?"

"You know, the spray-glue that comes in aerosol cans? Wardrobe's run out, and Britney needs her bikini stuck onto her so that when she does her fight scene, it doesn't shift and give a nip slip."

"Now I've heard everything."

The short walk into town is peaceful once I'm past the small crowd watching the shoot, and it's good to be away from the constant hubbub of the set. Becka's gum is easy to find, her spray glue not so much. I'll have to improvise.

I find a seafood restaurant and order a take-away platter of sushi and sashimi, and by the time the siren sounds for the lunch break, I'm back on set with Logan's lunch — fat slices of tuna, salmon and butterfish, smoked eel maki, California rolls, small mounds of shaved pink ginger and emerald wasabi, and several prawn nigiri stretched out like sunbathers on a beach.

Cilla, Phillip, Britney, Becka, Logan and a couple of others relax on folding chairs around a long trestle table set out under a shade awning with a canvas back to provide some privacy from the watchers. The sun has burned off the cloud cover, the wind has dropped, and it's getting hot — Cape Town is living up to its reputation for having all four seasons in one day.

Logan has abandoned his jacket in favour of a faded T-shirt and polarised sunglasses. We haven't spoken since our charged moment behind the van this morning. When I place the sushi platter on the table in front of him, along with a pair of chopsticks and sachets of soy sauce, he looks a question at me.

"I thought you could use something different to eat."

"They didn't have lasagne? Or fries? Or ice cream?" His lazy smile is back.

"All of the above. You want me to go get you some?"

"No he does not," Cilla snaps from the other end of the table.

"Sit," Logan says to me, dipping his chin at the empty seat on the other side of him. "I'm going to need help finishing this."

I pass the packet with my other purchases to Becka. She pulls out the pack of gum and hands it to Britney — who takes it without thanks — then holds up the stick of glue. It's the kind schoolkids use to stick their notes into exercise books.

"And this?"

"Best I could do, I'm afraid."

Britney, who's been watching our exchange, shakes her head. "No way are you putting that on my skin."

"Okay, Miss Vaux," Becka says, hiding a smile. "I'm sure the crew and crowd won't mind a wardrobe malfunction."

Logan snickers. He's already gobbled most of the sashimi and is now unravelling California rolls, separating the salmon and crab from the rice and avocado, which he pushes away to the side.

"Don't you think this is just the tiniest bit crazy?" I ask him, speaking softly. "A teaspoon of rice won't make you fat."

Logan peels a slice of tuna off its bed of rice. "It's just for today. Soon I'll be able to eat cheeseburgers if I want."

"You're all obsessed," I say, looking around the table.

Only the cinematographer, Becka and I are eating normal food. Britney toys with a garden salad (no dressing), Logan nibbles at the last of his raw fish, and Cilla eats half of her grilled chicken breast and steamed vegetables — perhaps she's trying to set a good example. Phillip eats nothing; what do polyps feed on?

In a low voice, Logan asks me, "What are *you* obsessed with?"

Apart from you?

"Um, endangered species, I guess. Rhinos, whales, marine turtles. And sharks, of course. You know, all the creatures that need our help."

"Yeah, you're good with helpless beasts," he says, with a slight emphasis on the last word. "You've got a good touch." His lips curve in a smile. "Can I ask if you find them appealing? Interesting?"

Are we still talking about animals? I sneak a glance at him, but his eyes are hidden behind his Aviators.

"Very much so. I'd like to get to know … them … better, find out all I can about them, see how I can get involved in their plight."

I quickly check the faces around the table. Cilla's holding forth about the Actors' Equity Guild to the man on her right, and Becka and Phillip are listening in on that conversation. Britney, however, has her sharp eyes fixed on Logan and me.

"Yeah, I also think that would be an interesting area of … exploration." Logan puts a slice of ginger into his mouth, then delicately lifts a pink sliver between his chopsticks and offers it to me.

I badly want to take it between my teeth straight from the end of his chopsticks, but I can't have Logan feeding me. Not in full view of everyone.

"Thanks," I say, taking the ginger with my fingers and popping it into my mouth.

The ginger burns sharp and sweet on my tongue, as it must be on his. We're tasting the same thing at the exact same moment. It's like a long-distance kiss.

Britney cocks her head and gazes at Logan suspiciously. If she were capable of frowning, there would definitely be lines furrowed between her eyes right now.

I smile innocently at her. "You should try some — it's good."

"May I?" Britney asks Logan.

She dips her lashes and opens her mouth like a baby bird waiting to be fed. He snags another piece of ginger with his chopsticks and deposits it playfully into her mouth.

"Yum!" She giggles and licks her lips. "More!"

I swallow and look away. Cilla smiles with satisfaction at the flirty little tableau of her two stars.

"So … sharks," Logan says to me. "What can you tell me about them? I probably should have researched them for this role."

"You mean you haven't?"

"Um, not really," he admits.

"I would've thought you'd want to know how they move and behave — for your performance, I mean."

He grins and ducks his head, as though embarrassed. Cilla and Britney are both listening to us now.

"You've missed out on something special — they're awesome creatures."

A great idea pops into my head. Not only could Logan study sharks for his craft, but maybe a close-up encounter with them might sensitise him to their plight. Maybe he could use his fame to help raise awareness.

"You know what, you should go shark diving!" I say.

"Do I even want to know what that is?" Logan replies, pushing his chair back from the table.

"I don't think our insurance would cover that," Cilla says.

"It's perfectly safe," I reassure them. "Well, there was that one case where — but never mind about that. What happens is you get into a huge, steel cage, and it's lowered into the water where the sharks are. They do it in False Bay — near where you had your birthday party yacht moored."

"How do you know where we were for his birthday?" Britney asks.

Crap. She's sharper than she looks.

"It was all over the Twitterverse," I say.

"Oh, really."

She scrutinizes me as though she suspects I'm fishy in some way.

"Are you saying there were sharks in that water?" Logan sounds mildly alarmed.

"Oh, yes. Well, Seal Island's close by, isn't it?"

"Seal what now?"

"Seal Island. It's this massive, breeding colony of seals on a chunk of rock in the middle of the bay. Sharks feed on them all around there. Every so often, a swimmer or a surfer gets bitten — or worse."

Even when he curses, Logan sounds chilled.

"Anyway," I continue, "the cage dive operators chum the water with blood which brings the sharks, and you can see them from right up close. I should probably mention that not everyone thinks chumming the water is a great idea, because it attracts predators to the bay. But it doesn't hurt the sharks, and it would be great research for you. And aren't you a qualified scuba diver?"

"Yeah. Well, I can't really swim properly — like lengths and such — but I can mosey around under the water. I had to learn it for the underwater scenes," he says, and adds significantly, "I'm talking about the scenes in tanks with green screens and mechanical models. Not the ones with real live predators sniffing at my flesh."

"I think it's an excellent idea," Cilla says unexpectedly.

"You do?" Logan says in disbelief. "You won't even let me do my own jump-and-roll stunts, and now it's okay to go shark diving?"

"What are you, scared?" I challenge.

"And you wouldn't be?" he counters.

"Me? Scared of a six-metre-long predator with several rows of serrated teeth? I'm made of stronger stuff."

"Good, then you can go down with me."

I swallow. This is more than I bargained for, but on the other hand …

"Sure," I say, grinning.

"*Really?*"

"Hey, Africa's not for sissies."

"Make it happen, Romy!" Cilla says. "What day is it today?"

"Monday," Polyp answers.

"Do it on Friday," Cilla orders. "Photography are doing aerial shots of the coast and beaches on Friday, and Logan will be free. Philip, contact publicity — tell them to liaise with Romy, here."

"Aw, Cilla, you're not going to turn this into a whole publicity stunt, are you?" Logan says. "I thought this was about method."

"Method, schmethod. This is about the movie. But it'll just be a few photos, Logan, no need to get uptight. You should be happy about it — you didn't get into acting to stay invisible. Now" — she claps her hands twice — "everybody back to work. Britney, your scene is up after this one. We'll be done in about thirty minutes, make sure you're ready and waiting."

Cilla stalks off back to the cameras with Polyp close behind her. Logan gives us — me? — a lazy salute and strolls off after them across the sand.

"We'll be done in about thirty minutes, make sure you're ready and waiting," Britney mimics Cilla's words, though only once the director is well out of earshot. She captures the flat, nasal tones perfectly.

I make to start clearing the table, but Britney stops me. "Catering will get it. You sit tight, I want to chat with you a bit."

CHAPTER 20
BEAUTIES AND OTHER SHARKS

I sit back down at the table opposite Britney, tensed for what she might want to discuss.

"Becka, go ask wardrobe if that glue will even work," Britney says. She takes a long sip from her glass of diet soda and says to me, "Now, you appear to know an awful lot about sharks and such."

"I guess so. They're such amazing creatures!"

"Such amazing creatures," she repeats, nodding. "Tell me about them, the ones down here in the Cape."

I'm surprised by her interest, but also relieved. For a moment there, I thought she intended to grill me about Logan. I'm in safer waters talking about sharks.

"Well, in False Bay we mostly see great whites, and thresher sharks, the odd hammerhead or hound shark, and raggies — ragged-tooth sharks."

She watches me intently, ignoring the catering staff who clear the table around us. "Tell me about the great whites — they look like beauties!"

"They *are* beautiful," I say, pleased by her enthusiasm. Maybe I've misjudged her — she seems genuinely interested in hearing more. "Too many people misunderstand and fear them — *Jaws* and all that — but they're the most perfectly designed predators on the planet."

"The most perfectly designed predators?"

"Yes! For example, they're grey on the top half of their bodies so that when they swim below their prey, they fade into the darker water and seabed. But they're white underneath, so that if a seal swims under them and looks up, the shark fades to pale against the sun coming through the water."

"Amazeballs! And they eat people?"

"Well, no. They eat Cape fur seals mostly. But from underneath, a surfer on a board looks a lot like a seal with flippers, so sometimes people get attacked. Honestly, humans are more of a danger to sharks than they are to us."

"We're more of a danger to them than they are to us." She tuts and takes another sip of her drink. "And they're an endangered species?"

"Not officially, but shark populations everywhere are under threat because of the practice of shark finning."

She motions for me to explain, her eyes drinking in my every word.

"Finning is when fishermen catch sharks and slice off their dorsal fins." I see Britney silently mouth the words *dorsal fins*. "And then they toss the sharks back into the water, where they can't swim properly, and so they die from suffocation, or are eaten by other predators. The fins get dried and sent to the Far East, where they're used a little in traditional medicine, but mostly to make shark fin soup."

"What's so special about that?"

"It's obscenely expensive, so people order it at banquets to demonstrate how rich and successful they are. Shark populations are being decimated just so some fat cat in China can show how prosperous he is. It's outrageous that a species which has been around for millions of years should now be threatened because of mere vanity!"

"Outrageous — because of mere vanity."

"And the irony is that the fins have been found to have such high levels of toxic mercury, that it can't be doing the people who eat it any good."

"Serves them right!"

"And sharks are such slow growers, too. The males only reach maturity at about ten years, the females even later, so we don't yet even know the full impact of killing off immature sharks. It makes me so mad!" I thump a fist on the table, nearly overturning Britney's soda. "I'm sorry, I'm probably boring you. I know I get a little crazy about this, but I'm just passionate, you know," I add, with an embarrassed laugh. "Not enough people get it."

"I get it," Britney says, patting the back of my hand reassuringly with one of hers and giving me a bright, super-white smile. "I've got you exactly. Oops, looks like they're calling me, I'd better go. Thank you for telling me all about sharks, I just know that information is going to come in handy."

"Sure, my pleasure," I say to her departing form. I'm pleased — I might just have made another convert to shark conservation.

By the time the shoot wraps for the day, it's almost eight in the evening and the light is dimming. The cast and crew piling into the vans and buses are tired, hungry and grumpy.

Logan slides the door of the VIP bus closed on Britney's surprised face, saying, "I think I need to hear more about those sharks before I go swimming with them on Friday."

Then he ambles slowly over to where Becka and I wait at the crew bus, climbs inside, and stretches out across the seats at the very back. Logan's bodyguard, who's scrambled out of the VIP transport, trots over to our bus, but when he boards, Logan gestures to him to sit up front. I stand in the aisle, uncertain.

"Romy," Logan calls. "You're still on company time. Come and confess — what's the likelihood I'll become human sushi for a shark?"

I laugh and pause to ask a favour of the driver before walking down to sit beside him, all the while studiously ignoring Becka's raised eyebrows and *just-what-is-going-on-here-girl?* expression.

"Right, what would you like to know?" I ask him.

"What I'd really like to know, Romy, what I urgently need to know is, have you got anything tasty for me?" A smile stretches slowly across his face.

"I beg your pardon?"

"I am so hungry, Romy, haven't you got a protein bar or some of that jerky stuff you guys have here?"

"You mean, *biltong?*"

"You have some?" he asks eagerly.

"I do not."

"You're a cruel woman, Romy. Pitiless." He gives a deep, regretful sigh then pins me with his cobalt gaze and asks softly,

"Do you have anything tasty to satisfy my appetite?"

I laugh, still not sure of the game between us.

Just then, as I'd arranged with the driver, the bus stops outside a general-store-cum-café on the outskirts of the village.

"I'll be right back." I move quickly to the front of the bus where the driver is already making an announcement.

"Last stop before Cape Town, if anyone wants to buy any food or smokes," he says.

I hop off the bus and run to the café to place my order. While waiting, I walk around the store, examining the shelves packed with an eccentric assortment of wares — fishing rods, packets of fudge, dangling mobiles made from seashells, jars of marinated mussels, and a strong-smelling type of dried fish called *bokkom*. A corner of the store stocks a selection of movie DVDs for rental, and in the window is a poster of Logan. *Beast: Sun. Release the tiger within!*

Ten minutes later I return to the bus with my contraband in a brown paper bag.

"These," I say, giving Logan the large greaseproof packet filled with steaming hot, golden chips doused in salt and vinegar, "are what is known locally as *slap chips*."

"Fries! You are a good woman, Romy. And a merciful one," he says, already cramming the hot potato into his mouth. He groans and rolls his eyes in pleasure.

"Do you two need to get a room?" I motion to him and the chips.

He grins and eats several more.

"Wonderful," he says, looking straight into my eyes.

Flustered, I drop my gaze. The bus lurches into motion, and I pull a bottle of beer out of the paper bag.

Logan's grin widens. "They sold *you* that?"

"We can buy and drink alcohol when we're eighteen here," I explain.

"Nice."

"But we can only drive when we're eighteen, too."

"You've got to admire the lawmakers who think it's a good idea for those two things to coincide," he says, laughing.

Logan has a great laugh. Every time he laughs, somewhere a unicorn is born.

"So can I have it?" He tries to take the beer, but I hold it out of reach.

"You get this" — I tap the cool, green glass where tiny droplets of condensation bead — "if and when you can pronounce the word *slap* correctly. *Slap*, spelt S.L.A.P."

"Slap," he says at once, rhyming the word with "clap."

"No, sslupp."

"Slurp." He's beginning to sound desperate.

Watching his lips move in slow exaggeration of the sounds, I have to hold myself back from leaning over to kiss the stray grains of salt off them.

"It rhymes with pup, not burp. S-l-uhh-p," I say.

"Slup?"

"Very good!"

I twist the cap off the beer bottle, hand it over, and watch how his Adam's apple moves when he swallows deeply.

"There was a poster of you in the window of the shop back there." I gesture back to the village we've left behind. "Weird that even in a remote little place like this you're famous."

"Yeah, there's no escaping the *Beast*," he says, with something like regret in his voice.

Not sure how to reply, I tuck into my own packet of chips, though they taste nowhere near as good as watching him eat his. Finally, he licks salt off his fingers, downs the last of his beer, and sighs.

"Okay, so now that you're fed, what did you want to know about sharks?" I ask.

"Nothing, really. I'm sure I'll find out lots on Friday."

"But … you said that's why you wanted to come on this bus."

"I lied." He rests his head against the seat, closes his eyes, and yawns.

"Why?"

"Cilla and Britney talk a whole lot of nonversation. Besides" — he opens one eye to peer at me — "I *need* my PA. I must have her."

My breath hitches. "What for?"

He pauses for a long moment before replying. "Forbidden food, obviously. And music — you have an iPod, don't you?"

"Don't you?"

"We could share yours."

I get it out my bag and offer him the choice of music.

"Y'all have some good music on here, Romy, but also some strange stuff. I've just got to try this *Whalesong Lullaby*."

I move up close to him and give him one earbud, plugging the other into my ear. And we drive back through the deepening African night like that, listening to the otherworldly songs of whales calling to each other across vast oceans. Before long, Logan dozes off. His head rests on my shoulder, and our arms, sides, and legs touch in a dozen points of heat and awareness.

Without moving anything except my eyes — I don't want to

jostle him off me — I look down at his face. His hair has fallen over one eye again. My fingers itch to push it back, to comb through his hair to the back of his neck, but I'm very aware of who all might have eyes on us. Anyone in this bus might carry tales back to Cilla, so I keep my hands folded in my lap, prim as a nun, and whenever anyone glances our way, I shrug my other shoulder, slide my eyes in Logan's direction, and make a "stars — whatcha gonna do?" sort of face.

But I do allow myself to breathe deeply. No one can see that, and Logan smells great — kind of sweaty, but in a good way.

I could happily sit like this for a few more weeks, but all too soon the bus slows to take the exit from the highway. When we stop at a brightly lit intersection of traffic lights, I look out of the window. Straight into the eyes of Britney Vaux.

The VIP minibus is idling alongside us in the next lane, and Britney — barely two metres away from us — spots Logan's head on my shoulder. Her mouth drops open in shock, and her eyes fill with outrage. Oh, crap.

I tug at the earbuds, point at Logan, twist my mouth, and roll my eyes — trying, with this frantic mime show, to convey that his head is only so close to mine because of the listening arrangement. Glaring at me with eyes narrowed to slits and lips pulled into a thin line, she touches a forefinger to her chest, points with a backwards V at her own two eyes, and then points back at me.

The bus rolls into motion, and I can no longer see her. But her warning stills rings in my ears, as loud as if she'd shouted it: "I've got my eyes on you!"

CHAPTER 21
SILENCE AND SECRETS

The movie set is about as far away from my parents' world of the sea as you can get, but I soon feel like I'm finding my land legs. I bust a gut to be quietly capable, well-organised and competent, and surprise even myself with occasional flashes of super-efficiency.

On Tuesday, I karate-chop and kick the dying air conditioner in Logan's room back into life, earn Polyp's gratitude by finding a local supplier of live insects for the dragons, and source diet Dr Pepper sodas for Logan. To my own delight, I discover a brand of mineral water that comes in a bottle with a pointed sipping nozzle and smile-inducing sound effects. Every time Logan takes a sip, his lips make a kissing noise against the nozzle. Sweet melting heaven!

When Becka asks me where she can find some penguins for a hastily-arranged photo shoot, I direct her to the aquarium at the Waterfront. Britney, she tells me, is jealous of the shark adventure planned for Logan and wants to get some animal publicity shots of her own — though she's going for the *aw-how-*

cute! look while Logan is still on track for the *aah-look-fearless-action-man-has-face-off-with-savage-shark!* photo opportunity.

In lulls between takes, I try to tell Britney more about sharks and whales, but she merely shakes her pretty head.

"I know enough, thanks."

"Enough for what?"

"Shh, Ronnie."

"It's Romy."

"Whatever. Whoever. You're giving me a headache. Becka? Aspirin."

Strangely, having directed me to organise a shark dive for Logan, Cilla gives me the brush-off when I attempt to give her more information about it.

"Cut the chatter, Romy, I don't need to hear all about it. Just put it in a memo," she says.

So I do, staying up late Tuesday night to make sure all the details are clearly spelled out. But when I give it to her on Wednesday morning, she merely passes it to Polyp, saying, "You know where to put this."

I doubt she even reads it. I suspect Polyp might use it to line the bottom of the chickabiddies' tank.

I spend the rest of Wednesday morning sourcing a new Gucci tuxedo and a pair of black dress shoes for Logan to wear to an important function the next night. He's ecstatically delighted with the new shoes.

When I tell him, "I *thought* you'd be happy about those," something like recognition flickers across his face, but total recall still eludes him.

It's not all fun, of course. There's the daily irritation of reading the rubbish printed about Logan in the tabloids and on the Net and not being allowed to speak up to set the record straight, the morning ritual of slathering on make-up and blow-drying my hair straight and sleek, and continuing to totter around in smart clothes and toe-biting heels in case any paparazzi are lurking about, ready to take a photograph of Logan in my vicinity.

On Thursday, I spend several frustrating minutes trying to stop the two animatronics guys from inaccurately crafting a blinking eyelid on their shark's head.

"Great whites don't blink, and they don't have a nictitating membrane on their eyes. That's why they roll their eyes backwards into their sockets to protect them during attacks."

"Cilla wants this shark to blink," says Techie One.

"Even if it's inaccurate?"

"This isn't *National Geographic*, sweet cheeks."

"But —"

"Pass me that mini-screwdriver, will you," says Techie One.

"Sorry, were you saying something?" says Techie Two.

"Oh, never mind!" I snap.

Perhaps Nana is right about body language, though, because they seemed to have no problem hearing *that*. As I walk off to find Logan, I hear one of them say, "That's a nice piece of tail," and the other agree, "Oh yeah, she can nictitate my membranes anytime."

Lovely.

"Sometimes," I grumble to Logan after his sparring session with his trainer, "I feel like everyone is trying to shut me up. It's like no one can hear me."

"I know how you feel," he says, wiping the sheen of sweat off his chest with a towel.

"What do you mean?"

"No one wants to hear me say anything except my lines from the script."

It's true. Whenever Logan suggests a different way of playing a scene, or tries to ad-lib a line, Cilla shuts him down immediately. It makes me grit my teeth, because I'm on his side, and because I want to see and hear more of the real Logan Rush.

The best moments of my job are spent watching Logan act, which he does better than anyone gives him credit for, and peering over Cilla's and Logan's shoulders to see the emerging magic of the day's rushes. I also enjoy getting a sneak peek of Britney before hair and make-up transform her from a pale-lashed, wan, bland set of features to her blonde bombshell "normal" self.

That's a balm for my wavering self-esteem.

Because there are bad moments, too, when reality slaps me in the face and the magic and the glamour vanish quicker than you can say, "That's a wrap." Like seeing the daily countdown on the shoot schedule — knowing that the day when the production wraps and the whole circus leaves town is approaching inexorably. Like watching from the hotel corridor as Logan disappears into the penthouse suite for a private function with visiting Hollywood money-men and a clutch of impossibly beautiful supermodels. And with Britney hanging on his arm and smiling smugly over her shoulder at me.

Masochistically, I replay these moments to remind myself of rules one, two and three, because it's getting harder to remember about the two different worlds, and not to confuse fantasy and reality, and never to dream that Logan might possibly be interested in me.

It's harder because the times when we are together are so sweet and easy and, unless I'm in the grip of a psychotic-grade delusion, *flirty*. We touch each other far more often than can be accidental — fingers grazing as we exchange script pages and coffee cups, bodies brushing as we squeeze past each other in the kitchenette of his star room, thigh pressed up against thigh as we sit at a table, going through each day's schedule. And when we talk, our gazes linger and there's an undercurrent of something else, something that makes my body yearn and my mind forget all the rules.

But hope alternates with worry. Perhaps Logan is just amusing himself — heaven knows that the hours spent before, between, and after takes are mind-numbingly boring for him. It's also entirely possible that I'm imagining the electricity between us. Britney's all over him — flattering and giggling and preening — and the rumours about them are stronger than ever. And every evening they leave together for their hotel, while I head back to the other side of Cape Town — the other side of the world —readying myself for the almost nightly confrontation with my overprotective father.

I'm careful to keep Friday's expedition a secret because if Dad finds out about that, he'll have a complete conniption. After supper with my parents on Thursday night, I go online to catch up on the latest rumours about Logan on the fan sites — it's enlightening to compare what's being reported with what I know is actually happening in his life. I discover that my favourite sites are in a frenzy because a British tabloid has reported that Logan and Britney are secretly engaged. In deep disgust, I switch off my computer and decide on an early night.

In less than twelve hours, I'll be in a steel cage, several metres under the sea, standing beside one beast while staring into the terrifying jaws of another.

CHAPTER 22
ONE MAN'S TRASH ...

At eight o'clock on Friday morning, I'm on my way to collect Logan from his star room — our transport to False Bay Adrenalin Adventures is waiting in the parking lot — when I hear a shout.

"Romy! Romy!" Cilla's calling to me from across the lot.

She'll probably have something uncomplimentary to say about how I'm dressed today, but I refuse to go on the shark-diving boat in anything but jeans, sneakers, and the bare minimum of make-up (coloured lip-gloss, waterproof mascara). I'm wearing my bikini beneath my clothes, and I've stuffed my wetsuit into my tote bag.

As I walk over to Cilla, I slip on my sunglasses and tug a floppy straw sunhat down low on my forehead to disguise my mostly naked face.

"Good morning," I say.

"What are you wearing?" she asks, frowning.

"Great weather for a dive, isn't it? Are you coming out with us?"

Cilla hands me a thick stack of post. "This is forwarded mail for Britney and Logan, it arrived with the courier package today — make sure they get it. Tell Logan to check his because it includes mail for Levi," she says with an odd smile.

"Who's Levi?"

"And tell him there's been a change of plan for today. We'll be doing his shark shoot at the aquarium on the Waterfront. Philip's organised everything."

"At the aquarium? What about —"

"Yeah, they do shark dives there. Britney put us onto it. She's getting pics done with penguins there today, so we'll have double the bait for the media."

"But —"

"Logan can do the dive safely in the fish tank there. They say it's great — glass all round, seaweed, colourful little fishes. And none of the bother of having to go out on a boat. It's perfect."

"But he'll be disappointed that —"

"Wise up, Romy. The insurance would never have covered him out at sea."

"Did you try?"

"What did I tell you about backchat on your first day here? Besides, we need to get full publicity from this little stunt, and how would we get all the media onto a boat and underwater in the middle of the effing ocean? No, it's much better my way. It always is." She cackles evilly. "You run along now and break the good news to Logan."

With a sinking heart and heavy feet, I walk back across the lot, slip Britney's mail under the door of her room and, when Logan opens his door, silently hand him his. He tosses the letters onto the dining table.

"Hi, all ready for our expedition I see?" he says, flicking a finger at the brim of my hat. "What's with the long face, Romy? Getting scared for the cage dive?"

"There isn't going to be any cage dive."

His smile vanishes. "What do you mean?"

"Cilla's canned it. She's turned it into a shoot in a fish tank at the aquarium, so you can get 'full publicity' from the stunt."

Logan's face tightens. Then he curses and bangs a fist on the table.

"She *always* does this! Every single time I have a chance to do something real, or authentic or interesting, she turns me into a performing poodle for this three-freaking-ring circus. Every time! You remember when I went on the elephant-back safari in India to see tigers in the wild?"

"No, I wasn't with you then."

"What?"

"I wasn't working for you back then."

"Oh, right."

"But I saw the photos online — awesome!"

"Faked and photoshopped." He stares down at the palm of his hand, scratches something there.

"*What?* How?"

"That elephant I was 'riding' on? It was the trained, tame animal from the shoot. Make-up added some scars to make it look different — wilder, I guess. And I wasn't riding, but just sitting on it in the sound stage, in front of a green screen. They added the jungle background and the monkeys later."

"But the tiger — the tiger that was prowling into the picture? That scared the elephant into rearing on its hind legs and you nearly fell off and broke your back, but you stayed calm and soothed it? Like … like an elephant whisperer?"

"The elephant was standing up on command from its trainer, and I was strapped to the saddle. And the tiger was a mangy, old, toothless cat from the local circus. I mean, literally — he had no teeth. And *his* trainer was just outside of the frame holding out a leg of goat or something to get him to walk past. They superimposed that image, taken at the circus, onto the pic of me. We weren't even on the same sound stage at the same time. But all the newsfeeds picked up the pictures and the waffle-copy that publicity had written about me being out on safari in the wild when a dangerous man-eater appeared. Total crap, it's all bullshit."

I say nothing. It's an appalling deceit, but there's no point in saying that — Logan already knows. There would be no point in telling Cilla either, she not only knows, she also doesn't care. And she would only tell me to zip my lip or lose my job.

"You go on ahead. Tell her I'm on my way." Logan leans both his hands on the table and stares blindly down at the pile of mail.

"I'm sorry," I say quietly and leave.

I make a quick detour to hand in my completed time sheet at the pay office, and I'm about to set off for the main gate when I notice Logan emerging from his room. I hesitate, wondering if I should wait for him, but judging from the way he slams the door shut behind him and storms across the lot, his mood has turned foul and he might want to be left alone for a while.

He's carrying a trash bag, and when he gets to the line of wheelie bins behind the next sound stage, he flings it into one of them, bangs the lid down, and stalks off. Strange. Logan doesn't usually empty his own trash. Also, I've never seen him move so fast off-screen. I'm about to shrug it off when I notice a man sneaking over to the row of dustbins. I recognise him at once — it's the gum-chewing, bald, weasel-faced paparazzo from the night I rescued Logan.

I break into a run, grateful for my sneakers. The paparazzo already has his camera up to his eye and is lifting the lid of the bin when I reach him and smack his hand away.

"Hey! What are you doing, lady?"

"What are *you* doing?" I counter, resting my hand on the closed lid of the bin.

"I just wanted to throw my gum away. You got a problem with that?"

I take a tissue out of my pocket and hold it under his mouth. Reluctantly, he spits his gum into it.

"Now you can go. You shouldn't be here — unless you can show me your permission slip to be on the lot?"

He says nothing.

"I thought so. Who did you bribe to get in?"

He merely stares at me speculatively while he unwraps another stick of gum and shoves it into his mouth. He crumples the silver wrapper and makes to put it in the bin. Again, I hold out my hand and, sneering, he drops the little foil ball into it.

"What's in the bin?" he asks. "What did he want to get rid of that you don't want anyone to see, hey? What are you covering up for him?"

I lift the lid and peer inside the packet Logan dumped, frantically trying to think what I can say that will put the reporter off wanting to see.

"What is it, man? Used syringes or crack pipes? Photos of him wrapped around an underage nymphet?" He hops from one foot to the other in excitement. "Is it something sick?"

That gives me an idea.

"Eww, yes. It's puke."

"Huh?" He cranes his neck to try and get a glimpse of the contents.

"It's vomit. That's all it is."

"You trying to tell me Logan Rush has morning sickness?"

"Oh yeah, he's pregnant. That's hilarious," I say, not smiling. "Maybe he ate a bad oyster or something. He obviously didn't want it stinking up his room."

"An oyster? For breakfast?" he says suspiciously.

"Hey, he's a star, he eats what he wants, when he wants."

"If he had food poisoning, he wouldn't be walking off to go film."

"Ah, but he's such a pro — he knows the show must go on, and he doesn't let anything get in the way of that. You can write that in your rag."

I stick two fingers into my mouth, whistle piercingly to get the attention of a security guard patrolling near the pay-office, and beckon him over.

"Come on, girly, you must have some juicy stories. We pay our sources well, you know." He gives me a grubby business card and stares at me hard. "Hey, are you also someone famous? I can't tell with all the —" He waves an irritated hand at my sunglasses and hat.

"This person does not have permission to be on the set," I tell the burly security guard who trots up to us. "Please take him outside."

"Alright, alright," the reporter says, trying to shrug off the guard's grasp. "You've got my number, lady. Call me. I want to hear what you have to say."

Keeping a sideways eye on them, I dump the tissue, gum wrapper and business card in the bin, wipe my hands on my jeans, and walk away unconcernedly, just in case the weasel is still looking back over his shoulder to see what I'm doing. But I can't leave anything Logan's keen to get rid of lying in the bin if there's even a remote chance the reporter might find a way to get it.

As soon as he and the guard are out of sight, I dash back and retrieve the trash bag. Stuffed inside are empty soda cans, protein-bar wrappers and tossed call-sheets. And a narrow white envelope.

It's been torn in half, but not opened — the back flap is still sealed under two ink stamps: *Unprivileged mail* and *Inspected.* I turn the halves over. The letter, marked *PRIVATE AND CONFIDENTIAL*, is addressed in small cramped hand-writing to Logan Rush care of the production company's postal address. Next to the postmarked US stamps in the corner, is the sender's name and address: *Mr. J Peabody, ID 32/02/3666-781, Louisiana State Penitentiary, General Delivery, Angola, L.A. 70712.*

Not stopping to think whether I should, I pull the letter out of one half, and get as far as seeing that it's dated October 29 and begins, "Dear Levi," when a shrill call from across the lot makes me snap my head up guiltily.

Shoot! Philip is frantically waving me over — they must all be waiting for me. I shove the letter into a back compartment of my tote bag and run.

CHAPTER 23

CIRCLING PREDATORS

I wait impatiently at the Predator Exhibit tank located smack in the centre of the aquarium. I'm suited up, with my diving mask perched on the top of my wetsuit hood and my feet in their flippers. I've tested my breathing apparatus and need only strap on my tank before I'm ready to go. Logan, however, is nowhere in sight.

On the drive over from the lot, he'd insisted that I go on the shark dive with him.

"I never did fancy dying alone. Besides, this was your bright idea — and those who have the vision …" he'd said, still looking irritated at Cilla's switch of plans.

"*I* had a very different vision," I said. But I said it quietly so Cilla wouldn't hear.

She was muttering instructions to the photographer. "And for God's sake, don't get *her* in any of the shots. Try to make some of them look like he's out in the wild. And you, Thabo," she addresses the bulky bodyguard, "make sure you're not in any of the pictures either. If the Rushers are there, I want them to have access to Logan for autographs and such, but no touching. I don't want him losing chunks of hair again. Not before we've wrapped filming."

"Cilla, I'm touched by your concern," said Logan.

Every time the minibus stopped at traffic lights, Mindy, the make-up artist, made adjustments to Britney's face. Britney was bubbling with excitement over her upcoming shoot.

"I'm so pleased we're doing this in the same place, at the same time! You're going to be right nearby, and I can keep an eye on you." She spoke to Logan, but her eyes flicked to me on the last phrase. I was tempted to tell her to be sure and pet the sweet, harmless penguins, but I bit my tongue.

Now I climb onto the elevated walkway above the top of the predator exhibit. Sunshine streams through the glass roof above, down to the massive circular tank below. We've been told that it's six metres deep and holds over two-million litres of water, as well as a couple of turtles, several mantas and stingrays, and a variety of predator fish — yellowtail, garrick, giant kob, mussel-crackers and stumpnose.

And of course, five ragged-tooth sharks.

Dave, the divemaster who'll be going down with us, joins me on the walkway. He holds a long-handled, two-pronged fork in one hand, and a flip-lidded bucket of food for the fish in the other.

"Is Rush still not ready?" he asks me.

"I'll go see what's keeping him."

Walking like a cross between a duck and an astronaut in the large flippers, I go in search of Logan and find him in the changing room, just strapping on his tank.

"What are you …?" I begin, but my voice dwindles to nothing as I switch from verbal to visual mode.

Logan's wearing his low-slung denim cut-offs again.

"She who must be obeyed forbade me from wearing a wetsuit," Logan says. In an exaggerated imitation of Cilla, he continues, "If you're in a wetsuit, nobody can see it's you. It could be anyone underneath that. They'll say we faked it. Besides, if no one can recognise you, if we don't give them a show that's worth seeing, then what's the point of doing this?' I told her I thought the point was for me to study the sharks to improve my acting, but she told me to shut my pie hole and be sure to come right up to the glass for the close-ups."

"Right," I say.

"She wants me on full display in a goldfish bowl."

My fingers itch to touch him — they actually twitch, but I disguise the movement by grabbing his diving mask from the counter and handing it to him. "Well, whether you're going in a suit, shorts, or buck-naked, it's time to get this show on the road. Follow me. The divemaster's waiting for us."

For a moment, he looks mutinous.

"Can't you get me out of this, Romy?"

He sounds serious, and I want to help him, I do, but his problem is bigger than this rigged photo-op. And there's nothing I can do. I try to lighten the moment.

"Fwightened of the big fishies?" I taunt.

"Trust me, they're the least of what scares me. It's the predators outside the tank that'll eat me alive."

"Look, Logan, there's no escaping today. Cilla's already got the whole juggernaut in motion. You need to suck it up. Time to put on your big-boy panties."

He grins. "Big boys wear panties? For sucking up?"

"And put on your mask and flippers already," I order and march out, hoping that Logan follows. Actor-wrangling for public appearances is definitely in my contract.

"You're so bossy," he mumbles from behind me.

"You've told me that before."

When we get to the shark tank, Dave, the divemaster, gives us final instructions while we strap on our oxygen tanks, adjust our diving masks, and insert our regulator mouthpieces. Then we slip into the water and I can hear only the loud sound of my own breathing. At once, we're surrounded by shoals of glittering tiny fish. Then the bigger predator fish swim right up to us, knowing that the presence of divers means food is on the way.

Dave opens the flip-lid on his bucket, pulls out a large, dead fish, carefully spears it onto the end of the feeding fork, and passes it to Logan. An enormous black fish, big as a bathtub, swims right up to the fork, pulls the fish off the prongs almost delicately between its sharp teeth, and cruises away.

I check Logan's reaction — this is, after all, more my element than his. He meets my gaze, and even through the barrier of the mask, I can see the surprised delight in his eyes. If his mouth wasn't wrapped around the mouthpiece, he would be grinning from ear to ear.

When Dave threads another fish onto the prongs, Logan offers the fork to me so that I can have a chance, but something makes me pause and look up. Outside the glass wall of the tank, Cilla is furiously gesticulating. She points a finger at me and then swings her arm in the opposite direction. The message is clear — *get the heck away from my star*. Then she crooks her finger at

Logan, beckoning him closer to the glass, closer to the cameras.

I hand him the fork and place a hand in the small of his back to push him gently forward, before swimming away from him. A swarm of reporters presses up close to the glass, their massive lenses like large staring eyes. A crowd of waving fans jumps about excitedly on the tiered mini-amphitheatre of seats beyond, holding up signs, phones and cameras. Flashes pop in small explosions of light from all sides.

Logan is indeed on display in a glorified goldfish bowl.

Two manta-rays the size of hula hoops, their curved sides moving like slowly beating wings, glide over to me, softly grazing the top of my head before floating down to where Logan holds out handfuls of squid taken from Dave's bucket.

They scoop it into their wide mouths and circle back for more, gracefully pushing and shoving each other in a slow-motion fight for food. The mouth of one closes over Logan's fingers, and he snatches them back, shaking his hand and wrinkling his face in laughing pain.

Then the sharks come, gliding towards us in their ceaseless circuit around the massive tank. Adrenaline kicks through my body, setting my heart racing. Every instinct urges me to back up and flee. But I'm frozen in place, mesmerised. Because they are extraordinary.

For a moment, I forget about the circus beyond the glass and just gaze in wonder at their alien beauty — spotted grey on top, white beneath, with vertical gills and fins, and tails that move slowly from side to side, propelling them through the water. Rows of sharp, serrated teeth splay outwards and sideways from their gaping jaws. The biggest of them is over three metres long, and its primeval eyes — blank white with a black dot of a pupil — track our every movement. Logan's hair floats in a dark halo around his head as he turns to stare back at it, clearly awestruck.

When Cilla's frantic hopping on the other side of the glass cues him to start his performance, Logan moves nearer to a shark, and a flurry of lights flash.

Keen to stay clear of the media feeding frenzy, I disappear into the forest of tall, floating kelp in the centre of the tank where a cloud of small fish enfolds me in a tight circling throng of flashing silver.

When the huge shark moves on, Logan returns to feeding the fish. He can't swim properly, not more than a few metres at a time, but he doesn't need to — the fish come to him. A fat white one, like an old man with a bulbous forehead and thick lips, keeps coming back for more. When a cream-and-tan loggerhead turtle at least as big as me approaches, Logan holds out a treat — being careful, this time, to pull his fingers away quickly before its beak snaps shut. As it sails up and away through the clear water, he trails a hand along its underbelly.

The photographers outside the tank trip over each other to get the best vantage point. One fan breaks rank and runs right up to the tank to press a hand-drawn sign against the glass.

Logan, dive MY tank!

Security escort the Rusher back to her seat before Britney descends on the scene, wearing a revealing, aquamarine dress of semi-transparent fabric. She poses for a few pics and then half turns to press her hand up against the tank wall. From Cilla's laboured sign language, it's clear what she wants her stars to do. Logan mirrors Britney's movement, pressing his own fingers against hers, with only the barrier of the glass between them, and Britney gazes back lovingly at him. The photogs go wild.

The vivid white light of the popping flashes lights Cilla's face in strange ways, giving her an almost unearthly look of feral satisfaction as she looks on, gaze riveted greedily on her star attraction. Logan's right — she *is* scarier than the sharks. And not half as pretty.

After another fifteen minutes, the divemaster indicates that our time is up. Logan looks relieved but also, as we haul ourselves out of the tank and remove our masks, high on excitement.

"That was incredible!" He shakes Dave's hand. "Thank you, man. It was awesome!"

"Out of this world!" I agree.

We rave about the experience all the way to the changing room. Logan's face glows with a wild, free joy. His cheeks are flushed and his eyes electric blue with excitement.

"I thought it would be tame, but it was wild! I mean, not wild-wild like in-the-wild kind of wild, obviously. But still *wild!* How were those rays — the way they crowded over each other to get the food?"

"Are your fingers okay?"

"They'll be fine."

"How 'bout those sharks?"

"They were crazy-beautiful! I can see why you like 'em so much."

"Yeah, they're magnificent creatures." This seems like a good moment to slip in my suggestion that he could help raise awareness for the species. "You know, you could really —"

I'm cut short by Polyp, who's waiting with Thabo at the door of the changing room. "Logan, you need to get dressed ASAP. Cilla's set up a Q&A with the press, and they're already waiting. She sent me to help you."

"From a tank to a zoo," Logan grumbles. "I'm no freer than those fish."

"Don't be a drama queen, you're hardly a caged animal."

Polyp lays his pale, limp hands on Logan's shoulders to unfasten the catch on the harness, but Logan shrugs him off.

"That's okay, thanks. Romy'll help me, won't you Romy?"

"I *am* your personal assistant," I say, following him into the changing room and nudging the door closed behind me with my hip.

Logan curses under his breath. "How am I supposed to go from that adrenalin rush to sitting behind a table, smiling and answering questions about my love life?"

"You poor thing," I say, though I also want to ask him questions about that. "Now, if you knew more about sharks, you could talk about *them* instead of yourself."

"Couldn't you —" he begins.

"Logan, get real. Cilla didn't set up a press conference for little Miss Nobody to talk about endangered species."

I pull off my hood, spilling my wet hair down over my shoulders, turn my back on him, and unzip the top of my wetsuit.

"Can't you help get me out of this?" he asks plaintively.

"There's only one exit to this place that I know of, and Cilla's probably got it blockaded." I peel the wetsuit to down around my hips.

"No, I mean this harness. Well, for starters this harness."

"Oh, sure." I turn back to him. "But then you'll need to stop whingeing like a wuss and go face the crowds."

I reach forward to unclick the clasps on his shoulder harness. Logan steps back and stares at me, agog. The tank slips to the ground with a loud clang.

"Well, I'll be … It's *you*! Miss Bossy-pants from the cemetery, and with the bunnies. It's you, isn't it? Why didn't you tell me who you were?"

"I figured you didn't remember much of that night."

"I guess the details *are* a bit hazy, but I remember … your mermaid hair." He waves a hand at the wet strands. "And your bikini, and your" — his gaze travels the length of my whole body — "your eyes! How the hell did I not recognise you before?"

"Well," I hedge, remembering the plucking and high-lighting and blow-drying and make-up, "I do look a little different now."

He lifts a lock of my wet hair in either hand and gently tugs me closer. Suddenly, despite having spent most of the last hour in a tank of chilled water, I feel hot and breathless.

"Yeah, it's a huge improvement," he says and before I can get annoyed, continues, "You look natural, more like yourself. Mu-uch better," he draws out the word, and my eyes move to his lips. "I like you like this."

"You — you do?"

He traces his hands over my shoulders and down my arms, leaving a wake of goose bumps on my blushing skin.

"I do."

His hands move from my sides, travel along the line where the black wetsuit curls over at my waist, meet at my navel, and then continue up in a straight line until they break apart to cradle my face.

"I'm going to kiss you now, Romy."

Yes! says my body.

At last! says my heart.

I mute the warnings of my brain, as his face bends down to mine.

My lips part. My eyes close. Perhaps they roll back into my head like a shark's do when in danger, but the bite of his mouth on mine is warm and soft, with the slightest tang of salt from the seawater, and gentle for long moments beyond the reach of time.

Then the kiss becomes something else. Hard and fierce and hot. He pulls me against the whole of him. His hands hold me as tightly as if I'm again rescuing him from the bottomless ocean. His back muscles move under my hands. He groans deep in his throat.

I cling to his body. His chest is cool against my own, and his thick hair is wound around my fingers. I'm beyond thinking, beyond breathing — just a breathless core of here and now. I'm clicking into my place in the universe, finally finding my true element. Nothing has ever felt so good. Nothing has ever fit so right.

We come up for air, breathing raggedly. He's gone from holding me close to holding me up. My bones are made of hot liquid, my knees of air, my head of spinning light. I stare up all the way into the blue depths of his eyes. His pupils are huge, hypnotic. He cups both hands behind my head and draws me in again. This time, the groan is mine.

There's a sound from somewhere far away. I dimly realise that it's a knock at the door. I drop my arms, step back reflexively, and nearly collapse without his support — I've literally gone weak at the knees.

"Logan? Are you coming?" Even through the door, I can tell that Polyp is peeved.

"Yeah, on my way," Logan calls back. His voice sounds rough.

For a long time, he doesn't move. And neither do I. We gaze at each other with speaking, searching eyes.

"I've got to go," he says eventually.

I just nod. Even if I had breath to speak, my words would be drowned out by the loud gallop of my heart.

I wish that it could also drown out the tiny corner of my mind registering the fact that Polyp did not enter. Is do-not-disturbing when Logan's behind a closed door with a female something he's used to doing?

CHAPTER 24
NEED TO TALK

Logan Rush Pregnant!

A representative of the Starlight Studios production company today denied that teen heartthrob and star of the Beast series of films, Logan Rush, is secretly pregnant.

Rush, currently filming Beast: Stars on location in Cape Town, South Africa, is rumoured to be pregnant with co-star Britney's Vaux's baby following a top-secret, hi-tech experimental fertilization procedure at a private medical facility in the city. On-set sources have confirmed that Rush has morning sickness but is keen to hide the evidence. Whereas most moms-to-be crave foodstuffs such as pickles and ice cream, Rush can't get his fill of oysters. Eye witnesses confirm he is suffering from severe mood swings ... (Continued page 5)

Holy guacamole. My daily Google alert for Logan-related news items has delivered up some doozies over the years, but this takes the cake. The weasel-faced reporter has turned yesterday's nonevent into the most bizarre tabloid story of the year. It's beyond ridiculous, it's insane. Honestly, I don't know how Logan hasn't come off the rails with all the rot that gets written about him.

As expected, there are scads of articles online about his swim with the sharks. Cilla will be pleased to see that many of them make no mention of the little fact that the dive took place in a tank in an aquarium. Most show pics of him swimming half-naked between sharks and rays, others use the Britney hand-smooch pic. According to one tabloid, Logan was attacked by a giant stingray and now needs reconstructive surgery on his hand. Accuracy is clearly not a requirement of celebrity reporting.

One article, obviously written by a reporter at one of the major international news agencies and then reproduced word for word across multiple sites, irritates me even more than the pregnancy story.

At Friday's news conference, co-stars Britney Vaux and Logan Rush would neither confirm nor deny rumours that their on-screen romance was an off-screen reality. Miss Vaux merely laughed and said, "That would be telling," while Rush said he would prefer to answer questions about the movie rather than his private life.

Logan had gone straight from our moment of heaven in the changing room to that press conference with Britney. It's upsetting enough to bring me down from the high I've been on since our kiss.

That kiss! I can still hardly believe it happened. There was no chance afterwards to talk to Logan — it took him hours to autograph and photograph his way through the throng of fans waiting outside the aquarium, and then Cilla whisked him straight back to his hotel. I watched the cloud-cuckoo land craziness from a distance, then cadged a lift back to the studio to collect my car, and floated home on a crazy-hopeful cloud nine. I don't know what I dreamed last night, but I felt great this morning — until I started reading the newsfeeds.

I log onto Twitter, check the usual Rusher hashtags, and learn that a sixteen-year-old girl, whose arm Logan signed outside the aquarium yesterday, got a tattoo artist to needle over the autograph with ink. She's posted a photo of Logan's signature — now forever tattooed on her arm. Madness.

My phone beeps an incoming message, and I snatch it up.

We need to talk. L.

Crap. That's what people say when they want to end a relationship, not begin one. I answer cautiously.

—

Ok. Where? At your hotel? R.

—

*No, not pvt enough. On set? Have costume fitting
at 11am — see you after at my room?*

—

See you then.

—

☺

—

I want to type x's and o's, a series of hearts and kissy-lips, or at least three smiley faces, but I rein myself in.

☺

On my way out, my father waylays me.

"You said there wasn't going to be any filming today," he accuses.

"There's been a change of plan, but I only have to go in for an hour or so."

"We never see you these days, Rosemary."

"You're seeing me now, Dad." I grab my car keys and head for the front door.

"Just make sure you're home for family lunch tomorrow. Your mother is going to a lot of trouble to make Nana's day special," he calls after me.

Shoot, tomorrow is November the seventeenth — Nana's birthday. I'll have to go gift shopping this afternoon. On the way to the studios, I try to brainstorm ideas for a present, but my mind slips sideways to dwell on Logan.

What is he going to say? That the kiss was a mistake and we should stay clear of each other? Maybe even that it will be better if I quit and he gets a new PA? My mind keeps returning, like a shark circling chum in the water, to the 0.1 percent possibility that he's going to tell me he's never felt this way before about anyone, and pull me into another wild kiss.

At half-past eleven, Logan strolls into his room on the lot, pulling the door closed behind him. We hold each other's gaze for several long, uncertain moments.

"Come here, you," he says.

I move as if in a trance, and then we're hugging and kissing, and giggling like kids. As the minutes pass, there's less hugging and giggling, and more deep, languorous kissing. When finally he pulls away, Logan kisses each of my eyelids and then steers me over to the bed. Uh-oh. I'm nowhere near ready for that yet. But he just sits down and gestures for me to do the same. I climb onto the bed and sit cross-legged, facing him. His lips curve upwards in a slow grin.

"Why so worried?" He envelops one of my hands in both of his.

"You wanted to talk with me?"

"I *want* to do many things with you." My breath catches at that. "But I *have* to talk. We need to keep this, *us*," he gestures to me and him, "a secret."

"Oh," I say, not sure whether to feel relieved or disappointed. This is neither as good as I hoped nor as bad as I feared.

"If Cilla finds out, she'll blow … not so much a fuse as her entire freaking motherboard. She'll fire you on the spot."

Yes, but the job isn't what matters most to me. My main reason for taking it was to get close to him. Be cool, I warn myself, no confessions of love. Remember rule number whatever.

"But Romy, your job's not the point here, trust me."

Although I've just thought the very same thing, it bothers me to hear him say it. This job may well have mattered enormously to me. For all he knows, I'm planning a career in the film industry.

"Oh, it isn't, is it?"

"No, trust me."

Zeb's warning comes back to me: "You only really need to worry if he begins saying 'trust me.'" And now he's said it twice.

"Romy, it's your *life* that matters here."

That brings me up short.

"My life? Cilla wouldn't kill me, would she? Not literally?"

He laughs. His eyes are shining amethysts today. "Actually, I wouldn't put it past her, but that's not what I meant. No, I'm talking about your way of living, your privacy, your freedom to come and go and do what you like."

"I can't do that anyway. My parents —"

"Your parents are just trying to protect you. That's what parents do. Or should do. Loving parents want the best for their kid."

"But I'm not a kid."

"Oh, I know that," he says, and there's such heat in his eyes that I blush. So much for playing it cool. "You've had a glimpse into my life. Whatever I do, wherever I go, the whole world watches and comments and judges. Everything I say is twisted and misquoted. If I cut my hair, it's front-page news. And when there's no news, they make it up."

"I've noticed. Did you know you're pregnant?"

"*What?* Never mind, I don't want to hear." He waves his hands in the air as if to erase the story. "The point is, I chose this world because I love acting, it's what I want to do. But I didn't know, back then, that I'd be trading my life for fame. Are you sure you want that for yourself?"

"I'm not sure I understand what you mean."

"Romy, if people see us together — even just here on set — if there's even the slightest suspicion of something between us, the crows will descend on you and peck your life to pieces. They'll camp outside your house, hassle your family, track down your friends and your enemies — especially your enemies, anyone who dislikes or is jealous of you — and pump them for details. They'll hassle your old school teachers for embarrassing stories, they'll bribe people you thought were your friends to take photographs of your bedroom, they'll trawl the web for any grain of information on you, any comment or photo you've ever posted. They'll snoop through your family's mail and garbage, hide on the beach when you go swimming, follow you wherever you drive. And if they can't find anything interesting enough, they'll invent some juicy, delicious scandal."

As he speaks, I can see it. I've been an anonymous presence on the periphery of his life these past weeks, protected by my clipboard and the fact that I'm so obviously not a part of his world. But if people suspect that there's a romance brewing, all of that will change. I've seen it, up-close — witnessed how the fans, the media, and the industry itself is a ravenous monster, insatiably set on gobbling up his life. And after him, the next person's. I think about my parents, my sisters, Zeb.

"You're young, Romy. Your whole life lies ahead of you."

"What are you? *Old?*"

"It sometimes feels like that," he says with a small, self-deprecating laugh. "I've been doing the same thing, playing the same role for four years now. I'm kinda trapped in the *Beast* thing." His fingers trace an unhurried pattern on the palm of my hand, distracting me. "You can do anything, become anything, go anywhere. And I want that for you — you deserve that and so much more. Are you sure you want *this*?"

I'm pretty sure I don't. I want him, yes, but not the life he's forced to lead. From the outside, his world seemed so free and exciting. From the inside, it seems a lot more restricted and a lot less satisfying. Besides, I've never yearned to be famous myself.

"And we — you and me — if we go public, we'll never have another moment alone. And I want moments alone with you. Many more of them," Logan says, studying my face.

"You're right," I sigh.

He waits, completely still, for me to explain.

"We're going to have to do this in secret," I say.

He smiles his slow, lazy smile. "What, this?" He outlines another pattern on the palm of my hand, around my wrist.

"Yes, and this," I say. I lift his hand to my mouth. Press my lips to a knuckle.

"And definitely this." He leans over to nibble on an earlobe.

I draw an uneven breath. "And most especially this." I kiss him, and he kisses me, and then we kiss each other some more. In secret.

We keep our clothes on, but we shed our reserve, sharing bits and pieces of our lives and families, what we dream of, and what we fear. I add more information to my mental files on Logan: he seriously admires and respects his mother, he seriously doesn't want to talk about his father, he wishes he could be considered for more serious and challenging roles, and if he winds up on death-row, he'll want his last meal to be boiled crawfish, fried green tomatoes, and something called collard greens. He hates prejudice, hypocrisy, and narrow-mindedness. (He gets so worked up when he speaks of these that I have to kiss him calm again). He loves hugs and quiet and the ocean.

"And Toffee, don't forget Toffee," I prompt.

"Nah, I don't have much of a sweet tooth."

"I meant your dog!"

"What dog?"

"The beagle that you adopted from the animal shelter four years ago."

"I don't have a dog, Romy, not even one called Toffee."

I perch up on one elbow and stare at him, horrified.

"You mean that's just a story, it's just —"

"B.S.? Yeah. My publicist at the time invented it. He said it would make me appear more sympathetic and increase the aw-shucks factor."

Wow. Something to delete from the Rush files, then. I must look woebegone, because he kisses the tip of my nose and says gently, "It's all just a show, Romy."

A few minutes later, he and I put on quite the show as we cross the lot. He plays the role of a spoilt movie star, issuing orders for the most difficult requests he can imagine — coffee made from beans which have passed through and out of the digestive tract of a civet (who knew?); a helicopter ride to the top of Table Mountain — which is to be cleared of everyone for his visit; five personal bodyguards in black suits; and a bucket of M&M's from which all the blue ones have been removed by hand. My hand. No one could guess, from his poker face, that he isn't entirely serious. After a while of this, even I begin to wonder if he's acting.

"You *are* kidding, aren't you?" I ask in a whisper.

In answer, he rolls his eyes at me.

"Okay, just checking," I say. "You're a very good actor."

"One tries."

"One succeeds. Right … so," I read loudly down my list as we pass the crew who're working on repairing the shark model that was damaged in Thursday's filming, "poop coffee, exclusive rights to a World Heritage Site, an Incredible Hulk quintet, and lucky-colour sweeties. That about it in terms of your needs and desires?"

"Not even close, I have plenty more needs and desires. I'm insatiable."

The words are innocuous enough, but the heat shimmer in his eyes as he says them causes me to stumble. He catches me by the elbow to steady me and gives it a squeeze when we part at the gate — Logan heading back to the Hotel, and me heading out to find a present for the woman who already has everything plus a feather boa.

CHAPTER 25
TWO LETTERS

On Sunday, at the family lunch held for her birthday, Nana pronounces herself delighted with my gift — a coffee-table book on the history of London's West End — and regales us with long anecdotes about her life in the footlights.

When the family's attention is on the massive lamb roast Mom brings to the dining table, Nana turns to me and whispers, "And how's it going with your prince?"

I smile and give her the thumbs-up. She crows with glee and pats my hand with her knobbly one, but there's no chance to give her any details — which is probably a good thing. Logan and I have agreed to keep our relationship private.

"So, how's the new job, Romy?" Meriel asks, dropping a spoonful of mint sauce onto her plate.

"It's good. You know, fine."

"They certainly keep her hopping — we've hardly seen hide nor hair of her lately," Mom says. "She's been as elusive as a *coelacanth*."

"Have you learned anything about the world of business?" my father asks.

"Loads."

I describe life on the set, being careful to keep my voice casual and my face neutral whenever I mention Logan. I tell them about my duties and all about the shark dive, but none of what happened afterwards in the changing room.

"Fancy making you go down with him into the tank — where you might have been in danger," my father says, frowning.

"She was never in any danger from the *Carcharias Taurus*, Rex," Mom says. "I'm glad you got to see an *Argyrosomus japonicas*, though, and some *Dasyatis chrysonota*, Romy. Aren't they impressive creatures?"

"Oh yeah, I was dead impressed by the creatures in the tank. Great specimens!" Especially one of the *homo sapiens*.

"And running around for food and coffee and scripts," Dad continues. "It sounds like you're nothing but a dogsbody."

"I'd be that wherever I worked my vac. Interns always start at the bottom."

"I must say, the world of moviemaking sounds like a whole other world — utterly foreign and very strange," Mom says. "More potatoes, Rex?"

"It sounds self-indulgent and crazy," Marina says, her lips tight with disapproval.

"I can't help thinking all that money would be better spent on helping uplift children from impoverished communities." Genna declines the second helping of roast potatoes Mom offers her, as if to underscore her belief that no one should have too much while others have too little.

"It's a business, not a charity. And it injects a lot of money into the local economy, and employs loads of people," Cordelia says. "Plus, it has better profit margins than you get in the seafood industry. Sorry, Dad, but it's true."

"Life is not all about profit, Cordelia," he replies.

"I'm glad to hear you admit that, Dad, really glad." I'm tired of everyone giving me a go about this. "Is no one happy for me?"

"Darling, of course we are. It's just such an odd job. Are you sure you enjoy it? A bright girl like you — what do you actually like about it?"

There's no way to answer my mother's question honestly without declaring my big secret. What I like about the job begins and ends with Logan. I've been in the position for long enough to know that my mom and dad aren't wrong about a personal assistant being a glorified dogsbody. Fetching and carrying don't make for much mental stimulation or job satisfaction. Even my sisters have a point — the movie industry might appear to be glamorous and magical, but in reality it's mostly a superficial, self-obsessed and self-indulgent moneymaking machine.

I don't know what to say, but thankfully Nana comes to my rescue.

"Well, I think it all sounds fabulous and magnificent! So enchanting and" — she gives me a big wink — "*romantic*. Follow your passion, Romy!"

After lunch, I finally get a chance to relax and catch up on the emails that have been piling up in my inbox since I took the *Beast* job. Among the solicitations from Nigerian princes, urgings to buy products guaranteed to enlarge my manhood to splendid proportions, and mail from friends, there are increasingly tetchy notes from Zeb, who takes exception to not receiving daily updates on my life and reminds me that he's moving to his new digs in December.

I type a quick reply, promising to help him decorate — he may know shoes, but he's completely ignorant about curtains and bedding — and ask him about his plans for New Year's Eve. I hit Send, trying not to think about how Logan will be back in the States by then. And I'll still be here.

My phone beeps an incoming message. It's from Logan.

Meet up tonight? Xo

My spirits rising, I reply at once.

Where and when? xo

While I sit in textpectation, my email inbox pings the arrival of a new message — one that immediately catches my eye. I read it three times to make sure I'm not misunderstanding anything.

From: Captain@Syrenka.com
To: OceanGirlR@gmail.com
Subject: Vacancy on voyage to Southern Ocean

Dear Romy

One of our crew has unfortunately had to return home to the US due to a death in the family. This leaves us with an open position on the Syrenka's *December voyage to the Southern Oceans to disrupt Japanese whaling operations there. Since you live in Cape Town, and since we'll be stopping there on our journey south, I wondered if you would like to join our crew? You'd be signing on for a four-month term, and your duties would include working mostly in the galley, preparing meals, and washing dishes, but as you know, it's all hands on deck when it comes to taking on the whalers. My cautions and warnings (as set out in my initial information email), still apply, as do the terms of being a crew member, as set out in our original correspondence and your signed application.*

Please let me know as soon as possible whether you would still like to join our mission. We are due to dock in Cape Town on December 14th to restock our supplies, and plan to leave Dec 16th.

Awaiting your response,

Kind regards

Keith Murphy
(Captain)

"We know that when we protect our oceans we're protecting our future." - Bill Clinton

P.S. Attached please find a Volunteer Waiver of Liability Form for you to sign.

Now they accept my application? *Now?*

Just as things with my other passion are taking off, I get the letter offering me a once-in-a-lifetime opportunity on the other end of the world, the one thing I've wanted to do since forever? If I spend the last few weeks the film production is in town with

Logan, I'll have to turn down this berth. If I take up the *Syrenka* opportunity, I'll have to cut short my time with Logan. I'm screwed. I have to choose between my two loves. How can a letter with such good news leave me feeling so bad?

Then I remember the other letter, the one I rescued from the bin and shoved into my bag on Friday. I retrieve it and place it on the desk in front of me, fitting the edges of the torn halves together. Should I, or shouldn't I? I'm burning with curiosity to know who it's from and what it's about, especially after Cilla's cryptic comment about mail for Levi. But it's Logan's private business — I have no right to read it. Sighing, I toss the torn letter into the rubbish bin and send Captain Murphy a reply asking him for the latest I can give him my answer by. I'm playing for time. Really, what could possibly change by then?

My phone beeps again.

> *Sorry, won't be able to make it — Britney wants to*
> *do a read-through of scene 68 with me. L.*

And what Miss Vaux wants, Miss Vaux gets, right? My mood takes a nosedive.

Without consciously deciding to, I fetch the letter. I extract the two pieces of paper from the torn envelope, smooth them out, lay them side-by-side, and begin reading. When I finish, I feel, if anything, worse.

Dear Levi,

I hope your well. I'm well as I can be in this place. Which is hell on earth for a just man falsely accused and railroaded by the system. You and Wynette have forgot all about me. Its shameful how I bin treated. Not even to speak of that bitch who turned me in, then divorced me. A woman should stand by her man.

I know your doing well and rolling in cash like a hog in mud. Probly think your too good for me now. Im sure you still don't want anyone to know bout me so best you send some more funds for another appeal, and to make my life better in here the screws wont do nothing for you unless you can give them cigrettes.

Best you write me soon boy.

Jonas Peabody

CHAPTER 26

HIDING IN PLAIN SIGHT

Two weeks later, sitting on a plush chair in a high-end restaurant, I study the man seated opposite me with distaste.

His hair is the colour and texture of straw, and his skin is sallow and wrinkled, with dark shadows beneath his eyes. A scraggly handle-bar moustache droops over his mouth. He attracted some odd looks when we arrived at this posh place — good thing I booked a private dining room.

When asked, "Caint y'all jes do me some hominy grits, back bacon and fried bread?" the waiter had fought giggles while suggesting that a *tian* of roast warthog with polenta and a gooseberry *jus* would be just the thing.

The restaurant is trendy, but I'm not here for the fancy food, or the gigantic chandelier made of dangling wine glasses, or even the magnificent views of the Franschhoek valley vineyards from our window. I frown at the tower of food stacked on the outsize, herb-sprinkled plate the waiter places in front of me, and turn my attention back to the man. He tucks the starched linen

195

napkin into the collar under his chin and looks set to climb into his food with his hands.

"I'm sorry," I say, "I can't face you while I eat. The sight of you will put me off my food."

"Well bless your pea-picking heart if you ain't a feisty lil' lady! And right purty, too."

I move chairs, slipping into the one next to him so that I won't have to look at him unless I turn. He interprets the chair swap as an invitation.

"If I said you hed a beautiful body, would you hold it against me?" His hand reaches over to cop a feel. I smack it away. "Ah, snuggle up sugar-britches, I won't eatcha."

"You eat your hog, please. I'm only sitting here so that I don't have to see your face."

"Is that any way to talk to a friendly fella?"

"Whatever." I eat a delicious bite of duck breast, and add, "The hair has to go."

"You don't like my mullet? I think it's the best hairdo that ever was — all business in the front" — he touches the short fringe — "and party at the back." He tosses his head and winks lecherously at me.

"Well I think it's gross."

I reach over and yank off his hair. When I rip off his moustache, he yelps in pain.

"You know," I say, cocking my head as I contemplate him critically, "you'd think that would be an improvement. But somehow it isn't."

The sallow skin and age -effects look bizarre under his tangle of thick, black hair, and shreds of glue still adhere to his upper lip.

"Here," I say, pulling off the wrinkled latex "skin" from under his eyes and handing him a wet wipe, "clean your face. We're in a private room, and we're going straight home afterwards, it should be safe to shed your disguise."

Wiping the thick layer of make-up off with a few experienced swipes, Logan sniffs in mock injury and says, "I think you only love me for my handsome face."

A thrill goes through me at the forbidden word, but I remind myself of rules one, two and three, and opt for humour.

I gasp melodramatically and clutch a hand to my heart. "How can you say that? I'm not that shallow. I do not love you *only* for your handsome face." I think there's a glint of something intense in his eyes when I say that — but it might just be residual pain from the moustache removal. I grin and add, "I love you for your gorgeous body, too."

I give his biceps a squeeze. He pinches my waist playfully then tickles me into giggles. The laughter somehow becomes a kiss.

It's the perfect moment in a perfect day. Apart from the mullet disguise, that is.

I've spent the last two weeks on set and on location — fetching, carrying, and generally running my feet off in my now-scuffed high heels. Contact between Logan and me has been restricted to long text conversations on WhatsApp, hidden hugs in deserted corners, stolen kisses in his room and, once, some passionate canoodlery in the "hold" of the fake trawler, muffling laughter with kisses as Cilla stalked about, a chickabiddy on each shoulder, calling out for Logan.

"Where is that boy? Someone find Romy. Tell her to unearth him."

We finally came up with a plan to spend this free day alone together in the Cape winelands. Logan begged Ed to create a disguise for him, saying he just wanted a normal day sightseeing in the Cape without being recognised. Ed was delighted at the opportunity to uglify one of the stars he spent his life prettifying, and set to with gusto, offering Logan a selection of wigs, moustaches and make-up effects. When he was finished, not even Logan's mother would have recognised him.

"No fair that you don't have to wear a disguise," Logan grumbled as we drove north out of Cape Town.

"It comes with the fame and fortune, cupcake, so suck it up."

I wore my comfortable jeans with a simple cotton shirt and sneakers, minimal make-up and un-styled hair. I loved that I could be myself with him. Loved that he preferred me that way.

We spent a glorious Sunday morning riding horses on a trail winding through the Franschhoek valley nestled beneath craggy granite mountains, admiring the Cape Dutch architecture of the wine estates and the undulating mauve lines of lavender fields, revelling in the freedom to speak and touch without fear of being discovered.

It turned out that Logan wasn't a complete dud as an action-man. He could horse-ride very well — far better than I could, even though I'd had a few months of lessons back when I went through a preteen phase of crushing on horses. He rode like a lazy cowboy, stirrups long and low, and the reins held casually in one hand.

"Where'd you learn to ride so well?" I asked him, as we splashed through a shallow stream.

"They got me an instructor for my horseback scenes in *Moon*.

But that was just to smarten up my style — I could already ride when I was a kid."

"That's the first thing you've told me about your childhood."

A shadow of wariness passed across his features.

"It was just a normal small-town Southern childhood, I guess. Going to the local school with my sister. She was smarter'n me, I was always catching flack for staring out of the window and daydreaming. We spent summers playing down by the river, catching craw-daddies and making tree houses, and getting into fights with Dwayne Jackson and his gang. There was a farmer down the road that had a horse that would come up to the fence. We'd feed him sugar cubes stolen from the diner and try to sneak rides on his back. He was an ornery mule of a horse, too, nothing like these sweet darlin's," he said, patting the neck of his bay.

I noticed that he had slipped into a deeper Southern accent as he spoke about his childhood. "Tell me more."

"We were pretty much dirt poor, especially after my father … died. Well, y'all have read the stories, I'm sure. Sometimes we even went to school with holes in our shoes."

Finally — an explanation for his loving obsession with shoes.

"One time the counsellor bought me a new pair and sent a note home asking if we needed any help. I can still remember the shame on my momma's face." When next he spoke, pride replaced the embarrassment in his voice. "My mom was a waitress in a diner; she worked harder'n anybody I ever knew."

"Did she really leave you near a sewing machine that fell on your baby toe?" I asked.

Since the revelation about the elephant picture and the non-existent pet beagle, I half-doubted all the stories I'd read about him.

"Now, strangely enough, that story is one-hundred percent true. My poor mother still feels guilty about that."

As well she should. "And she lives in Atlanta now?"

"Yeah, with my sister."

"Is it true that you bought them a house? And cars?"

"What is this, twenty questions?" he said, ducking his head in embarrassment. "Let's ride!"

We jumped over a small drainage ditch between lavender fields, and he urged his horse forward with a click of the tongue and a slap of the reins. I caught up soon enough, though — his wig flew off as soon as he went faster than a sedate trot.

"Let's talk about you for a while," he said, once he was back in the saddle with his mullet back on his head.

"I've told you about my childhood. Nice, normal and happy — pretty dull stuff."

"Hey, don't knock nice, normal and happy. It sounds amazing."

There was a note of longing in his voice, but before I could ask him about it, he carried on. "And what about your future — any ideas what you'd like to do?"

"You sound like my father," I stalled.

This discussion was a minefield. I was as uncertain and undecided about my future as a kid in front of a sweet counter. And so much depended on what happened between Logan and me. Picking my words carefully, I explained to him about the offer to crew on the anti-whaling craft.

"I don't know what to do. On the one hand, I deeply want to join the *Syrenka* and do something worthwhile to help whales. But I don't think I'd want to do that forever. A four-month mission would be an adventure, a chance to escape my protected little life and see something of the world. Maybe I'd even learn a few things about myself. But to do it indefinitely? I don't think that's for me. On the other hand, though, when I think about my other options — a degree in business if my dad has his way, or in marine biology if my mother gets hers — I'm totally not enthusiastic. I want to sink my teeth into something worthwhile, something that changes the world."

"So, not more celebrity PA'ing then?" he said, his tone light. "You could crew on the good ship Hollywood, you know. We wrap in under three weeks, and I'm not ready to let you go. You could leave home and come with me back to L.A."

"And be a film-set flunky forever?" I paused, but he offered nothing more. "No offence, but no thanks."

"That's the gratitude I get for introducing you to the world of wigs, and CG'd jigs and chickabiddies!" He laughed.

And I laughed, too. Though suddenly I felt like crying.

CHAPTER 27
ENDANGERED SPECIES

Earlier, riding in the vineyards and lavender fields, it had seemed like a relationship between Logan and me was a sheer impossibility. But now, kissing in our private room in the restaurant, anything seems possible. That's how it is with Logan. Every time I'm in his arms, all my concerns fade to background noise.

"So," he says, pulling away just far enough to look me in the eyes, "you love me for my face *and* my body?"

"Yup."

"Well, I am definitely a person of greater depth, Miss Romy Morgan, because I love you not only for your golden eyes and mermaid hair and delicious body." I hold my breath, because his face is earnest now. "I love you for your kindness and your honesty, for your integrity and even your danged bossiness. I love how you want to save the world, and how you want to save me."

I stare at him, lost in those pools of blue, drowning in the words.

"I love you, Romy."

My heart stops, along with the rest of the universe. When it starts again, I say, "And I love you, Logan. I love you for your sense of humour and the way you laugh, for your chill —"

"My chill?"

"You are very chilled. You make me more chilled."

"Go on."

"I love your loyalty and cute Southern manners. I love the slow way you walk and how this lock of hair always flops over this eye. Oh, did I mention your eyes?"

"I notice we're back to my face," he says wryly.

"Right. But I also think you're a seriously talented actor and a great — and I mean *gifted* — kisser."

"It's been said."

I laugh and shove him back. "Plus," I add, "I loved you before I met you, so I win."

"It's a competition?"

"*Life* is a competition. And I must win."

I want this day to last forever. I wish we could run away together. But Logan needs to be back at the hotel by five, for a read-through of the next day's scene. He'll be spending the evening with Cilla and Britney. I'll be spending the evening at home. Alone.

"Come with me," Logan says.

"To the hotel?"

"To L.A. — I'm serious."

Could I do it? It would be like running away from home, turning my back on my parents, betting everything on a relationship which has lasted just over two weeks, with a guy I met in the flesh for the first time just a month ago. And if I went, I'd be doing … what?

"What do you plan to do in L.A.?" I ask him. "Cilla told Polyp that —"

"Who?"

"Philip — who told Becka who told me that she's pitched for another two *Beast* sequels after this one. Are you going to sign on for more of them?"

"Nobody seems to think I can do anything else," Logan says, pushing his over-priced pork and grits around on his plate, trailing patterns in his gooseberry *jus*.

"What do you mean?"

"Back when I'd just landed the role in the first *Beast*, I was so happy. Man, I was over the moon! Fame, money, travel — all of it was mine, and it was more than I could ever have imagined. And I'm still grateful. It changed my life, you know? But now it feels less like an opportunity and more like one of the Beast's traps. I'm tired of doing the same thing over and over. Chase Falconer gets to punch and kick and spout clichés — it's not too much of an acting challenge, except for trying to find fresh ways of saying the same old things and having to wear different face fur. Or scales."

"Sharks don't have scales, Logan, you should know that after the dive." I point a fork at him in admonishment.

"You're not going to give up trying to educate me about sharks, are you?"

"Nope. I happen to think you could do some good with your fame, raise awareness, change attitudes."

"Nah, who would listen to me? I'm not a scientist, I'm just an actor."

"They'd listen to you *because* you're an actor. But don't get distracted now, you were telling me about your future. Go on."

"So bossy!"

"Huh. You should be used to it in your profession — you spend your whole day being ordered about by everyone from the director on down. Say this, say it this way, that way, stand here, speak louder, softer, sit still, don't eat that, do lift this. I think they pay you the big bucks so you'll let them boss you around."

He gazes at me, astonished, as if I've said something profound or pointed out something he's never noticed before.

"Your future?" I prompt.

"So, there are a couple of things I'd like to try."

"Tell me more."

"I … Well, for a while, I've been wanting to do some writing."

"Becka *said* you wanted to write a scene."

"She's right. I've actually re-written one of the scenes for this movie, and I've begged, pleaded, and half-threatened Cilla into agreeing to shoot it."

"Wow!"

"Wednesday morning — if you want to give me some moral support."

"I'll be there. I'd love to see you doing something deeper, working with better material."

"You don't know that mine's better," he warns.

"Yes I do," I say simply.

"Aw shucks, you're just as sweet as syrup on a Sunday. Y'all got me grinnin' like a possum eatin' a sweet 'tater."

"You know," I say, "it hasn't escaped my notice that you do an excellent rednecky trailer-trash accent."

He shrugs. "What can I say, I'm a great actor."

"Where did you learn it?"

I watch him carefully, thinking of that letter now hidden at the bottom of my underwear drawer and feeling a pang of guilt. He takes a last bite of his food and closes the knife and fork on the plate.

"From *Here Comes Honey Boo-Boo*, and *Jerry Springer* reruns," he says smoothly.

Right. "Have you written anything else?"

"I've started working on an original screenplay."

He looks at me warily, as if expecting me to mock him

"But that's fantastic! What's it about?"

"The Freedom Riders."

"The who?"

"In April 1961, a group of thirteen civil rights activists boarded a Greyhound bus in Washington, D.C. and headed south for New Orleans in Louisiana in a protest to challenge racial segregation laws."

I roll my hand in the air, motioning for him to continue.

"The bus was for whites only, but the riders were both African American and white, and they used — or tried to use — restrooms and lunch counters designated as being for the opposite race only, which did not please too many people in those places."

I nodded. "I can just imagine."

"More riders joined, and as the rides grew and spread across the South, the opposition grew, too. They were met with violent white mobs, beatings, bombs, and even imprisonment. But the movement drew national and international attention to the racist policies, and in September, they achieved victory. Segregation on buses and trains was prohibited."

His face is alight with excitement. I can tell he's passionate about this project.

"It sounds like an amazing story."

"Yeah, it's important, you know? It needs to be told, and I feel like maybe I owe —"

There's a loud knock at the door. The waiter, who's come to collect our plates, does a double take at the sight of me with a completely different, and undeniably hot, man, but he's too well-trained to betray his surprise with more than a raised eyebrow. He clears the table and promises to be right back with our desserts.

"What was the other thing?" I ask, removing the napkin from Logan's collar.

"What other thing?"

"You said there were a couple of things you'd like to try."

"Well, I *would* like to try different roles, something more edgy, not all action or romantic leading man. My agent doesn't like it, says it's too risky. He says I should cash in on the heartthrob dollar while I still can. Bu-ut," he draws the word out on a sigh, "they're doing a production of *Equus* on Broadway next year, in February. And ..." He pauses, shoots me a quick glance and then finishes in a rush, "And I'm busting a gut trying to land the role of Alan Strang. Do you know the play?"

"Yes!"

I *do* know it. Zeb dragged me to see a production of it earlier this year. It was hectic — a roller-coaster ride of raw emotions — and afterwards I felt like a wrung-out sponge. The role of Alan

Strang is incredible. It's possibly the most demanding role there is for a young, male actor. It would totally give Logan a chance to show his talent.

"That would be awesome. *Awesome!*" I'm bouncing in my seat with excitement at all his amazing plans.

"Yeah, I think so, too. But the producers and the director don't seem to think I can hack it."

I stop bouncing. "What do *you* think?"

"People don't usually ask me what I think."

"I'm not usual people."

"No sirree, that you aren't."

"You're avoiding the question."

"Okay, then. I think I could. I think I could nail it."

"Then you should totally go for it."

The waiter returns with our desserts — gooseberry sorbet for Logan and crème brulée for me. We linger over the sweet treats, reluctant to end the day, but as we're finishing our coffee, we become aware of a rising noise from outside — slamming car doors, loud voices, and then, unmistakably, the high-pitched mating call of the hunting Rusher.

Logan sighs and rocks back on his chair to peer out of the window.

"Yup, it's over — we've been made."

Damn. I'll bet it was the waiter who ratted us out.

My fingers are already flying over the screen of my phone, checking the #RushTo hashtag on Twitter. I groan.

"The word is well and truly out," I say, showing Logan the rolling stream of incoming tweets. "We need to escape now — the crowd's only going to grow bigger."

Logan peeps out of the window again.

"It's like a scene from that Hitchcock film, *The Birds*. Every time I look, a few more have gathered, and they want to peck pieces out of me."

I suddenly feel irresponsible for helping Logan ditch his bodyguard.

"Wait here," I tell him.

I'm back in less than five minutes.

"Where did you go?" he asks.

"Can I boss you around a bit more?"

"Will you wear black leather while you do it?"

"Pervert."

He laughs. "Is that a yes?"

"I have a plan. You're going to go to the men's room. I've reconnoitred it, and —"

"You checked out the men's room?" He whistles.

"A good PA doesn't know the meaning of the word 'no,'" I say. "And in the men's room, there's a window in the right-hand cubicle that'll be big enough for you to squeeze out of. I'll exit via the front, and get the car. Unfortunately, there's no way I can get it to the back of the restaurant where the restrooms are, but I'll get it through the boom gate and be waiting, engine running, in the road. You just need to cross the road, preferably without the Rusher pack seeing you, and we'll take off."

I shove my phone into my bag and stand. But Logan is still sitting back, completely relaxed, in his chair. As usual, he isn't moving fast enough for me.

"What about the check?" he asks.

"I've already paid the bill."

"But … nobody ever pays the check with me." He looks bemused.

"What, you sneak out without paying? That is so not okay, Logan Rush."

"No. I meant, *I* always pay the check, not anyone else."

"What, always?"

He shrugs. "Pretty much."

"Then your friends have no manners." I sneak a last peep out of the window and grab my bag. "Okay, so I'll initiate diversionary tactics, and you proceed to the escape module. On three … two … one … Go! Go faster, Logan!"

I stride through the main dining room and stand just inside the entrance of the restaurant. The flock of Rushers has gathered a little way outside the front door. Behind me, I hear Logan asking someone the way to the restroom — that's my cue. As I walk slowly out the door, all faces turned towards me, and for a moment I feel like a movie star on the red carpet. But they look away as soon as they see who I'm not.

"Hey, are you guys waiting for Logan Rush?" I ask, loud enough for all of them to hear.

"Yes!"

"Is he in there? Have you seen him?"

"I'm gonna faint."

"I'm gonna die!"

"He's just behind me," I say. "He should be out any moment now."

Squealing, they get out their phones, focus their cameras on the doorway, pull the caps off their permanent markers, wipe their teary eyes, and spray their mouths with breath freshener. Are they expecting to kiss him?

While their attention is riveted on the restaurant entrance, I hurry to my car. I drive it to the security boom, where I hand the guard on duty my token.

"Does this boom work?" I ask him.

"Of course, yes," he nods.

"Maybe, when all those screaming girls want to get out, it will be broken."

The guard frowns at me, puzzled.

"Just for one or two minutes," I say, handing him a R100 note.

He nods again, smiling in perfect understanding this time.

Tactical-delaying deal done, I turn into the main road that runs alongside the restaurant and wait with the engine running, my eyes fixed on the back corner of the building I've just exited. The gaggle of girls is still clustered around the front, craning their necks, and taking pictures of the maître d' now flapping his gloved hands at them as if to shoo off a flock of troublesome pigeons.

Finally, Logan emerges from the back corner of the building, rubbing his head. Has he hurt it? Again?

He strolls casually away from the building, but just as he reaches the road and is about to cross, he's spotted. Shrill screams rend the air, and the pack of crazed fans hurtle towards him. He glances back reflexively and only then notices the car headed directly at him. He leaps backwards and is well out of the way by the time the ancient Peugeot, driven by a tiny old lady barely tall enough to see above the steering wheel, drives slowly by. Logan dashes across the road and leaps into my car.

"You took your time," I say.

"I had an altercation with a drain and a pipe. And the ground. Where's a stuntman when you need one?"

As we screech off, I see the Rushers are scattering for their cars, but the security guard is out of his booth and examining the boom as if there's a fatal fault with it.

"So long suckers!" I yell, waving a hand out of the window.

Logan laughs at me. "You know, you could always become a getaway car driver. There's lots of work for those in L.A."

CHAPTER 28
KEEPING QUIET

Logan Rush in hit-and-run!

Demented pensioner hits Logan Rush, condition stable

Tightwad Logan Rush makes his dates pay for lunch!

Logan Rush killed in car accident!

Logan shrugs when I tell him about the outrageous headlines early on Tuesday morning while we wait to start filming a romantic scene with Britney on sound stage three.

"Logan, Logan! We need to rehearse the scene," Britney calls from where she sits on a large leather sofa on the dressed set. A dimly lit lamp and a vase of lilies grace a side table. High bookshelves stacked with fake books stand behind the couch, and a blood-red Persian carpet covers the floor. The contrast between the warm, luxurious feel of the set and the jungle of wires, lights, cameras, and hubbub of action that begins where the carpet ends, is stark — almost surreal.

"I'll be right there," Logan tells Britney. With his back to her, he gives me one of his lazy smiles. "Don't worry, sugar — as Mark Twain said, reports of my death have been greatly exaggerated."

"It's ridiculous. Will you look at this!" I pass him my phone so he can see the tributes pouring in on the Twitter feed. Today's top trending topic is *#RIPLoganRush*.

"Places, please. I'm looking at you, Logan," the assistant director calls.

"Logan!" Britney is starting to sound petulant.

"At least I'd be free and have some peace then," Logan says, his expression something between humour and longing.

"Um, yes, but you'd also be *dead*!" I say.

"Ah, good point. Maybe I could just fake it and disappear." He ambles off to join Britney, who flashes her Hollywood whites at him in a sparkling smile.

"Cilla would track you down," I call after him.

"Did someone say my name?" Cilla has arrived.

She comes to stand next to me, plucking one of her pet dragons off her shoulder. She cradles the critter under its belly and strokes its back as if it's a cuddly kitten.

"Yeah, me," I say. "I was just pointing out to Logan that I don't see the retake of scene thirty-one, his new rewritten version of it, on the schedule for Wednesday's shooting."

Cilla stares at me in disapproval, her eyes glittering like the reptile's.

"You still haven't learned to shut up. Dear."

"No, I admit I am still struggling with that."

"Here, speak to him." She thrusts the pet dragon into my

surprised hands, where it squirms, digging its sharp little claws into my skin. "*I* don't want to hear anything you have to say and neither, I think, does anyone else."

Mouth twisted in an evil smile, she turns to survey her two leads on the set. Britney is nestled in Logan's arms on the sofa, and they're cuddling. He strokes her hair, and she kisses the base of his throat.

My stomach clenches painfully. They're just practising for the scene, I tell myself. It's just acting.

But it looks very real.

Logan whispers into Britney's ear and they giggle intimately. She caresses his arms and shoulders, and I'm suddenly — viciously — jealous. Not just of her hands on my man, but of the freedom she has to touch him openly, when I have to keep my hands firmly in my pockets. When I have to watch my every word and guard my every look.

I can't bear to stay and watch once they start filming the scene — it's one in which they kiss passionately. I'd rather be outside, even if it is raining, so I palm the repulsive reptile off on Polyp and head out. I walk around the lot for a bit, tidy Logan's room, and worry about that letter again. I wish I'd never read the damn thing.

When I return to the sound stage in time for the lunch break, I stay outside, leaning up against the warehouse wall, studying the pillowy grey clouds overhead, and enjoying the feel of the soft, cool rain on my face.

Our day in the sunny vineyards — laughing, kissing, talking freely — now feels far away and long ago.

Time is running out fast. In two and a half weeks, on the twenty-first of December, filming in Cape Town will wrap so that the US contingent of the cast and crew can be back stateside well in time for Christmas with their families. The week before that, the *Syrenka* will arrive in Cape Town, and depart two days later. I want to be on it. But I also want to be with Logan.

I know he wants me to join him in L.A., but as what? He's made no promises about our relationship. What if I go to the opposite end of the world only to discover I've merely been a passing fling for him? He can have his pick of any woman on the planet — why would he possibly want me? Every ounce of logic says our relationship won't, *can't*, last.

Even if I risk the wrath of my parents and the uncertainty of a relationship with Logan, I don't know what I would do for a career in L.A. any more than here. Will I just continue to trail around after him from set to set, watching him kiss Britney Vaux, all the while doing nothing that matters with my life?

Something about that seems like a betrayal of myself.

Captain Murphy is holding a berth open for me on the *Syrenka*. "If you don't take it, we'll put out the word and somebody else will. I've been doing this for fifteen years, and I've learned that it always works out somehow."

A gentle touch on my arm interrupts my troubled thoughts. Logan leans against the wall next to me. His arms are folded across his chest, but the fingers of the hand underneath caress my arm where other eyes can't see.

"You shouldn't be standing in the rain like this — you'll catch a cold."

I stare down at my sweater. I'm pretty much soaked through.

"Better out here than in there." I jerk my chin back at the sound stage.

"Sorry about that," he says softly, staring straight ahead. "It's just acting. It's part of the job."

"I know that. But I didn't want to watch."

After a while, he asks, "Still up for watching the scene I wrote?"

"Has Cilla put it into the schedule now?"

"Yeah. When I confronted her, she said the omission was just an administrative error. She's put it for tomorrow afternoon. We'll film scene sixty-five at the docks, as scheduled, then my scene at the same location afterwards."

"I'll be there, but I'm taking this afternoon off, if that's okay with you," I say.

I have no desire to hang about while he films the rest of the lovemaking scene with Britney all afternoon.

"Sure — it's a closed set, anyway. Britney insists on it for those scenes."

"Oh, I somehow don't think she'd mind me watching."

"Are you okay? You seem ... upset."

"I need to do some thinking." I push off from the wall. "See you tomorrow."

"Hey," he says as I start to walk off. "There's a cast dinner tomorrow night, at the hotel, for Britney's birthday. Will you join us?"

"As your date?"

"If you're ready to go public, Romy, then so am I. But once the story's out, there's no going back."

"Fine," I say grumpily. "I'll be there. As your not-date."

My crabby mood lifts the next afternoon as Becka and I stand together, watching Logan act the section he rewrote. In the scene, Chase Falconer passionately begs a bunch of poor fishermen to stop the practice of finning sharks. He speaks of understanding their hardship, but warns them of a greater poverty — a poverty of the soul, a poverty that follows in the wake of killing their mother the earth, a poverty which will leave us all orphans to empty oceans and sterile fields.

The new dialogue is beautiful, poignant, almost musical in its rhythm. And Logan's acting is incredible. He disappears into the character so completely that I forget who I'm watching, forget that these are lines in a script, that this is all make-believe.

When he finishes speaking, there's a long moment of stillness before someone yells, "Cut." Then everyone — cast, crew and extras — break into applause.

"He was actually crying — did you see the one perfect man-tear?" Becka says, clearly impressed. In a whisper, she adds, "And he didn't even use a cry-stick! Britney always has to."

I'm choked up myself. My voice is a little croaky when I tell Logan afterwards, "You can act!"

"Um, yeah. It is my job."

His hand strays as if to tuck a strand of my hair behind my ear, then falls. We're not alone.

"No, I mean you can really act."

He grins at that.

I already knew that Logan was a good actor, but I hadn't, until today, known exactly *how* good. He's astonishingly — bewilderingly — good. Suddenly I get it. This is his craft and his passion. This is what he needs to do. There's no way I could ever ask him to give this up, even if it would make it easier for us to build a real relationship. Losing this would damage and diminish him. And the world would be the poorer without his gift, especially if he's able to do better, more complex projects.

The selfish and the loving parts inside of me are at war.

I want to yell, "Run away! Give it up. Get a normal job — something where we can stay together and go public."

I need to urge, "Go for it, live your dream. Be the best damn actor you can be!"

And another part of me urges me to put myself first. "Letting your life revolve around a guy is crazy-stupid. If you sacrifice your own dreams, you'll regret it forever."

Perhaps my throat can't decide what I want to say and settles for a choked, confused silence, because by the time the cast dinner rolls around that night, I have full-on laryngitis.

CHAPTER 29
LOSING VOICE

"Gotta say it, Romy. I prefer you like this. It's a huge improvement," Cilla says at the party that evening.

I'm not sure if she's referring to my appearance — black cocktail dress, stiletto heels, full-hair-and-make-up — or to my lack of a voice.

"Hey, Cilla," Logan greets his director with the usual air-kisses on either side of her cheeks. "I had a look at the rushes from this afternoon, and I think they're pretty good! Have you had a chance to see them yet?"

"Oh yeah. Not too shabby at all. Maybe we can use that scene in the extended edition, or as a bonus feature when the DVD is released."

"What do you mean? Are you cutting it?" Logan's face is neutral, his voice polite, but there's anger in the tensing of his shoulders, and in the stillness of his hands.

"Oh come now, Logan, get real. I can't put that in the film, it's way too much of a downer. It slows the action right down. We can't change the winning formula now. That would *not* make the producers happy. Besides, the Screenwriters' Guild would have my guts for garters if I included a scene written by a non-member."

I try to protest, but only manage to croak a few words. "But … 'portant message … Art …!"

"The *Beast* audience don't want to see *art*. They want to see action, romance, and of course" — Cilla chucks Logan under the chin — "eye candy."

Logan jerks his head back. "I thought we could do something deeper, maybe make them sit up and think for a change."

"They don't come to sit up and think! What part of this don't you understand? They come to kick back, stuff their faces with popcorn, and be entertained." She shakes her head at Logan and completely ignores me.

"Ah, here's Britney. Britney, darling, happy birthday!"

Britney wears a scarlet Dior dress that clings to her curves, and killer heels by Jimmy Choo. As she turns from side to side to accept good wishes, her blonde hair swings in waves around her face, and her laughing voice tinkles like wind chimes. I suddenly feel very plain. Nana's earrings pinch my ears, and my feet are already aching.

Our party is escorted to a secluded section of the hotel's dining room, and I find my place card at the corner of one end of the long table. Britney is seated at the other end, with Cilla on her right and an empty chair on her left. A dozen actors fill the spaces between us, including the hunk that Zeb thinks is drool-worthy. I'm going to have to break the news to my friend that his crush is Austrian, speaks almost no English, and looks to be as straight as an arrow.

Logan comes to sit next to me at the foot of the table, but Britney's having none of that.

"Logan, your seat is right here," she coos, patting the empty chair beside her.

"But —" Logan begins, flicking a glance at me.

"That's the *assistant's* end of the table, Logan. Becka and Philip and Ronnie can all chat together quite happily without you. Well, perhaps not Ronnie, who's lost her voice, poor thing."

She gives me a dazzling smile of utterly false sympathy, then comes over and tows Logan back to the seat next to her. No doubt she'll have her hand on his leg under the table before long.

I wish I was at home, in bed, drinking hot water with lemon and honey. My throat hurts, my head throbs, and I can do nothing but nod or shake my head at the conversation swirling around me.

To my right, two of the actresses in supporting roles are debating the ideal size for boob jobs, and comparing names of plastic surgeons.

"Not Lobos, Sherry, you'd be loco to go to Lobos! He positively botched Lindsey's nose, and he left Keira's eyes uneven. Which is not something you want at her age."

"Isn't she only, like, twenty-four or five?"

"As if! She's pushing the big three-oh — maybe even older. Mindy has a friend who worked on that last period piece of hers that bombed, and swears she saw a passport proving she's over thirty."

"No way!"

Across the table, Zeb's hunk and a starlet are chatting about where in Cape Town they might be able to "score a line." They look at me hopefully, perhaps hoping I can give them some local tips. I turn my back on them and face Polyp, who is telling Becka about his plans to travel to London the minute the production wraps.

"I cannot wait to get back to civilization. This continent is not for me."

"Are you crazy?" Becka says. "It's beautiful!"

"Nope, it's way too wild." He drinks deeply from a goblet-sized glass of red wine, and smiles slyly, showing teeth stained red. "Have you heard the latest? They've given the next *Beast* movie the green light. Pre-production is slated to start in February, and first filming in March."

He carves a slice of nearly raw meat off his slab of a steak, places it in his mouth and chews. A drop of bloody juice trickles down his chin.

"What's it called?" Becka asks.

"*Beast: Mars.*"

"What?" I squawk.

"Yes." Polyp nods at me and takes another gulp of his wine. "Bit of a departure. Chase Falconer gets to travel into outer space and fight alien lizards, or something like that."

Becka laughs. "I reckon Cilla fancies the idea of giant chickabiddies trying to kill the talent. This movie would be her dearest fantasy come to life."

I push my plate away from me, food untouched, as Polyp describes what he knows about the plot. The movie sounds awful. It doesn't have anything to do with the original books, and there's no deeper message about nature and conservation. A brief vision of Logan at age forty, still spouting Chase's clichés in an umpteenth sequel, flashes through my mind.

"Sounds like complete crap on a cracker," Becka says. "Wonder if Britney will still be in it?"

"Well of course! She's the main star, she's the one who signed on first."

"Forget that! Listen, Phil, Logan may have been an unknown when he first signed on, but if you think *she's* still the bigger star, you're fruit-loopingly delusional."

At the head of the table, Britney chats animatedly. She has the rapt attention of everyone around her and keeps them spellbound as she speaks — in an intelligent and informed way — about sharks!

"They are such beautiful creatures. Far too many people don't understand that they're the most perfectly designed predators on the planet."

My mouth falls open.

"But they're terrifying and dangerous," says Pete from the pay office, who's hanging on Britney's every word.

She pats his hand playfully.

"Honestly, we're more of a danger to them than they are to us. Entire species of shark are at risk because of the practice of shark finning. The poor sharks get their *dorsal fins* sliced off, and then they're tossed back into the ocean to drown. The fins are used in the East, mostly to make shark fin soup for banquets because it's such a fabulously expensive dish, that it shows everyone how rich and successful you are when you order it."

What the hell!

I glare at the faces of those listening to her. The accountant is entranced, and Cilla's nodding like this is vitally interesting to her. Even Logan looks dead impressed.

"Entire shark populations are being decimated just so some fat cat in China can show how prosperous he is. It's outrageous! That creatures who've been around for millions of years should now be threatened because of mere vanity. It makes me so mad!"

She thumps a fist on the table to emphasise her last line — *my* last line — and the clique around erupts in a little burst of applause. With a self-deprecating laugh, she says, "I'm sorry, I'm probably boring you. I know I get a little crazy about this, but I'm just passionate, you know. Not enough people *get it*."

Logan says, "I never knew you cared so much about them, that you even knew so much about them, Britney. You put me to shame."

Bitch stole my lines! I try to scream. All that comes out is a loud, raspy squawk which turns everyone's attention to me.

Britney looks me straight in the eye and smiles sweetly. "Don't strain your voice, Ronnie, I know exactly what you want to say. And thank you so much."

CHAPTER 30
INTENTIONS

A week later, my voice has returned, but even though I'm over the flu, I'm feeling miserable. A fistful of deadlines looms, ready to pound me into misery.

Time left until the *Syrenka* docks in Cape Town: three days.

Time left until *Beast* wraps and Logan leaves town: ten days.

Time left until my university prison sentence starts: two months.

Time left until the family dinner to which I've invited Logan and at which I'll have to pretend there's no romance between us: six hours.

Time left until I smack Britney Vaux upside the head: any minute now.

Following the excellent reaction of her audience to her birthday dinner speech, Britney has set herself up as some kind of eco-expert and is doling out tidbits of information about the species of shark that live in False Bay and how surfers look like seals to a shark. She'll soon have to do some research of her own if she intends maintaining the pretence, because she's running out of my material.

I've said nothing — for the first few days because I couldn't, and afterwards because what's the point? I'd only look petty. Besides, I want the message about shark-finning out there, don't I, so does it really matter who says it? You can accomplish lots if you don't mind who gets the credit. And anyway, people will be more likely to listen to her than to me.

Britney's smugger than a cat swimming in cream because reports of a romance between her and Logan continue to circulate. The rumours have been fuelled by the pictures of her clinging to him that were taken the night of the birthday dinner by the studio's own photographer and 'leaked' to the press. Cilla has also released stills of "Chase and Fern" from the smooch shoot — of Britney in his arms, them kissing, him gazing at her with what looked a whole lot like love in his eyes. There's even a new name for the Logan-Britney hook-up that fans are shipping online: Logney. *Logney!*

I try to stay away from the celebrity news sites — these days they only make me miserable. But when I'm with Logan, I'm blissed out, happy, content. I feel like I belong by his side, like I've come home to myself in some way.

My parents keep asking me why I'm in such a good mood, why I seem so happy. I credit the job — "I'm working in the movies. I've got stars in my eyes." That makes them worry even more, like I might run off to become a Holly-gofer.

I still haven't ruled it out. I haven't ruled anything out, but I haven't made any decisions, either. Should I please Logan, my folks, or honour my dream? What am I waiting for? A burning bush? Writing in the sky?

Zeb says he's worried about my sanity, but he offers no

advice, only support. "Whatever you decide — and it is *your* decision — I'm on your side."

I've invited him to tonight's dinner, too, to help smooth any atmospheric rough seas. My parents approve of Zeb, who's unfailingly polite and respectful towards them. My Nana adores him — I suspect because he always flatters her wildly.

"Just help keep the conversation flowing, okay?" I give Zeb his last-minute instructions. "Crack a joke now and then. And distract my father if he starts giving Logan a hard time. Sidetrack him with talk of Mozart — you know he always likes that."

"You don't ask for much."

"I will reward you, Zeb. I'll take you as my companion to the wrap party, and you can try and sway the Austrian ox from the straight and narrow."

"Take me as your disguise, more like, so no one catches on to the fact that you and Logan are …" He twists his fingers together.

Zeb is up to date on (most of) the details of my relationship with Logan. He understands the reasons we're keeping it hush-hush, but he also worries that I'm being used by a Hollywood player in search of a little fun while out on location.

"He loves me, Zeb. He said so."

"Sweetie, saying it don't make it so."

Don't I know it?

Dinner starts well enough. Logan is charming, friendly, and polite. He calls my parents "sir" and "ma'am," praises my mother lavishly for the delicious food, and Nana is won over from the moment Logan kisses the back of her hand with a whispered "Enchanté." He delights her with spicy little stories from

Hollywood, and she winks and nods at me repeatedly to show her approval. Lobster sits on top of Logan's feet under the table, devouring the bits of roast beef he manages to sneak in her direction. Another female heart is conquered.

My father, however, is determined not to be charmed. He interrupts an anecdote to ask Logan about the business and financial aspects of movies.

"Shucks, sir, I guess I don't know much about that side of things. I'm concerned with what goes on in front of the camera. I never did want to be a bean-counting accountant."

Crap. I've never mentioned to Logan that while my father is now the head of Poseidon Industries, he originally qualified as a C.A.

Nana cackles and Zeb hides a grin behind his napkin, but I can tell the comment has put my father's back up. He immediately goes on the offensive, as if trying to prove to me how pathetic the movie industry is — just in case I have any ideas about creating a career in that world.

"I see. Not arty-farty enough?" my father challenges, his head lowered between his shoulders like a belligerent turtle.

I glare at my father. He ignores me.

"So what are your intentions, then?" he demands.

"Dad," I say, in a warning tone.

With the merest flicker of a glance towards me, Logan says, "My intentions, sir?"

"Yes, your intentions. What do you intend to do with your life?"

"Um, act?"

"Is that all?"

"Isn't it enough?"

"I would think that there comes a time when a man gives up play-acting and make-believe, and settles down to something more secure."

"Dad!" I'm getting angry.

Under the tablecloth, Logan gives my hand a squeeze to let me know he's okay. From over the table, Zeb watches the interchange between my father and Logan like a spectator at Wimbledon, delighted by the volley. I frown at him and aim a kick at his shin but crunch my toe on the chair leg instead.

"Well, sir, after the movies I've completed, I find myself in the fortunate position of being financially secure."

"Yes, but for how long?"

"*Dad!*"

"For life, I guess. Unless I start throwing my money around like a complete fool."

My father seems stumped for a comeback. I frown at my mom, telling her with a hard look to stop my father's rude inquisition, and she rushes to fill the silence.

"Tell us about your dive in the predator tank, Logan. Romy says it was fascinating. Was that the first time you've seen a shark up close?" she says, offering him second helpings of baked butternut.

"Yes, ma'am. Romy here was determined that I learn more about the creatures I portray in my films. But I gather you're the real expert?"

Logan deflects the attention from himself and allows my mother to wax lyrical comparing raggies to hammerheads. Nana nods off, having heard all this before, but Logan is either truly fascinated by the informative little lecture, or he's delivering an Oscar-worthy performance.

That's the thing about dating an actor — you never can be entirely sure.

Over dessert — home-made custardy *milktart* — Logan engages Zeb in a discussion about computer-generated technology, describing how the graphics artists use actual footage of sharks as the basis for the effects. Zeb, who's probably been suppressing the urge to ask all evening, finally pops the question.

"And do they ever do CG effects on, um, the actors' bodies? I'm just asking because they don't always look real."

"Zeb!"

I want to find a sinkhole, preferably twenty thousand leagues under the sea, and disappear into it. I've never been this embarrassed in my life.

Unoffended, Logan laughs and says, "Yeah, sometimes they do."

"See?" Zeb says to me.

"But not mine," Logan adds.

"*See?*" I say to Zeb.

Logan grins at me. "Have you been defending the existence of my abs?"

My mother, who's been watching the exchanges between Logan and me intently all evening, now looks positively worried.

"Logan, tell us about Britney Vaux," she says bluntly.

But I've had enough.

"That's it. Logan's got to go now. He's got an early call time tomorrow, and he needs his beauty sleep. The transport to take him back to the hotel is probably already waiting outside."

I hustle him away from the table amidst many *thank yous* and *you're welcomes* and even a *nice to meet you* from Zeb.

The hotel transfer car is indeed already waiting in the street in front of our house, and as soon as we step outside, Thabo climbs out and opens the rear door for Logan.

"I'm so sorry about all that. You must think my family's insane. And so rude!" I apologise to Logan.

"Don't worry about it. They love you. They're not wrong to be suspicious of some smooth-talking stranger from the other side of the world."

I glance back at the house, just in time to see a curtain at the front window twitch.

"You look so lovely tonight, I'm battling to keep my hands, and my lips, off you. But if we're trying to keep this secret, I'm guessing I'd better save my goodnight kiss for tomorrow," Logan says.

"I think they may already be on to us," I say glumly. They're probably already lying in wait, preparing to give me a lecture. "See you in the morning."

"See ya."

I wave forlornly at the disappearing car, then notice that Zeb has come outside and is standing next to me.

"You know, I think he might be okay. The real deal," he says.

I give him a hug for that.

"Do the right thing, Romy. The right thing for *you*," he says, before heading off home.

I trudge back to the house.

"Well, that was an enlightening evening!" my father says crossly as soon as I'm inside.

"What do you mean?"

"Your mother tells me that you and he ... that you are romantically inclined towards this Logan Rush. Is that true?"

"Thanks for that, Mom," I say.

"He's going to break your heart," my father says. "He's just amusing himself with you until the circus leaves town. He's probably already tried to get you into his bed."

"How dare you? You don't even know him!" I can feel an angry flush rising up my neck.

"And he's much older than you."

"Two years, Dad. One and a half, actually."

"Are you sure he hasn't lied about his age? They do, these actors."

"Rex, dear, *please*. Romy, what your father means to say, is that he's worried you'll wind up getting hurt, because there can be no long-term prospects for this relationship."

I've thought the same thing more than once myself. But hearing them say it makes me furious.

"Why shouldn't there be?" I turn on my father. "Why do you immediately assume he only wants one thing from me? That he couldn't possibly really care for me? Am I such an unappealing person?"

"I never meant —"

"He likes me. He. Likes. Me! And he's a good guy, alright? He's kind and genuine and talented."

"Oh, he's a real prince alright. And you can bet he intends to marry a princess, not you." My father flings himself into his recliner chair and swallows a large gulp of his brandy.

"Marry! Who even mentioned marriage? I'm only eighteen years old, for fu- for fudge sake."

"It's all over the papers and the Net that he's going to marry this co-star of his," my mother says.

"Those are just stories invented to generate publicity for the movie. They're not true. The 'romance' between Logan and Britney is not real."

"Are you so sure? Are you so certain that what's between him and you is real?" my father demands. "You should settle down with someone of your own kind, like Zeb."

"He's gay."

"Good Lord!"

"We're just worried that this is going to end in heartbreak, sweetie," my mother says softly.

"Why can't it work? Why shouldn't it?" There's a catch in my voice when I say the words. Tears aren't far off.

"You're not from his world," Mom says.

"I could join it. I *have* joined it."

I feel beleaguered, the more so because they're giving voice to my deepest fears.

"You don't belong there. It's all acting and faking and partying," my father says dismissively.

"You don't know anything about it!"

"I know it's all smoke and mirrors, show without substance. I know that you're an intelligent person who wants some purpose in her life." My father sounds almost weary now. "You'll never be satisfied with make-believe, Rosemary, with a life where there's nothing real or significant for you to do, and no way for you to make a difference."

This, too, resonates with me more than I like.

"We just want you to choose your course wisely, love," Mom

says, giving me a hug which I'm too angry to return. "Time's running out and you haven't yet decided what you'll be doing next year."

I haven't told my parents about the *Syrenka* offer. Initially I wanted to avoid my mother's inevitable protests about safety and my father's lectures about the need to settle down and study. Now I'm too afraid to mention it in case they urge me to go as a way of prying me away from Logan.

Zeb is right. I need to make a decision based on what *I* want. I need to choose a world not because other people want me to fit in there with them, but because it's where I truly belong.

"I'm going to bed," I tell my parents.

Upstairs, I close my bedroom door. I want some privacy. Not to think — I'm sick and tired of thinking. All my conflicting thoughts and feelings are jumbled and tangled up inside my head like wet washing in a tumble dryer.

I send Logan a goodnight text, with three kissy faces. Sometime in the silence afterwards, while waiting for a response, I fall asleep and dream I'm running and running, in shoes that are too small. And I can't tell if I'm running from, or running to.

CHAPTER 31
A WEDDING

Logan, who's checking emails on his phone, gasps.

"What is it? Not bad news?" I ask.

We're perched on our usual canvas chairs in sound stage two, waiting. This is how I spend half my life these days. Light, sound and photography techies bustle about, and the set dressers add final touches for the next scene — when Chase Falconer weds Fern Lightly.

Logan is costumed in a deep charcoal tailcoat with matching trousers, a silver embossed satin waistcoat, and a loosely-knotted cravat the precise blue of his eyes. Wardrobe has styled him down to the last detail — silver cufflinks in the shape of a shark. His floppy hair is swept back smoothly, and Ed has threatened him with death if it gets mussed.

Twenty minutes past the call time, we're still waiting for Britney. A pair of photographers are set up in prime positions to take stills of the wedding ceremony. The actor playing the priest paces up and down the faux flagstones at the front of the 'chapel.' Extras squirm restlessly in the pews — custom built and 'distressed' to look old and worn — on either side of an aisle fitted with dolly tracks for the camera.

"What is it?" I ask Logan again, trying to read over his shoulder.

"I got the part." He sounds stunned.

"What part?"

"Alan Strang," he says softly.

"*Equus*? In New York?"

He just nods, apparently dumbstruck. I glance around, see that Cilla is safely on set, shaking the priest's hand, and no one is within earshot. Still, when I speak, it's in hushed tones.

"That's so awesome!" I desperately want to jump up and hug him. Never has the need to keep us secret chafed as much as it does at this moment, when I have to settle for a whispered, "Congratulations!"

I'm as relieved as I am excited for Logan. This role will be a wonderful opportunity for him to stretch his talent and break out of the Chase Falconer mould. Logan, however, doesn't seem as over-the-moon as I am.

"What's wrong?"

"I can't do it. The timing — it conflicts with the next *Beast* shoot."

"You've signed for that?" I ask, dismayed.

An image of Logan in a spacesuit, doing battle with giant lizards, momentarily sears my eyeballs. Even *he* won't be able to pull that off and make it look like anything but franchise-milking junk.

"Not yet," he says, but before I can breathe a sigh of relief, he continues, "but I will. Probably."

"Why in the name of all that's holy would you do that? You told me how much you wanted to play Alan Strang, how hard you fought for this role!" I whisper fiercely. "You said it would give you a chance to practice your craft, to grow yourself as an actor. You could do this" — I sweep a dismissive hand at the current set — "in your sleep."

"The series probably won't go ahead if I'm not in it. I'm not being arrogant, or anything, it's just that the producers and backers want a bankable name — my name." Logan fidgets with a shark cufflink, turning it around and around.

"Just because they want you in the next movie, doesn't mean you have to do it. Why would you even be tempted? It sounds like a chunk of junk."

He says nothing, merely stares ahead at the bustling set. There's a bleakness to the set of his face, and a tightness around his mouth that worries me.

"You don't need the money," I say. "And it's not like you need more fame — you've already got more than you can handle. Why do you need to keep going with the *Beast* movies?"

"Maybe I'm not good enough for anything else, have you thought of that possibility?" he says, finally turning to look at me.

"No. Because that's rubbish, and you must know it. You could do so much more with better roles and better material."

"No one thinks I can."

"I do."

"Thanks, but you're not the one that matters. No, wait," he says when I wince. "I didn't mean it like that. I just mean the people with the power to cast me in a different kind of movie don't — can't, maybe — think of me as a serious actor."

"Then kick down the doors and show them. You're Logan Rush, for goodness sake! Write your own screenplay. Make your own movie. Show them what you can do. Let someone else take the Beast to Mars. And take Britney with him," I add bitterly.

"I can't. Britney still wants, and needs, these roles. And I owe her."

"Owe her for what?"

He sighs and looks down at his hands.

"Back when I auditioned for the role of Chase Falconer, Britney had already been cast as the female lead. She was already famous. Without her signing on, the film wouldn't even have been made — it was a risky venture, and they needed a big name as a drawcard. I was a complete unknown, with no acting track record, and she chose me. Cilla and the casting director narrowed it down to five actors. Any one of them could have played this role at least as well as me, and three of them were power names in the industry. But Britney chose me. She insisted that Cilla cast me in the role, said she could feel the chemistry only with me."

"I'll just bet she did," I mutter.

I can imagine the scene — Britney looking forward to a rosy future in which she could sink her claws into Logan and keep him close to her. Britney knowing the massive appeal Logan would have for the female half of the population, and knowing that if she hitched herself to his star she would rise and rise.

Speak of the devil and she shall appear — at that moment, Britney glides regally onto the set, staggeringly beautiful and resplendent in a long-trained gown of raw silk the colour of the palest iceberg blue. A collar of realistic-looking diamonds circles her throat, and a tiara glitters in her upswept hair. Glowing with pleasure at the gasps and compliments coming from all sides, she's every inch the princess to Logan's prince.

"I owe her. Without her, I'd be nothing." Logan's eyes, like everyone else's, are trained on the dazzling bride.

"That's not true." I'm not ready for him to accept defeat. "You just might not be Chase Falconer."

"But being Chase Falconer is what has allowed me to rescue my mother from working as a waitress in a diner, having to bite her tongue and smile for her tips while she's hassled by free-fingered perverts and sassed by smart-mouthed trashy teens, living day to day from hand to mouth. Being Chase Falconer is what has allowed me to send my sister to college, so she can be something one day. And anyway, Cilla's insisting."

"So what? Cilla this, Cilla that. It's like she's got some kind of hold over you." I half-mutter the words under my breath, but Logan's head snaps up.

"What do you mean?" he says sharply.

"*Does* she have a hold over you?"

He looks away from me and exhales a frustrated sigh. "Britney has asked me — begged me — to sign on for the next movie. She wants to do it, and they won't do it without me. It's time to pay back what I owe."

"Send her a bunch of flowers and a thank-you card."

"Places, please," the assistant director calls.

Britney floats over to her mark at the front of the aisle and chats to the priest. The extras in the pews straighten their hats and smooth their hair. I put a restraining hand on Logan's arm as he makes to stand up.

"Logan, you yourself told me that you don't feel challenged anymore, that you're not satisfied. Can't you just *try* something new, something different?"

"Sounds like you've got plans for a new-and-improved Logan. Next thing, you'll be asking me about my intentions, like your father did. Asking me what I plan to do with my life when I give up 'play-acting and make-believe.'" He stands up, shoots his cuffs, and pulls his jacket down at the back. Up on the set, Britney beckons Logan with a finger and a smile which promises royal treatment.

"I just think you can do more, that's all."

"Let me guess, sharks? Spread awareness, raise money, change the world?"

"Is it so stupid to want to do something meaningful, to leave the world a better place?" There are tears in my eyes and a lump in my throat. It feels as if he's slipping away, like a handful of water in my fingers.

"No, it's not stupid. *You* should do it."

"I want *you* to do what will make you happy." I speak passionately, but I'm not sure he hears me. He's already walking towards the altar, towards Britney.

CHAPTER 32
HEADLINES

Logan Rush and Britney Vaux married — for reelz!

The Beast weds the Beauty!

Logan and Britney tie the knot in Africa

Representatives for Logan Rush and Britney Vaux, stars of the Beast *trilogy of films, have refused to confirm or deny reports that they are officially married.*

On Friday, the couple filmed a scene in which their on-screen characters took their vows. According to a confidential source, the priest who presided over the scene was no actor, but was in fact an ordained member of the ministry. This has raised the possibility that the couple may now, in fact, be married in reality.

For years, rumours have circulated that the on-screen lovers are also an off-screen couple. Their red-hot chemistry ... (continues page 3)

The crap-flinging tabloid monkeys have just made my mood — already bad after my tiff with Logan — even worse. I'm unsettled by our conversation yesterday. For one thing, I regret getting all preachy with him about his work. But what bothers me more is how he reacted to my throwaway comment about Cilla having some kind of hold over him. I only realised afterwards that he never actually answered my question.

She's such a witch, it wouldn't surprise me if she's trying to strong-arm him into more *Beast* movies. And something keeps niggling at me — the memory of her saying Logan should check his mail for a letter to Levi. *And* the strange smile on her face when she said it. The outside of the letter was addressed to Logan, and it was still sealed, so how did Cilla know about "Levi"?

I click the stupid news sites closed but leave my browser open. I'm due to have lunch with Logan this afternoon, but in the meantime, I could do some research. It's not something I'm especially eager to do — it feels a lot like snooping. But what if Cilla knows a secret and is using it as a weapon against Logan? I want to help him, to protect him from Cilla if possible. So I need to know what he's up against, don't I?

Ignoring my twinges of conscience, I retrieve the crumpled letter from my drawer and make a list of key search terms.

Jonas Peabody

Louisiana State Penitentiary

Levi and Wynette

My pen hesitates, making little ink dots on the paper, before writing down the final two words.

Levi Peabody?

I key the first term into the search box, hit the return key, and dive into the results, checking ancestry sites, directory listings, social security birth listings and obituaries, reading Facebook profiles and sifting through newspaper articles, eliminating false leads and clicking through hopeful-looking ones until I find what I really *wasn't* looking for.

Holy cow.

I print out some of the news articles, order them chronologically, and read them again carefully, trying to get my head around what I've discovered. The first article, dated fourteen years ago, is from the Picayune Daily Chronicle.

Fatal stabbing on Canal Street Bus

New Orleans: The New Orleans Police Department has confirmed that seventeen-year-old Clarence Washington, a senior student at nearby Jefferson High, was yesterday stabbed and killed during an altercation on a city bus in the French Quarter.

Washington and another man boarded the Canal Street bus at the Decatur Street stop. A confrontation over seats followed, in which the man taunted Washington with racist epithets. According to Miss Tanita Merrero (22), a fellow passenger on the bus, the man "called Washington a 'mongrel' and 'good-for-nothing n__r.' He used the n-word several times. He said that they were taking over the city and getting all the good jobs. He said that Washington should stand up and give him the seat because you should respect your elders and betters. Clarence told Peabody that he was hardly old, and what made him better? Next thing he shoved Clarence off the seat into the aisle, and began kicking him, telling him to go back to where he came from. When Clarence got up, they started fighting and the man stabbed him. There was blood everywhere."

Washington was stabbed four times in the chest and neck, and was pronounced dead on the scene by paramedics.

When asked if the stabbing was being treated as a hate crime, NOPD Captain Luiz Delgado refused to speculate. "We are open to all possibilities at this time."

The last article is from July of the following year.

Peabody convicted in Canal Street Stabbing

New Orleans: *Jonas Peabody (27), of Chalmette, New Orleans, was yesterday convicted of the second-degree murder of seventeen-year-old Clarence Washington.*

The jury took only three hours to deliberate the evidence presented over the course of the four-day trial and to return with a unanimous guilty verdict. Criminal District Court Judge Roberta Broussard dismissed Peabody's claims that he had acted in self-defense, noting that Washington had been unarmed and that Peabody had provoked the dispute between them.

Addressing Peabody, Judge Broussard said, "You ended the life of an innocent young man with a bright future, a young man whose right to sit on a bus like any other citizen was won many years ago. I find no extenuating circumstances in your actions or motivations."

Peabody seemed shocked by the verdict. As he was led away in cuffs for his transfer to the Louisiana State Penitentiary in Angola, he shouted that he had been "railroaded" and would be appealing his conviction on the grounds of "incompetent lawyering."

Under the 1979 "life means life" amendment to Louisiana law, he has been sentenced to a mandatory life sentence, without the possibility of parole. Peabody's criminal record includes previous convictions for DUI, domestic violence, assault and drug possession. It emerged in the trial that he has links to the Aryan Nation and KKK organizations.

Peabody's wife of seven years, Mrs. Nancy Peabody (nee Rush) (25) was in court to hear the verdict, but she declined to answer questions from the press.

Mrs. Arlene Washington, mother of the murder victim, has been in the courtroom for the duration of the trial, often weeping as she heard details of her only son's shocking death. When asked, after the conclusion of the trial, if she believed justice had been served, Mrs Washington said, "The law has done its job. But you can't call it justice when my boy is dead and that vile man is still alive."

Accompanying this article were two colour photographs. The first, a mugshot of Jonas Peabody, showed a scowling man with black hair, squinting blue eyes, and a mouth that was slightly sunken — as if he had bad teeth. Narrower, older and meaner, his face was like an off-kilter, distorted version of the features I know so well.

The second photograph was captioned: "*Mrs Nancy Peabody leaves the court building with her two young children, Levi (7) and Wynette (3).*" It showed a woman in a dull beige dress, clutching a toddler on one hip and holding the hand of a small boy on her other side. The toddler's and the woman's faces were half-turned away, but the small boy was looking over his shoulder directly at the camera. His black hair was neatly combed in a side-path, but one lock tumbled across the forehead of his thin, pinched face. His little hand was stretched out towards the camera — in appeal? In a wave? — and you could just see the resemblance, if you were looking for it.

So Logan Rush *is* Levi Peabody — the son of a good-for-nothing drunk and wife beater, who may well have knocked his little kid around, too. Logan's father didn't die in a car accident when Logan was seven years old. He's alive and kicking, serving out his life sentence in a high-security prison.

No wonder Logan wants to write a screenplay about the Freedom Riders. His own father was a racist, possibly even a white supremacist, who killed an innocent young black man in an argument over a seat in a bus.

More searching turns up nothing for the remaining Peabody family after the trial. It's like they vanished. I suspect Nancy and her kids left New Orleans and started fresh somewhere else because I do find a mention in a small-town newspaper of a Mrs. Nancy *Rush* winning employee of the year in 2007 at Donny's Dinette in Fairville, Alabama.

Maybe the kids took their mother's maiden name as a new surname, too. I spend another hour searching for Levi Peabody *and* Levi Rush, but I find nothing that relates to Logan until thirteen years after the trial, when stories of Logan Rush's discovery begin to appear. I spend another fruitless hour trying to track down his supposed music band, scan endless music reviews of gigs in Atlanta clubs from the time period, and search for a Levi or Logan Rush in Atlanta prior to his casting as the *Beast*. But I come up with a big, steaming pile of nothing. Perhaps the band story is just another fiction created for the new star by the studio's publicity department.

Or by Cilla. Because this must be what she knows and holds over him. She knows his real origin. Heck, she probably presided over the birth of "Logan Rush," complete with a good haircut and an even better backstory.

Thank God that scummy reporter never got his oily hands on that awful letter. It'll destroy Logan, or at least severely damage his career, if the news ever gets out that his father once killed a black teenager in a hate crime. I can just imagine the media descending on Jonas Peabody, offering him money, listening with phony sincerity and empathy to his racist rantings, his whines about being railroaded by the justice system, and his self-pitying stories of how he's been abandoned by his wife, daughter, and especially his rich, too-big-for-his-Hollywood-britches son.

All attention would be diverted from Logan's talent as an actor, to the sordid, sensational details of his childhood and speculation about whether he's inherited any of his father's character. The media feeding frenzy would make great whites look like genteel ladies at a tea party.

I can see why no one has ever connected Logan Rush with Levi Rush — nowhere are their names mentioned together, though I suppose if I searched through every single one of the millions of mentions of Logan Rush now on the Net, I might find something along the lines of, "I swear I went to school with that guy — but his name was Lionel or Levi or something like that," in a Facebook page somewhere.

I collect all my printouts into a neat pile, but I don't want to leave them where someone might find and read them. As I shove them, together with the Peabody letter, into the back compartment of my handbag, I catch sight of the time on my wristwatch.

I change into a red dress and a pair of strappy sandals and do my hair and make-up as quickly as I can, because I'm already running late for my lunch date with Logan. It's his last Saturday off. My stomach feels cold and hollow at the realisation that this time next week, they'll be wrapping the shoot.

I give the life-sized poster of Logan a quick kiss and hurry off to meet the real thing. Today is going to be difficult because I'll have to come clean and confess how I've been snooping and checking up on him. There's so much awful stuff to discuss and so much to ask that, even though I'm longing to see him, I'm also dreading it.

CHAPTER 33
APPETITES

Knocking on a door and having Logan Rush answer it? That never gets old. I laugh in delight.

"What?" Logan says, grabbing my hand and pulling me inside his hotel room, shutting the door behind us.

His suite is enormous — all polished wood furniture, thick brocade fabrics in muted greys and charcoals, black leather seats, and deep, soft carpets. Massive canvasses streaked with abstract splashes of red hang on the walls. Ceiling-high windows run the length of the room, looking out on the glittering, silver ocean of Table Bay. But my eyes are drawn inexorably to the view of Logan.

He's wearing faded jeans and little else. His feet are bare and his sky-blue shirt —which turns his eyes the azure colour the sea is where shallow water meets deep — is unbuttoned, as if he just slipped it on to answer the door. The sight of his chest and abs does funny things to the inside of me. The hug he enfolds me in, crushing me against that bare chest, compounds the effect.

I am lost. Funny how it feels like I'm found.

"What?" he demands again, in response to the goofy grin I can feel on my face.

"The first time I met you, you told me about this room. You were right."

He cocks an eyebrow.

"It *is* very nice. And big."

"I said that, did I?"

"You did."

"I always was one for the fancy words."

"Oh, you used a fancy word to describe the shower — you said it was massive."

"Did I describe the bed?" He walks backwards, towing me towards it.

My breath hitches in my throat. I shake my head.

"You could come check it out with me. Help me find the right word to describe it. You know, soft … hard … bouncy." He smiles slowly and lazily. His eyes are hot with invitation. "And afterwards, we could explore that shower together. See if it is … big enough."

I blush furiously, which seems to delight him. He grins and flicks the tip of my nose.

"I could just eat you right up, sugar-lips. But first I think I need to apologize for yesterday. Sorry I was such a grump."

"No, *I'm* sorry — I had no right to tell you how to live your life. And," I force myself to add, "I also want to apologize for something else."

"Let's have lunch first, okay? I'm starving, and there's only so much emotion a man can take on an empty stomach. There's a room service menu here somewhere." He rifles through folders and room files in the drawers of the room's massive desk, and finds a leather-bound menu. "So what do you fancy?" He flings himself onto one of the massive leather sofas and beckons me to join him. "How about some *fois gras*?"

"No! They force-feed those poor ducks, Logan!" I take a seat at the other end of the sofa. "Don't tell me you eat that stuff. Do you know —"

"Hmm, I'm guessing you wouldn't like the veal, then. How about steak tartare?"

I pull a face. "That's raw meat, right?"

"Yeah, but —"

"Yeah, but no. Thank you."

"*Bobotie*?" He pronounces it *boh-boh-tye* and reads the description of the dish with a growing look of disbelief. "Wait, there's a regional speciality over here which is actually a dish of curried ground meat and raisins, with a baked custard on the top?"

"It's an acquired taste," I say, shrugging. "Besides, don't they serve jello salad, and sweet potatoes topped with marshmallows in your neck of the woods? I watch the Cooking Channel, you know. Those who live in glass houses …"

"Vanilla smoked quail breast? Lobster bisque? Seared" — he does a double take and repeats — "Seared lamb's brains with pan-fried scallops?"

I snort and take the menu from him.

"Just something light and simple — I'm not too hungry."

That's the truth. This morning's discoveries and my guilt are sitting heavy on my stomach.

"How about a chicken club sandwich?" I suggest.

From what I can decipher from the fancy description, it sounds like a bog-standard, but extortionately expensive, toasted sandwich.

Logan rolls his eyes. "Anyone ever tell you you're a cheap date?"

He snags the room's phone, asks for room service, and puts in an order for oysters on the shell, caviar, and something called Bollinger. Then he lifts my feet, slips off the sandals, and swings me around so that I rest back against the cushions with my bare feet in his lap. He rubs his hands slowly down my soles, massages the balls of my feet, pushes deep circles into my heels. The worry that my feet might stink flashes briefly through my mind, but soon I'm lost in pure bliss.

"There you go," he says when I sigh and relax back into the cushions. His fingers rotate my toes in small circles and tug on them. "You always look like your feet are hurting you."

"They are. It's the heels," I murmur from deep in my sensuous trance.

"Then why d'you wear them, if they hurt?"

"Cilla."

"Ah, Cilla. She who must be obeyed."

I groan as he kneads knuckles into the flesh under my arches. All the tension locked into my body melts down into a puddle of delicious pleasure.

"You ever taste caviar, Romy?"

I move my head slowly from one side to the other. I'm beyond speech.

"Tastes of the sea. I think you'll like it."

The caviar, when it arrives and I can be persuaded to rouse

myself to take a look, is served in a round blue tin set on a bed of crushed ice atop a glass pedestal. A delicate mother-of-pearl spoon protrudes from the gleaming black mass of tiny eggs.

"Is this ethically sourced?" I ask, trying to wake my brain up. I realise I don't know how caviar is harvested. Do they kill the fish to get the eggs?

"Shhh." Logan's lips purse as he shushes me, and my gaze fixes on them like a limpet on a wet rock.

He scoops up a spoonful of caviar and holds it out to me, saying, "Just taste."

I open my mouth and draw the caviar off the spoon with my lips, then bite down on it. Tiny bubbles pop between my teeth and dissolve into a subtle brininess.

"Good, isn't it?"

In answer, I open my mouth for more and Logan obliges. This time I burst the delicate eggs with the tip of my tongue against my palate. They taste like buttery bubbles of salty sea air.

"Now a sip of this."

Logan pours a flute of champagne and hands it to me. Rising lines of fine bubbles sway up like miniature pearl necklaces through the pale golden liquid. I take a sip. Heavenly! If caviar is like eating the ocean air, then this is like drinking cold, gold, liquid sunshine.

"You know," I say. "I could get used to the finer things in life."

"You know, I could give you the finer things in life."

I elbow him. It bothers me that he's so rich, so good-looking, so talented, so *everything*. It makes us lopsided.

"The best things in life can't be bought," I say with a sniff.

"Don't I know it."

I load tiny piles of caviar onto triangular points of toast and mini-pancakes, and we gorge ourselves. Then we start in on the oysters. I've had oysters before, but these are delicious — plump and succulent. It feels decadent and faintly embarrassing to eat them, though that may be because of the way Logan is staring at my mouth.

We fall into a sated silence once we've finished the food. Oysters, champagne, and caviar, with chocolate truffles for afters — it's a long way from Donny's Dinette in Fairville, Alabama.

Almost as if he can sense my mind straying back to my online discoveries, Logan asks, "So, what have you been doing all morning?"

"Um …" Damn. And we've been having such fun. "Research." My voice breaks and goes up at the end, so it comes out sounding like a question.

"Research!" Logan looks puzzled for a moment, then his face clears. "More about sharks, I s'pose?"

"Well, actually —"

I sit up straight, moving slowly, heavy with a growing sense of dread. I can't figure out what to say next, which words to use. I can't just blurt out: "Well, I fished in your trash and read your private letter and then poked around into your background, snooping for details of what you'd rather leave buried. And I discovered that you're the only son of a good-for-nothing drunk, white-supremacist murderer and wife beater. And then I figured out that you changed your name and reinvented a different past. And now your vile father is blackmailing you, threatening to reveal the truth which would sink your rising star. But my goodness, isn't the ocean looking just beautiful today, and is there any more of that champagne left, by any chance?"

I'm aware of my heart beating in an unpleasantly fast way, and feeling sensitive around the edges — as if anticipating a painful strike. I wish I'd never stuck my nose into what was none of my business. That I hadn't found out any of it. I feel disloyal, scared, nervous about how he'll respond to me checking up on him, and knowing his secrets.

Will he be angry? Or hurt? Perhaps he'll worry that I might betray him and tell someone else. And if he just takes it in his stride, is his usual chilled self, will that be because he loves me enough to forgive me, or will it be just so I'll keep the secret?

These thoughts race through my mind while Logan smiles at me in unconcerned expectation.

"Well, no." I blow out a long breath. "My … research … wasn't about sharks."

CHAPTER 34
SHARKS, WHALES AND OTHER TALES

"Not about sharks? Whales then?" Logan asks. He knows about my rage at whalers, my dream to thwart them. "Wait! That reminds me — I got you a gift. Two gifts!"

He ambles over to fetch something from the bedside table, then strolls back, grinning widely, with both hands behind his back. For a moment, he looks so young and carefree — like an impish schoolboy about to surprise his teacher with a shiny apple, or perhaps a white mouse — that my heart contracts in a sudden spasm at what I have to tell him.

"Here!" He hands me a plain white rectangle of plastic, with a magnetic strip on the back. It looks like a blank credit card.

"Um, it's lovely. Just what I always wanted."

"You! Always joshing me. It's a key card for my room, for this room. I got it especially for you, Miss Morgan."

I just stare at him, my mouth slightly open.

"So you can come and go as you please. Now you can have easy access to me anytime you like." He winks and tosses the card into my handbag. "Just don't let Cilla catch you coming or going, or she'll hand me my ass."

"And me my marching orders," I say softly.

If he's giving me access to his room, anytime, even when he isn't in it, that must mean he trusts me. A lot. I'm touched and in danger of tearing up.

"Thank you, Mr Rush, but I believe you said there were two presents?"

Without a word, he pulls me to my feet and hands me a small black velvet box.

"Logan?"

"Open it," he says, as excited as someone about to *receive* a gift.

I do. I lift the trickle of silver nestled inside and examine it. It's a delicate charm bracelet — made of platinum, I think — with tiny, dangling charms of sea creatures: a turtle, a whale, a conch shell, a dolphin and, of course, a shark.

"You like it?"

"I love it! It's beautiful." My eyes are moist now.

He fastens the bracelet around my right wrist. "There, I knew it would be a perfect match for my sea-girl. And there's a necklace, too, see?"

He draws a matching chain of the finest links from the box and holds it up.

"Thank you, Logan," I say, looking deeply into his ocean eyes.

And we stand that way for a long moment, holding each other's gaze, saying so much in the silence.

Then Logan clears his throat. "Here, let me help you."

I turn around, lifting my hair up onto the top of my head so that he can fasten the chain. His warm fingers falter against my neck.

"Are you trembling?" My voice sounds breathy.

"Uh-huh. You make me tremble."

"Are you afraid you'll break it?"

"I'm afraid I'll break you."

Then he touches burning lips to the back of my neck, and I turn in his arms so that he can kiss the hollow under my collar bone, the pulse in my throat, the sea and sunshine on my lips. We cling to each other, mouths locked, hands running through hair, over hips, under shirts. When his lips tug gently at the lobe of my ear, my knees cave.

He slips his hands beneath my knees and scoops me up, lays me gently on the cool white linen of the bed. His hot eyes fixed on mine, he shrugs off his shirt.

I'm suddenly aware that Logan is a man while I'm something more than a girl but not quite a woman. He's twenty to my eighteen, he knows so much of the world I haven't even begun to explore. He's experienced and I'm a beginner.

I'll need to trust him. Really trust him. And be worthy of his trust.

"Logan, I need to tell you what I —"

"Later."

He silences me with a deep kiss and when his hands move lower, all thought leaves my mind. His hands pause on the top button of my dress, his eyes looking a question. In answer, I open the button and lie back on the pillows. Slowly, he opens my dress, one button at a time. Slowly, he kisses every inch of revealed flesh, murmuring against my skin.

"So soft. So beautiful. Ah, Romy, I've wanted to do this since the first time I saw you." His voice is deep and rough with emotion.

When his lips reach my navel, I begin trembling. Then his mouth is back on mine and we're kissing again. Deeper. Longer. My head is spinning. I can't catch my breath. I cling to him as though I might be washed away.

Then his weight is on top of me, the bare skin of his chest burning against mine, his hands loosening the catch of my bra, exploring and caressing. My body rises up towards him. My hands pull him tight against me, his hardness against my softness. I'm hot as fire, liquid as water, light as foam on an ocean wave. And aching with a hollowness that begs to be filled.

Logan pulls his lips off mine, and I whimper, trying to reclaim their heat.

He stares down at me, his breath coming as rapidly as mine.

"Romy, I love you. I want you, I want to be a part of you. But … are you sure?"

"I want you, too. Now. Please," I beg.

I tug at him, trying to pull him down again, trying to keep cold, rational thought from invading my mindless bliss.

"You're sure, Romy, about doing this — here, now?"

My body is sure, and even my mind wants to grab this moment — for us to be fully together, to create a golden moment of ecstasy. I don't know what the future holds, and I want something I can hang on to. There'll be bad times ahead, I can sense it. Doubt and confusion, and maybe even heartbreak. He'll be gone in a week. And maybe I'll follow and maybe I won't. But even with the tide of uncertainty that pulls at our relationship, even though I've never imagined having sex with someone I've known for so short a time and may soon never see again, I want to do this with him.

Already I can feel the secrets of his past slinking into this moment, widening a space between us. I want Logan to close that space with his hands, his lips, his body. I want him to kiss away my insecurities and fears for the future, and make a memory I can keep forever. I want this moment of special. I might not get to have him, but I can have this at least, can't I?

But I've paused just a moment too long. Logan groans a sigh and rolls off me.

"Nooo." I reach for him again, my eyes prickling.

"Come here." He pulls me against the length of his side and into the crook of his arm, cradling my head on his shoulder.

"There's no rush, sugar, I can be patient." He kisses my forehead, the top of my head.

"But —" I feel panicky.

"When you're ready, when you're sure. This" — he points from himself to me and back again — "isn't over. And it's not going to be over in a week's time. One way or another, we *are* going to be together."

I want to cry at the tenderness in his voice.

"You're worth waiting for, Romy, don't you know that?"

He strokes my hair with a gentle hand, trails a finger over my shoulder and down the inside of my arm.

"But maybe," he says, clearing a husky rasp from his voice, "maybe you should button up, so I'm not tempted beyond my better nature."

I follow his gaze with my own and see that my breasts are pressed up against the side of his chest.

My face flames. I fasten my bra and the buttons of my dress, amazed that I can still blush after what we've just done. And very nearly just done.

I lie back down with my head on his shoulder, so close and comfortable. But I can't keep my hands off him.

"Would it strain your better nature if I do this?" I ask, trailing light caresses over his chest.

"I can just about keep myself in check," he says, smiling. "But don't let your fingers do the walking below the Mason-Dixon Line." He takes my hand and traces a line with my fingers along the skin below the edge of his waistband. "Wild beasts lie in wait there."

"Wild beasts?" I giggle.

"Of monstrous proportions." He holds his hands up, about a foot away from each other, to demonstrate the size.

"Yeah, right!"

We both laugh, and in that moment, the rising and falling waves of love inside me shift and solidify, anchoring themselves firmly in place somewhere in my core. Suddenly I'm sure: I cannot let him go.

Everything is clear to me now. I cannot — will not — let this end. No matter the risk and the uncertainties, I'm going to L.A. with Logan. We'll give us our best shot. Somehow, we'll *make* it work. So what if I have to keep our relationship secret and make his life the main focus of my own? So what if I have to leave my home and family and friends? My parents will have a conniption of tsunamic proportions, but they'll come around eventually —

they love me, they want me to be happy. And this will make me happy.

I feel a pang at the thought of the *Syrenka* sailing south to do battle against the whalers without me, but I tell myself it's just too bad. I can't have everything. Sometimes you have to sacrifice your personal dreams for love. Women do it all the time. Logan — this wonderful, loving, funny, tender man — is worth sacrificing anything for.

But first I'd better confess. I take a deep breath and push myself up on one elbow so I can look him in the eyes. "I need to tell you two things — one is good, and one is bad."

"Give me the good news first."

"No, I think I'd better start with the bad. You might not care about the other news once you hear that."

"Okayyy," he says slowly.

There's a loud bang at the door. We sit up and look from the door to each other. A series of sharp raps sounds through the room.

"Logan? Logan, let me in — we need to talk!"

The voice is loud, flat, nasal, and female. Unmistakably Cilla.

CHAPTER 35
HUSHED

Logan slips on his shirt and buttons it up while Cilla stalks around the room, a bearded dragon on each shoulder. Her eyes linger suspiciously on the remains of room service. As she passes the door to the bathroom, she suddenly thrusts her head inside.

"Looking for something, Cilla?"

"*Someone*, Logan. It wouldn't surprise me to find Brittany here."

"It would certainly surprise me," Logan says, casting a quick glance at the wardrobe where I sit hunched in the cramped and stuffy darkness, perched uncomfortably on a collection of Logan's shoes, trying not to make a sound.

I clutch my plate and glass in one hand and curl the forefinger of my other around the bottom edge of the wardrobe door, keeping it open two inches. I don't want to suffocate, and I do want to eavesdrop.

"Well, Logan, enjoying your day off?"

"Sure."

Logan flops onto the sofa, probably hoping she'll stop her sniffing around and join him. She does.

I can no longer see either of them, but I can hear them easily in the plush stillness of the room.

"So, about *Mars* …"

"About what?"

"Don't play dumb, Logan. You know exactly what I'm talking about. Contracts has informed me that you have not yet signed for *Beast: Mars.*"

"That's right."

"Well, when exactly *are* you planning to sign?" Cilla says, clearly irritated. "We need to get the ball rolling, and we can't do that if the lead hasn't signed on yet."

"You did once before, with the first film."

"That was different, and you know it. We were signing an unknown to star opposite Britney Vaux. Anyone cute and capable of being beefed up would have done well enough." I imagine her giving one of his biceps a sharp squeeze with her red claws. "It didn't matter who he was."

"Why thank you, Cilla, that makes me feel right special and valued."

"Now don't get pissy with me. You were a nobody, and my movies made you a star."

"You act like I had nothing to do with it."

"These movies *made* you a star," Cilla repeats. "Britney Vaux made you a star, she gave you a break. And now it's time to return the favour."

"I know what I owe Britney — you don't need to remind me of that — but I had a look over that script and, no offence Cilla, but it's bad. Real bad. There isn't a line in that script that isn't a cliché, a plot point that isn't a plot hole, a line of dialogue that isn't more corn than a boiled cob."

"Will ya listen to him? Scribbles one deleted scene and suddenly he thinks he's a writer." Cilla's tone is bitter and scathing.

I can feel anger at her building inside me.

"You're not a writer, Logan, need I remind you? And before you start whining some rubbish about wanting to do stage work on Broadway, let me also remind you that you're not an *actor* either. You're a *star*. A celebrity who happens to have landed his lucky ass in one of the biggest-grossing franchises of all time, and should be milking it while he still has the looks and the body and the fans. It doesn't last forever, Logan. A week is a long time in Hollywood. You can lose it all like that."

I hear the sound of fingers snapping and grow hot with fury. If I was a pet lizard, right now I'd be open-jawed and hissing. Cilla's planting doubts and feeding Logan's insecurities, all to serve her own money-grabbing ends. I want to kick the door open and give her a piece of my mind.

Why should Logan be held back from growing as an actor? It's not fair that he be forced to play opposite Britney Vaux yet *again* and pretend like they're a couple only so that Cilla won't be upset or inconvenienced. It's outrageous that people just cave in to her like this. That she manages to silence everyone. I want to shout at Logan to stand up for himself, to tell Cilla where to get off. Never has staying silent and keeping us a secret been so difficult.

"You owe me, Logan. You owe me and Britney and the cast.

And you owe your fans. We're all depending on you. So be a good boy and sign the contract."

There's silence for a few moments. Is her guilt-trip getting to him? Is he actually considering this? When Cilla speaks again, her voice is hard and flat.

"I've given you the carrot, don't make me use the stick. I made you. Don't forget that I know where you come from, *what* you come from, and I can send you back, *Levi*."

I hear the door of the suite click shut, and I launch out of the closet. Logan stands alone in the middle of the room, his shoulders slumped, looking down at the floor. He seems smaller, somehow, diminished in some way. I can't bear to see him like this.

I bang the plate and glass down on the coffee table hard, snapping the stem of the champagne flute.

"Logan!" For a moment, I can't say more — I'm choked with anger.

He looks up. His face is pale and his eyes sad.

"Don't believe a word she said, do you hear me? It's not true. It's all rubbish, self-serving lies!"

"Is it?"

"Yes!" Now I'm growing angry at *him*. I want him to put up more of a fight. It breaks my heart to see him feeling so hopeless and helpless. "Don't listen to her. How could you even let her talk to you like that? Insulting you and insinuating that you can't write or even act."

He walks over towards me, holding out his hands, as if he can soothe away my temper.

"Hush, sugar, it doesn't matter what she said about me. Don't get all riled up."

"Don't hush me!" I throw up a hand to stop him.

He looks surprised.

"I've had enough of people shutting me up. I am sick and tired of people shushing me and ignoring me and interrupting me, dammit! Everyone is always telling me to shut up, bite my tongue, be quiet, sit down and listen. I will not be silenced! I'm sick of it. I'm going to have my say."

"Well, out with it then." He crosses his arms and waits.

"It's time you stood up to Cilla."

"Great," Logan says, raking his fingers though his hair. "Another woman telling me what I should and shouldn't do, just what I need."

"The difference is, Logan, I want what's best for you. That — that witch of a woman only wants what's best for her. And what's best for her is your flushing any hope of a serious acting future down the s-bend by starring in sewerage! Why would you do what she wants, rather than what you want? Why *should* you?"

"I owe —"

"You owe her nothing. Nothing!" Now it's me doing the interrupting, and it feels good. Better than good — it feels wonderful to shout everything I'd been holding back. "And you owe Britney nothing! You've made them all millions! And they'll go on to make even more, whether or not you sign on. It's time you decide what you want — what *you* want — and fight for it."

"Are you sure you aren't talking about yourself, Romy?" He's not smiling now.

"What do you mean?" I say, taken aback.

"Just that if there's anyone who needs to figure out what they want, and stand up to the people who want to make them do something different — it's you. You're big on telling me what to do, but not so hot on making decisions for yourself."

He's right. Of course he is. It only makes me angrier.

"Do you really think the whole series will fizzle out if you're not in it? Do you really think they can't replace you? Maybe your problem isn't that you're insecure, maybe it's that you believe you're irreplaceable."

"Romy!" There's a warning edge to his voice.

"Nobody's indispensable. Maybe it's time for them to find a nice, new star. And maybe it's time for Britney to move on to a different role, too — trust me, she's no slouch in the acting department. And you're a big enough name to take some risks. I mean, would the world end if you acted in a play? Or if you came out and said the rumours about you and Britney were rubbish? Or even if — here's a thought — if *we* appeared in public, *together*."

"I gave you the choice on that, Romy."

"I wanted *you* to choose, to choose us."

"Then you should have said so!"

I'm dimly aware that I'm being unfair, irrational even, but I can't stop my fears tumbling out my mouth. "Why can't you tell Cilla that I'm your girlfriend, and that Brittany isn't? We sneak about, hiding, catching quick kisses in backrooms, wearing disguises."

"Is this about the mullet again?" He's trying to make me laugh, to distract me.

"It's not funny!" Tears are threatening now.

He sighs, obviously frustrated. "You agreed to keep us a secret. And I told you why I wanted it — to protect you."

"Yeah, I remember you saying that."

"What's that supposed to mean?"

"Is it really to protect me, Logan? Or to protect the media hype around you and Britney. Which matters more to you? *Who* matters more?"

Logan curses loudly. "You know I care about you. You know I love you."

"Love doesn't make the other person hide in a cupboard, Logan. It's humiliating. I deserve better than that."

He looks at me for a long moment, then his shoulders crumple and he looks away, all the fight drained out of him.

"Yeah. Yeah, you do," he says simply, sagging onto the sofa and examining his hands.

I walk over and sit down on the low table in front of him. "What are you saying?"

"You deserve better."

I wait, but he doesn't say anything more. He isn't going to fight for himself, and he isn't going to fight for us, either. My throat closes, my eyes fill.

He won't meet my gaze. "This is my life, Romy, this is how it is. You knew that when we started."

"You're right. You warned me. I was a stupid little fool to think I could change anything."

"Maybe you were."

His comment fires up my anger again, and before I know it, words I don't intend saying slip out. "Yeah, because I play fair, I don't blackmail you with threats about your father."

Logan's head snaps up at that. "What do you know about my father?"

"Everything. And you don't see me using it against you."

"How … How do you know?" Logan's eyes narrow, his face has gone pale, and his lips are tight.

My own anger fails in the face of his. I stammer out an explanation of what I discovered and how I tried to tell him.

"You had no right! How dare you read my private mail?" he yells.

"I was trying to protect you."

"By snooping? Researching my family and my past on the Net like some tabloid reporter?"

"I'm sorry! But I wanted to see what Cilla had on you."

"Is that what you told yourself? I can't believe you did this. It's a complete violation of trust."

He's taking this worse than I thought he would. He's taking it worse than he took Cilla's threat, and that pisses me off.

"*Trust?* Don't talk to me about trust," I say hotly. "If you really valued trust, you would've been honest with me. Told me who you really are and the reason why you'll always ultimately do whatever Cilla wants."

"I think you should leave now." Logan's eyes are blazing pools of fury.

"With pleasure!"

I stride across the room, retrieve my shoes, and squeeze my feet back into them, longing to throw them at his head instead. Then I grab my bag and head for the door, but when I yank it open, I fall back in surprise. Britney Vaux stands right outside, wearing nothing but a tiny gold bikini and matching dagger heels. What *is* with these people — walking around a fancy hotel half-naked or wearing lizards? Who do they think they are?

"What do you want?" I ask rudely.

"Manners, Ronnie," she chides, trying to peer over my shoulder into the room. "I'm here to see Logan, of course. We have a date."

"Oh, is that so? Well, let me not get in the way," I say, stepping aside to let Britney slink into the room on her long, golden legs.

"Not that I need an appointment," Britney says, giving me a smile as wide as a tiger's. "After all, we are *married*, aren't we, handsome?" Giggling, she holds up a white plastic card, just like the one Logan gave me. "I can drop in anytime."

"You …" Words, ugly and harsh, bubble up inside me. But they stick sideways in my throat and won't come out.

I just stand there trembling, staring with furious disgust into his blue eyes. They aren't the colour of deep water, or the eye of a peacock feather, or dark blue sapphires or any other beautiful thing. They're the colour of the Pacific Blue Tang, an exotic and peaceful-looking fish whose flesh poisons humans, and whose sharp spines pierce skin, leaving deep, painful wounds and lingering infection.

"Romy. I —" Logan begins.

"Save it."

I slam the door closed behind me.

CHAPTER 36
TEMPTATION

My anger wars with tears and rising panic as I ride the elevator down from the penthouse to the hotel lobby. My heart pounds in my ears, my tight scalp feels like it's crushing my head, and my mouth is dry as dust. What just happened? One minute we were holding each other, loving and laughing, and the next we were fighting. And now we're … over?

I swipe at my eyes, hating the weakness. Part of me wants to press the penthouse button and head straight back up, fall into his arms, and listen to his explanations, to his reassurances that Britney means nothing to him, that he loves me. To apologise and beg him to take me back — on any terms. But another part of me, a part that has to do with self-respect and pride, refuses to go grovelling.

When the door opens onto the lobby, I step out, rummaging in my bag with shaking hands to find my car keys. In the back compartment, I discover what I'd earlier been meaning to hand over to Logan. For a moment, I'm tempted to go back and throw his father's damn letter at him, but I don't trust myself not to cave once I see him. Or not to kill him if Britney's still in the room.

"Swine!" I mutter under my breath as I stalk across the lobby. "Jerk!" I'd like to shove *him* in a cupboard. I hope I crushed his new shoes while I crouched there.

This is how it is — you knew that when we started. Things can change, can't they?

We are *married, aren't we handsome.* Bitch.

I think you should leave now. Bastard.

I'm fuming so hard that I don't notice the small man standing in my way until I crash straight into him.

"Well, well, well. If it isn't the little lady who protects Rush's trashy secrets," says the weasel-faced paparazzo, studying my face closely. "What's got you all hot and bothered?"

"None of your business." I try to step around him.

"It *is* my business if it's about Logan Rush," he says, nimbly stepping in front of me again. "Is it him who's got you so angry? What's he done? Who's he done it to? Come on, you can tell me."

Why is it that the only person in the world who *wants* me to speak is the one person I don't want to talk to?

Or do I?

He notices my hesitation and pounces. "It looks like you've got something you want to get off your chest, hmm? They say confession's good for the soul."

Involuntarily, my hand dips into my bag. It's all there, inside — the letter, the newspaper articles, the photo of him at the courthouse. I'm suddenly aware of my own power. I could stab him in the back right now with the sharp truths I know, the secrets I've kept. I could get some blood on my hands to match the blisters on my feet.

It would serve him right if he was forced to come clean — it would do him good to be completely honest and open. *Plus*, it would finally end Cilla's hold over him. Yes, leaking what I know to this horrible little man, letting it go public, might bring Logan's career momentum to a screeching halt, but Cilla was right about one thing — a week *was* a long time in Hollywood. There would be a crazed media shitstorm when the news hit the tabloids, but it would die down eventually. It wouldn't kill him, just hurt him some.

And if I can't be happy, why should he be?

"C'mon girl, you know you want to. Tell me what you know," the reporter urges.

And so help me, I do.

When I finish with the reporter, I drive straight to Zeb's house. His mother answers the door but tactfully makes no mention of my red, swollen eyes and puffy face. She hands me over to my friend, brings us tea and cookies, and then leaves me to fall apart. I tell him the whole sad story, what Logan said and failed to say. What *I* said. What I did. He lets me vent my anger and my grief and my guilt. And I tell him in detail about Britney.

"She had such long legs," I wail.

"I think we might need to break out the ice cream," Zeb says.

Over spoonfuls of Rocky Road, I sob, "And I already miss him, Zeb, I love him, but I can't …"

"No," he agrees. "You definitely can't."

I slide over to nestle into his shoulder, and he puts a consoling arm around me, but my head doesn't fit — it keeps rolling off — and when he pats my back, it only makes me want to cough. It's the wrong shoulder, the wrong hands.

"It's a damn shame, I was beginning to like him. But he didn't appreciate what a catch you were. He needs to figure out what's important, and what isn't," Zeb says loyally when I eventually subside into sniffles and the odd hiccup. But he also adds, "And, sorry to say it, Romy, but you've got some growing up to do, too."

Feeling a bit queasy from all the tea and sugar, and the reality-check, I drive home. When I walk inside, the house seems strange to me — too small, different in some indefinable way.

Once, in my second-last year of high school, I went back to visit a teacher in my primary school, and I experienced the surreal sensation of the place being both completely familiar and yet utterly strange. The staircases, which had once been so wide and so high, were now narrow, the steps too shallow and too few. The teachers who loomed large in my memories, were now shorter than me and seemed too young, and the basins and toilets in the girls' cloakrooms were teeny and too low for comfort. Everything was different, alien. Nothing about the school had changed, of course — I had. I no longer fit there.

I feel like that now, here at 'home.' It's as though I'm looking at my world through new eyes.

I remember Cilla — cursed lizard witch! — telling me that working in the movies would spoil me for real life, and I sigh. It's going to be insanely difficult going from love and passion and magic, to a soulless vac job among the academic or commercial fishes. I broke the surface of my life, looked around, and had a taste of love and adventure, but soon I'll sink back down again. I'm about to settle, just like my sisters did before me. Maybe even worse — they at least had actively made their own choices, while I've been reactive, basing my decisions on the plans and actions of others.

"I thought I heard the door." Mom comes into the entrance hall, followed by my father. As soon as she sees me, she knows something's very wrong. "What is it, love, what happened?"

Both their faces — the wrong faces — are concerned.

"It's over," I say. "With Logan, with the movies — it's all over."

"My poor baby," Mom says.

"Did he …? What did that boy do to you?" Dad bellows.

"He didn't do anything, okay? It just didn't work out — it couldn't work out. You were right. There, happy now?"

"How can we be happy when you're so sad? We never wanted this for you," Mom says.

"It's what we tried to protect you against, Rosemary. I told —"

"So help me, Dad, if you say 'I told you so,' I won't be held responsible for what I do or say." I am through biting my tongue.

There must be something in my expression that warns him, because he stands aside without another word and lets me run upstairs to my bedroom. Nana is there within minutes.

"I've heard. Oh, my dear, my dear," she says, enfolding me in her arms, pressing me up against the sweet smell of her scent. The wrong arms, the wrong smell.

"It is better to have loved and lost, than never to have loved at all."

I grind my teeth. I love Nana and don't want to snap at her, but I can't stand any more advice on love.

"Never mind," she consoles. "It may not feel like it now, but your heart will heal. And, after all, there are plenty more fish in the sea."

"I don't want a fish — I want Logan!" I cry, perilously close to bawling my eyes out again. "But I can't have him. I don't fit in his world. And now I don't fit here anymore, either. I've changed."

"Of course you have. Life changes us, *love* changes us! And you've been living and loving with a passion. When I ran away from home, I was just a little younger than you are now, dearest, and there were oodles of gentlemen offering me … er … a room. But I turned them all down. I wanted to live alone — alone! — for a while, even just a little while, to find out who I was when I wasn't someone's daughter, or sister, or sweetheart. And I'm glad I did it because I grew up and learned an awful lot about myself. And also, sadly, about the breeding habits and virtual indestructability of cockroaches."

"Nana, you know I love your stories, but now? Really?" I fling myself on my bed, trying to blink away my tears, but everywhere I look, there are reminders of *him*.

"What I'm trying to say in my muddled way, is that you need to find your own element."

Huh. My own element. I *had* thought it was with Logan. But maybe not.

Nana comes over and bends to kiss me on the cheek. "You have a little nap now — I always find a broken heart to be odiously exhausting! I'll come visit in the morning, and we'll go shopping. Spending money frivolously invariably cheers me up, and my goodness," she says with a glance at my dolphin calendar, "it's the fifteenth already. There are only ten days left to shop before Christmas!"

Nana leaves and I glare around at my bedroom. This house is definitely no longer my own element, if it ever was. My room seems childish and silly to me now, decorated with reminders of broken, foolish dreams.

I spring off the bed and lunge at the posters of Logan, ripping them off the wall and tearing them to shreds, which float like confetti down to the floor. Lobster barks and tries to catch them in her teeth.

"Go away! Out!" I shout at her, and feel guilty when she slinks out of the room, tail between her legs. I know the feeling.

I grab the little figurine of Chase Falconer off the drawer handle and throw it against the far wall. It bounces off and lands in the rubbish bin — a broken-hearted slam dunk. I yank open my wardrobe door, snatch off the poster, and trample it underfoot. Then I descend on the whale and protest posters, crumpling them up and pitching them on top of the binned Beast. The calendar follows — it's been a craptastic end to a disappointing year, with nothing to look forward to in the future. I wrench the last remaining picture — the poster of the majestic *Syrenka* — off the wall and hurl it at the growing pile.

The room looks cleaner and airier. And emptier — like me. I feel empty of everything except regret. I have plenty of that.

But right then an idea bubbles up from my murky depths. I know what will make me feel much, much better. I know exactly what I have to do.

I pick up my phone — I have an important call to make.

CHAPTER 37
NEW WORLD

I examine my face in the bathroom mirror while I brush my teeth. My eyes are a little puffy in the pale dawn light, but not too bad considering how little sleep I got. I spent most of last night making calls, packing my bags, and arguing with my parents.

They told me my plans were rash, that I was gambling a sure future on a risky venture, chasing a girl's romantic dream. Mom begged me not to go, Dad suggested that I was mentally unstable, but — short of locking me up — there was nothing they could do. Being eighteen still counts for something in the world. It's time to stand on my own two feet, to make my own decisions, to choose my own world.

I do a final check on my packed belongings, zip my stuffed bags closed with difficulty, take a last long look around my room, and then head downstairs.

"Mom, Dad!" I call, eager to be gone now.

They insist on being the ones to drop me off — though Zeb volunteered when I called to tell him my decision. He was more supportive than my folks.

"We always regret the things we never did more than the things we did," he'd said. Wise boy.

On our way, driving through the mostly empty Sunday-morning streets of Cape Town, Dad asks, "Is there anything we can say to change your mind, Rosemary?"

"No."

"Maybe it won't be such a bad thing, after all," Mom says. "Fun, adventure, a whole new world."

"You've been listening to my mother, Sally," Dad says sourly.

After that we drive in silence until we get to the Cape Majesty hotel. Dad pulls into a bay for taxis right by the front door to drop me off.

"Are you sure about this dear?" my mother asks for what must be the hundredth time.

"*Yes*, Mom."

"Do you want me to come in with you?" my father asks.

"Dad, *no*."

"Good luck, Romy!" Mom calls after my departing back.

"It's not too late to change your mind!" Dad adds.

The hotel lobby is almost deserted except for a cleaner steering a polishing machine over the marble floor. I pause for a moment, checking that I'm still sure I want to do this.

I am. And I'm not. But mostly I am.

I head for the reception desk, hold up my large, padded envelope, and tell the clerk behind the counter, "I'd like to leave a package for Logan Rush, please."

"We have no guests by that name staying here," he replies automatically.

I suspected this might happen, that's why I haven't yet sealed the package. I fish out my identity card and hand it over for the clerk to check. "I'm his personal assistant. Please ensure he gets this directly."

When he nods, I replace the ID card in the padded envelope, peel off the sticky-strip protector, and seal the flap tight over the contents: the key card to Logan's penthouse; a letter of resignation to Cilla Swytch; the beautiful necklace and charm bracelet Logan gave me; and a letter from me to him apologising for the ugly things I said, and trying to explain my feelings and my decisions.

The receptionist takes the package and I turn to leave. My heart scrunches painfully inside me. Was it really only six weeks ago that I brought Logan here after fishing him out of the ocean? I'm way older than the girl I was then.

I walk across the lobby where yesterday I gave the reporter a piece of my mind.

"So you want me to tell you what I know, do you? Sure. With pleasure!" I'd said. "I know you're an oily, scum-sucking, bottom-feeding, life-destroying excuse for a hack. And I know I have nothing more to say to you. Now get out of my way before I kick you down and walk right over your miserable body. Mood I'm in, I could do it!"

I'd marched straight into the ladies' restroom, torn the Peabody prison letter and the news article printouts into the tiniest pieces of paper possible, then flushed them down a toilet. I'd kept flushing until the last speck of evidence was gone, and most of my anger along with it.

Now, as I exit the hotel I feel mostly a heavy aching sadness. But there's a glimmer of hope, too. I'll feel bad for a while.

Scratch that. I'll feel wretched — heartbroken and miserable — for a long time. But as Nana would likely say if she were here, you don't die from heartache.

Dad starts the car as soon as I climb back inside.

"Right, next stop — the Red Cross," I tell him.

"The Red Cross?"

"They've got a big bin outside, where you can deposit clothing donations. And I've got some shoes that no longer fit, and that I surely won't be needing."

When we get to the donation drop-off spot, I chuck the shoes, pair by pair, down the chute into the clothing depositary — the dagger heels I wore on my first day on the job, the black stilettos I wore to Britney's birthday party on the night I lost my voice completely, the strappy sandals I'd worn just yesterday for my date with Logan. I smile grimly down at the sturdy, waterproof running shoes now on my feet. Not elegant, not fashionable, but comfortable and fit for purpose.

On impulse, I spin around and karate-kick the chute closed with a bang that startles a foraging flock of seagulls into flight, screeching their protest to the skies.

"Right," I say firmly as I get back into the car. "Next stop, the docks. And floor it Dad, I've got a boat to catch!"

CHAPTER 38
CHRISTMAS PRESENTS

I need better shoes.

I've spent ten days on board the *Syrenka*, slipping and sliding across its wet decks while it carves its way through rough seas towards the Southern Ocean, and I can confirm that running shoes don't give you nearly enough grip, especially when you need to reach a bucket or a rail or a toilet in a hurry. Which I need to do all the time.

I'm permanently queasy. And when the seas are rough enough to set the ship rolling, like now, I spend loads of time kneeling beside the ship's toilet — which, I've learned, is called "the head." Maybe because your face is so often bent over it.

Another wave of nausea shudders through me, and as I heave, I cling to the white porcelain throne, so I don't go rolling across the tilting floor. I feel sick and miserable, and even though I'm dressed in jeans, thermal underwear, thick sweaters, a waterproof jacket, gloves, and a beanie, I'm still cold. I'm permanently, seriously, bitterly, bone-achingly cold. Having lived all my life in Africa, this is like nothing I've ever felt before. I'm a bit panicky because everyone says it's still going to get a whole lot worse. Crew members who hail from Sweden, Norway and Canada just laugh at me, but Libby — a twenty-four-year-old Aussie from Darwin with the foulest mouth I've ever encountered — feels my pain.

"Yeah, it's colder than a witch's tit, alright," she told me this morning. "But at least there're no bities out here, mate."

I think she was talking about mosquitoes. Yup, that's one thing I *don't* need to worry about out here.

When my retching finally stops, I wash my face and hands, brush my teeth, and head up onto the deck. It calms my stomach to breathe fresh air and to be able to see the horizon. And it reminds me why I'm here. At last, I feel like I'm in my element. Not physically — apart from being a wuss when it comes to the cold and seasickness, I don't much enjoy being a vegan or getting to shower only once every four days. And I seriously miss the sun. But I love knowing that what I'm doing is important, that it matters, and that we're making a real difference.

The main aim of this mission, Operation Zero Kill, is to disrupt and harass the fleet illegally hunting whales in the Southern Ocean sanctuary. Currently we're playing a cat-and-mouse game on a gigantic scale. We need to find the whalers before they locate us, and each of us is hiding from the other on an ocean 20.3 million square kilometres in size.

The Japanese whaling fleet consists of two harpoon ships, which sail out to slaughter the whales, and one factory ship to which they transfer the carcasses for butchering. If we find the factory ship first — we win, because by sticking close to the slipway on their stern, we can block them from receiving the dead whales, which in turn stops further hunting because there's nowhere to store the "meat."

But if a harpoon vessel were to find us first, then we'd lose — and so would the whales — because it would follow us and relay our coordinates continually to the factory ship, to help it stay out of our range. The harpoon ships are smaller, faster and more manoeuvrable than the old *Syrenka*, so outrunning them isn't an option.

So far, we haven't spotted them, or them us. It's a freaking big ocean out here.

We've been preparing for when we do encounter them, though — running drills and practice exercises, and training in everything from small-boat launching and radio protocols, to fire safety and abandon-ship procedures. So far, everyone's been very friendly, showing me the ropes (sometimes literally) and helping me figure my way around the old boat. The *Syrenka* was originally a Russian icebreaker built in the 1960s, but now she's equipped with all the latest in technology and communications equipment. There are forty-two crew members on board, and for the next four months, I'll be sharing a cramped cabin with three of them, including Libby.

Standing at the rails, I gaze out at the enormous vastness surrounding us — the endless grey-blue of the water, the 360-degree horizon, the floating chunks of ice, some as small as my fist, some as big as our boat. I've never felt so small and insignificant, yet I've never felt so real. I'm at the far end of the world, blissed out on space and wind and ice. My life on land, in my parents' world and on the film set, seems like another lifetime.

Because today is Christmas we each got one phone call on the satellite phone this morning — our first since we left Cape Town — along with strict instructions about not giving any clues to our position. I called my parents, just like a good daughter should. Dad wasted no time in telling me my matric results, and I was pleased to hear I'd gotten mostly A's and B's. They both sounded proud, and relieved to hear I was still in one piece.

Mom said she checks the ship's internet blog every day, and nagged me to send more emails. I explained that between a lack of time and internet restrictions, they were lucky to get anything at all. I had to laugh when Mom told me that Nana is spending Christmas with a new "beau"! Husband number six on her horizon?

It was great to hear their voices, even though I couldn't help wishing I was speaking to someone else entirely. I guess I'm more heartsick than homesick. I wonder how Logan will be spending his Christmas. Where will he be? And with whom?

It starts sleeting and I'm headed back inside — Libby needs my help in the galley to prepare the special meal we've got planned for the crew — when my favourite cry sounds out.

"Whales!" Mike, a Canadian who usually works in the engine room, points South-East.

When I squint into the distance, he offers me his binoculars. A sharp stab of pain reminds me of the time I scanned the sea, looking for human prey, but I push memories of Logan from my mind and train the lenses on a cluster of icebergs.

One is a huge flat-topped chunk of brilliant blue-white, with tapered edges and horizontal turquoise striations in the ice. The other has a crenelated top, like a castle, and as we draw near, it dwarfs us with its pearly massive bulk. A colony of snow-dusted seals lies on its edges, and when we pass — close enough to catch their pungent odour — several slip into the water and come closer to investigate us.

In front of the iceberg are the whales — a pod of Southern Rights, including a massive mother at least fifteen metres long, her calf, and some smaller males or females. They're beautiful, despite looking like they've been cobbled together from half-a-dozen different creatures. They have enormous, round black bodies, short stubby fins, wide triangular tails, and heads covered in patches of crusty brown growths called callosities. Their long, arching mouths begin at a point higher than their eyes and run all the way around, giving them a perpetual *hmmmph!* expression.

The mother and calf in this pod play a kind of tag — breaching alternately, one after the other. Their massive splashes back into the icy water boom like cannon blasts.

My eyes tear up. It's the best Christmas present I could ever have asked for. This is what I'm here for, this is what it's all about. I only wish Logan were here to experience it with me.

When the whales disappear around the back of the iceberg, I head back to the galley — a tiny kitchen crammed between two huge walk-in refrigerators, a freezer and a pantry, all packed to the gills with enough food to keep us going for months. The galley is the warmest spot on the ship, but it always smells like cooking, which is hard on my feeble stomach.

"Feeling better?" Libby asks. She's the chief cook and I'm her galley slave.

"Sort of."

"Well, at least *everyone else* is keeping your food down, and you're keeping the fishes fed."

Today's Christmas lunch menu is Thai coconut soup, vegetable and chickpea curry with home-made naan bread, spinach and mushroom lasagne, canned peaches with custard, and a vegan chocolate cake. There's lots to be done — peeling, grating, frying, stirring, and washing the endless dishes — but I volunteer to chop onions so I can have a good cry without anyone noticing.

I've shifted from anger to wallowing self-pity about the Logan-shaped hole in my life. Why me? Why didn't he? Why couldn't we? There are no answers. I'm just grateful that I'm kept so busy that there isn't too much time for pity-partying. I've discovered that when you miss someone you love, your heart actually does *ache*. Your bones feel hollow, your hands empty, and there's a longing in your skin. Your body knows something vital is missing. The anger fades, but the hurt remains, like the phantom pains of an amputated limb.

After lunch, I pull up a chair at the crew's computer in the common room. According to the rotating roster, it's my turn to post on the ship's blog — the main way we stay in touch with our supporters across the world. I describe today's whale sighting and our special festive menu, wish our followers a happy festive season, and end with the usual appeal for moral and financial support.

Our access to the internet is strictly rationed, and this is my first time since we left Cape Town. I can't resist the temptation of navigating to my favourite Rusher fan sites to check on the latest news.

Holy Crow!

Rushing Away from the Beast

Teen heartthrob and megastar Logan Rush today confirmed rumours that he has declined to star in the next Beast film, Beast: Mars.

"The Beast *movies have been very good to me, and I'm grateful for all the support I've received from fans and my colleagues along the way, but it's time for a change and a new challenge."*

Rush laughingly dismissed the idea that the Beast Saga *would tank without his name in the opening credits.*

"The series won't fizzle because I'm not in it. Britney Vaux will still be its star, and with Cilla Swytch at the helm, you can be sure it'll be a box-office success. Somebody very wise once told me that nobody is indispensable or irreplaceable."

I gasp when I read that last sentence. Mike, who's hanging about waiting for his turn on the computer, asks, "Good or bad news?"

"Excellent news!"

I angle the screen away from him and examine the online photograph of Logan, which even now, at this distance of time and space and possibility, does funny swooping things to my insides. There's a shadow of stubble on his square jaw, and his hair looks unkempt with its usual flopping black lock over one brow, but his face seems more relaxed, his grin more of a true smile and less of a pose for the camera.

"Indispensable, irreplaceable," I murmur.

I was wrong. He is both.

My jaw falls open as I continue reading the article.

This latest news comes on the back of startling revelations made by Rush earlier this week that set his fandom agog and blogging.

Rush confirmed that his next film project will be to star in the production of his own screenplay. Set in the American South of 1961, during the famous Freedom Rides of the civil rights movement, the story will be about a young man's struggle to overcome his early suffering at the hands of an abusive father, and to escape the lingering guilt and shame following his racist father's murder of a black teenage boy. Twitter, Facebook, Instagram and other social networking sites were ablaze with messages of support when Rush revealed that the script will be based on elements of his own life story.

"It's a story that needs to be told, not silenced," he said.

Watch this space for more details as they emerge, and follow the hashtag #RushToFreedom on social media.

Suck it Cilla!

My heart is hammering, my hands trembling, my eyes leaking. I'm speechless.

Logan, on the other hand, seems to have found his voice.

CHAPTER 39
FINDING VOICE

In Cape Town, early January is the height of summer, with long, hot days and a welcome southeasterly wind to freshen the air. Out here, things couldn't be more different.

We've crossed over into the "screaming sixties" of high winds and waves, and we've run into a force nine storm, with icy winds of over ninety kilometres per hour, and waves over seven metres high. The weather reports predict the storm will blow itself out in a few days, but right now the *Syrenka* rolls and lurches like a drunken pirate.

I'm sick as a dog, but I don't dare go up on deck. Peeping out the porthole, I see how we ride up one side of a high swell and plunge down into the deep trough on the other, and my stomach heaves. I can hear the storm outside — the crash of towering waves smashing violently against the hull, the wind howling like a monster in torment.

I could *so* use some steady earth beneath my freezing feet right now. And some warm sunshine on my face.

We're all spending the day preparing for our first mission,

because yesterday we located the Japanese whaling factory ship, the *Koshitsu*. From now on, we'll be sticking closer to it than a callosity on a Southern Right's head.

The *Koshitsu* is a big and ugly ship, with the word "RESEARCH" neatly stencilled on its grey hull, and "RESEARCH ACTIVITY PURSUANT TO INTERNATIONAL WHALING CONVENTION" on the back above the very slipway where whale carcasses are hauled up to be butchered in the on-board processing factory.

The whalers claim they're researching dietary habits, but what they're doing is not for science, it's for profit. Legally, no whale killed for "lethal research" can go to waste, so the meat gets sold on the open market and winds up on dinner plates, restaurant menus, and has even been found in sushi in California. It's big business. Captain Murphy says one whale will sell for between a quarter and one million dollars, and the Japanese alone have a permit to take about a thousand whales this season — mostly Antarctic Minkies and some Fin Whales, with the occasional Humpback if they can get it. They're prohibited from whaling in the Southern Ocean Sanctuary, but they do it anyway.

Libby has seen whales being killed. She says the grenade harpoons often miss the spine and don't get an instant kill. It can take up to an hour after the grenade explodes for the whale to die, and all the while it thrashes about in agony, getting shot repeatedly by high-powered rifles. Sometimes the whale is dragged backwards by its tail until it drowns.

We all know what the whaler really is: a floating abattoir. A death ship.

Our goal is to wreak such financial damage and operational havoc, that it makes it unprofitable for them to continue. As soon as the weather allows, we'll do an interception. In the meantime, we're planning our strategy for the assault and stocking our arsenal with homemade bombs — of the stink and slippery variety.

The disgusting smell hits me before I even enter the common room. Actually, "disgusting" doesn't even begin to describe the nauseating stench. It's like a blend of vomit, dog doo and rotten drains.

Some of the crew, wearing eye goggles and masks over their mouths and noses, are hard at work filling dozens of glass bottles with a disgusting-smelling substance.

"What *is* that?" I ask Libby, who works with the practised hand of long experience.

"Putrefied butter. It's non-toxic, but high in butyric acid — that's what causes the smell, and the smell's what does the damage."

"We try to lob these onto the deck and slipway of the whaler," Mike tells me. "When the bottle shatters, the muck spreads on the deck, and it sticks around for a really long time. Makes their work conditions deeply unpleasant. And even better, if the whale meat touches the stuff, it gets contaminated and it can't be sold. Cool, ay?"

Gagging at the smell, I volunteer for the other task — scooping a white powder called Methocel into brown paper bags, rolling them up, and securing them with tape. Pete, the second mate who is another plain-spoken Aussie and, at fifty, the second-oldest person on board, explains that the packages explode when they hit the deck, scattering the powder everywhere. When it comes into contact with water, the result is a deck-coating substance so slippery that it becomes nearly impossible to walk and go about the daily business of hauling in and hacking up whales.

"Slippery as roo-poo, mate. I love it when it sends them arse over tit," Pete says.

That afternoon, I get a twenty-minute slot on the Net and start by checking the reaction to my Christmas blog post. In amongst all the well-wishing comments from supporters around the world, as well as the occasional troll calling me a bunny-hugging eco-terrorist who should wash my stinky, hippie ass, eat a cow, and then die, is one that makes my insides leap — in a happy, thoroughly un-seasick kind of way.

Alabama_Hog (December, 25)
You go, girl! If anyone can save endangered creatures and other helpless beasts, it's you. Merry Christmas, Romy. ☺

It's him — I know it is. It's got to be.

I curse the fact that we get such infrequent access to the Net. His comment has been up for two weeks without my knowing about it. I type an immediate reply:

Romy (January, 8)
Thank you, Alabama_Hog, kind of you to say so. We welcome all supporters, even hogs and those who wear mullets. ☺

I stare at the screen for a full minute, grinning wider than a great white, and then I check the Rusher sites.

Rehearsals begin for Broadway revival of Equus

Movie megastar Logan Rush yesterday sat down between rehearsal sessions with veteran of the stage, Sir Nicholas Dwyer, to talk about their roles in the latest Broadway production of Peter Shaffer's classic Equus.

Rush will be playing the part of Alan Strang — an apparently mild-mannered young man who savagely attacks six horses with a metal stake. Dwyer plays the psychiatrist who investigates the inner demons which lead the boy to commit the atrocity.

"I've done several films now," said Rush at the Paladium Theater today, "but I'm a novice on the stage, so I'm extremely fortunate to be working with such an experienced and talented cast."

When asked about his feelings regarding the infamous nude scenes in the play, Rush quipped: "I guess I'm going to be asked about that in every interview from now on? Let's just say the play will be a challenge to me on many levels. But I'm excited by the opportunity to test myself as an actor, and to grow my craft."

Many in the showbiz community have dismissed the casting of Logan Rush in the play as a moneymaking ploy to pull in Rush's enormous fan base, but Dwyer disagrees: "I've been highly impressed with what I've seen of Logan's ability so far, and I believe he has only just begun to tap his talent. People are going to be surprised."

An assistant director agreed. "Guy can act, you'll see."
Theatre-goers will be able to judge for themselves
when Equus *premieres at the Paladium on February*
first.

I am so proud of him. So. Freaking. Proud.

Quickly, before I run out of my allotted time, I type a note to Logan — his personal email address is still burned in my brain. I apologise again for reading his letter and snooping into his past. I tell him how impressed and excited I am about all his amazing news, adding, "Finally you're saving a creature that was endangered — yourself." I share a little about what my life's like on board the *Syrenka,* and tell him that I'm finally learning the value of a good pair of shoes, because mine aren't. I can imagine him smiling when he reads that. I end by wishing him a happy New Year, hesitating over how to sign off. I settle for, "Romy xoxo."

I hit send, and when I rise from the computer, my heart is lighter than seafoam on a cresting wave.

CHAPTER 40
CONTACT

Two days later, the sea is finally calm enough for us to tackle the whalers. At mid-morning Captain Murphy draws the *Syrenka* in close to the *Koshitsu*, and we lower the inflatable dinghy and its small crew into the ocean.

They race off towards the whaler, loaded with stink- and slippery-bombs, and dressed in orange protective suits, helmets, gloves and goggles. I can clearly make Tiny — a six-foot-three good-looking American giant of an ex-marine — limbering up on board the dinghy, rolling his shoulders and windmilling his long arms around in sweeping circles. Though he doesn't hold a patch to another tall, good-looking American of my acquaintance, he once played college football, and Mike says he has a killer throwing arm. A short figure, who I reckon must be Libby, flings her arms wide open in what looks like *I-must-I-must-improve-my-bust* warm-ups.

Up on the whaler, a line of crew members now holds up large printed signs.

Animal research

We conduct marine mammal research
Scientific enquiry vessel
We add to scientific knowledge

Irate, I hurl myself below deck to the common room and with a fat, black marker make signs of my own on the back of some old *Syrenka* posters and banners. I race back on deck, hand out the signs, and we hold them up facing the *Koshitsu*.

We speak for the whales.
We watch, we witness, we tell!
We won't stop until you do!

Our dinghy, looking small and vulnerable, zooms alongside the monstrous factory ship, bouncing over the *Koshitsu*'s swelling wake, trying to match its speed.

"Warning. Warning. You are too close!" a loud female voice sounds out from the whaling ship's speakers.

Then all hell breaks loose.

Tiny, Libby, and the rest of the dinghy crew hurl their bombs up onto the whaler. Every time a puff of white powder signals a slippery-bomb hitting its deck, those of us watching from the *Syrenka* cheer loudly. But soon the whaling crew fires up their powerful water cannons and aims them at the small boat below.

"They're going to crash!" I yell, as the dinghy zigzags at top speed, trying to avoid the pummelling force of the jets.

I watch in horror as two of the *Koshitsu* crew lean over their rails to drop objects down onto the dinghy below them. Grappling hooks! One bounces off Tiny's helmeted head and flies into Pete's leg, leaving a long gash. Another hits the outboard motor, and the dinghy slows, then stops, marooned. The whalers take full advantage of this, directing all cannons onto the helpless crew as they crouch in the small boat below.

To rescue the crew and retrieve the boat, we have to pull up alongside the dinghy. For heart-stopping minutes, the *Syrenka* and the *Koshitsu* are abreast of each other, closer than I would have thought possible without colliding, or without squashing the small dinghy on the water between us.

Some of our crew climb as high as they can on the superstructure of our ship and launch the remaining bottles and packages towards the *Koshitsu*. I don't kid myself that I'm strong enough to get one onto their deck, so I make myself useful passing the filled bottles to the pitchers.

But then the whalers lift their cannons from the dinghy, turn them towards the *Syrenka*, and aim them directly at us. At me.

A blast of water punches my gut and flips me over (arse over tit, as Pete would say). I skitter across the deck, smash into something hard and sharp, and bang my head. Lights pop behind my eyes, and I space out.

An hour later, I exit the doctor's room, holding one hand gingerly to the golf ball-sized lump on the back of my head, and the other to my left side. Libby and Mike are waiting outside to check I'm okay.

"Well? Will you live?" Libby asks.

"What did the doc say?" Mike asks.

"She reckons I cracked a rib."

They make me show them the bruise, which is the size of a dinner plate and the colour of squashed mulberries.

Libby whistles appreciatively, gives my ribs a none-too-gentle prod, and when I don't die, declares, "No worries, mate, you'll be apples."

Mike gives them a gentle stroke and volunteers to give me a "therapeutic massage." I'm beginning to think he has the hots for me. I decline, because his are the wrong hands. What wouldn't I give for a (very gentle) hug from the right hands, right now. I wish I could take a long, hot, soaking bath, but I'll have to settle for getting some pain meds down my throat and rubbing anti-inflammatory gel onto my ribs.

What a day. I don't know whether to laugh or cry. And I'm too sore to try do either.

The final score of the *Syrenka-Koshitsu* face-off? Five-one to the whalers, I reckon. In addition to my ribs, Pete's leg, and assorted bumps and bruises all round, the dinghy is out of commission and something blew in our ship's main engine. And in the meantime, the *Koshitsu* has slipped away, though we landed some good missiles, so hopefully they'll be spending the next while scrubbing and cleaning their ship, rather than whaling.

The *Syrenka* is limping to Fremantle for repairs and replacements, and we'll stock up on fresh food and fuel at the same time. The captain has put out an appeal for donations to repair the dinghy, as well as to purchase supplies and fuel — I hope Australia comes through for us.

That afternoon, Captain Murphy gives me an extra slot on the computer.

"I posted on the blog about the assault on you. So perhaps you better send your family a reassuring note," he tells me.

I email my folks and Zeb, telling them not to worry, that it's not as bad as it may look. Though it freakingly-well *is*. My ribs hurt like a sweet-suffering swan in a ditch. I can't yawn, laugh, cough, hiccup, sigh, sit, climb stairs, or lie down without wanting to whimper.

I read Captain Murphy's official account of the mission on the blog and see that in addition to posting some gruesome photos of my side, he's "upgraded" my probably fractured rib to "several broken ribs." I'm sometimes uncomfortable with the slant put on our version of events, and I guess I could object to being used as an exhibit in the propaganda war, but when I think about what gets done to those gorgeous creatures I saw playing in the ocean, I figure I can probably live with the spin. Hey, all's fair in love and war, right? And this *is* war — a whale war.

I wish I'd put up a better fight in the love war.

I should have taken that line-and-love-stealing bitch Britney on headfirst. I should have stood up to Cilla, should have found my voice even if it lost me my job. Instead of trying to change Logan, I should have focussed more on trying to change *me*. And I should have fought for us.

I should have spoken up for us. I lost my voice, then I found it enough to say no, to protest against what I didn't want. But now I know that's not enough. You also need to speak up for what's right, for what you *do* want.

I sigh and scroll down to read through the comments to the Captain's blog. There's already a crapstorm of reaction. Some comes from the usual trolls — this time lamenting that the grappling hooks didn't crack open our heads — but most slate the whalers and applaud our efforts.

One comment, though, means more to me than all the rest.

Alabama_Hog (January, 10)

Now I'm angry.

Romy, are you okay? Does it hurt?

I reply:

Romy (January, 10)

Only when I breathe. Miss you.

CHAPTER 41
GIFTS

Nine days later, exhausted from the journey through wild seas and rough weather, we drop anchor in the port of Fremantle, just outside Perth, Australia. The crew smiles and waves at the small crowd of cheering supporters holding welcome banners and posters, and at the contingent of press with cameras and microphones at the ready. But what catches every eye on the *Syrenka* is the brand-new fast-boat resting on a trailer on the pier.

It's a Gemini hard-bottom inflatable — a long, sleek, black craft with powerful twin outboard motors, dual consoles, and six jockey seats. Wrapped around its middle is a giant-sized, red ribbon tied in a bow.

"Well stone the crows!" Libby says. "Somebody came through for us, big time."

Some of the Aussie members of our crew have family and friends waiting to meet them, but the rest of us make straight for the fast-boat as soon as we disembark. My legs feel odd, and I list to starboard as I walk. It's like the ground is swaying beneath my feet and sucking at me with double its usual gravity.

"Need an arm until you find your land legs?" Mike offers.

"I'll manage, thanks." I follow the gang to the new boat.

"This is military grade," Tiny says, stroking an appreciative hand over the aluminium keel protector.

Captain Murphy laughs in glee when he spies a length of thick blue nylon rope threaded at intervals with red buoys lying in the bottom of the boat, though I don't understand what's so amazing about a rope. The Captain plucks a card off the wide ribbon, and I swear there's a tear in his eye as he reads the message aloud.

"To the captain and crew of the brave *Syrenka*, I salute your efforts to protect our planet and its creatures. I hope this helps in your war against whalers. I only wish I could be there to shake your hands in person."

"Who's it from?" Tiny asks.

"It's just signed, 'Best Wishes, L.R.'"

"What? *What?*" I say. It comes out way too loud, but everyone else is exclaiming in delight and too busy checking out the fast-boat to notice that my jaw is on the floor. Could it possibly be from him?

"Awesome, man!"

"I wonder who this L.R. is."

"We'll be able to run rings around them in this!"

"What shall we name her?"

"It's already got a name," says Libby, popping up from the other side of the boat. "Come see."

We all walk around to the other side of the inflatable to read the name written in large white script: "*Romying Free.*"

I grin so widely it feels like my face might crack. It *is* from him.

"Roaming Free?" says Tiny. "It's a good name, but they've spelled it wrong."

"Perhaps it's a pun, named it after someone special." Libby fixes me with a suspicious stare. "Anything you want to tell us, *Romy?*"

I'm saved from answering when a man in the uniform of a courier company approaches our group and says he has a package for Ms Romy Morgan of the *Syrenka* crew.

I claim the parcel, find a quiet spot away from the crew, tear open the wrapping, and peep inside the box. Lying on the top of the contents are two envelopes — letters from my folks and Zeb. I'll read them later. Under a layer of pale pink tissue paper stamped *bio-degradable*, is a pair of comfortable, sturdy, undeniably inelegant technical deck-shoes — boots, really — in my size. The laces of one are threaded through a note in Logan's handwriting: "I can't recommend the right shoes highly enough." Ha!

I unroll the soft bundle packed beneath the shoes to find two sets of high-tech thermal underwear and thick socks, with another note: "So you don't need anyone else to keep you warm." Then there's a bottle of homeopathic Arnica ("for bruising," according to the label), lying alongside slabs of dairy-free vegan chocolate ("sweets for my sugar").

My heart swells and tears well in my eyes. The gifts are so thoughtful — he must have followed our blogs, researched life for crew on the ocean, carefully read my email, and contacted my parents and Zeb. Anyone could have sent a bunch of roses or a bottle of champagne. This gift is an act of consideration and care.

Lying at the bottom of the package is a small box and a sealed letter.

I open the box to see my platinum chain and charm bracelet nestle inside. Attached to the delicate links of the bracelet is a new charm — a pig. I laugh through the now-overflowing tears, and immediately put the necklace and bracelet on. They aren't best suited to life as a galley slave on the *Syrenka*, but they feel so right resting against my skin, like a soft touch from him, that I don't care about the practicalities.

Finally, I open his letter.

Dear Romy,

I was so glad to get your email.

I'm sorrier than I can say at how things ended. Sorry as a one-legged cat eyeing a canary in a tree. Sorry as a fish without fins. Sorry as a man with a heart cracked plum down the middle - which is what I am.

I've woken up since you left, Romy. As you know, I've refused to do any more Beasts. (When I told Cilla, she threw one of those damned lizards at me and the thing nearly took my eye out.) And Equus opens on the first of February. I feel excited, terrified, way out of my depth, but alive!

I'm looking at ways of putting something back into the world, "leaving it a better place" you called it. I used to think there was only one way of being in this business, but as my momma says, "There's always more than one way to skin a cat" — *even a one-legged one. And I'm going to find a way of doing this, living this, without selling my soul.*

I wish you were here, so I could show you what you taught me, how you inspired me. You made me see what matters. I'm heartbroken that the only one that mattered, was the one that got away.

I miss you! I want to scream it into the night, up to the stars.

But you are where you need to be, and I hope you're loving it.

Love you, always,

Logan

I feel warm for the first time in a month, and it has nothing to do with the blazing Australian sun. I connect my phone to the port's free wi-fi and start typing my reply.

Dear Logan,

Thank you!

When we set sail again next week, I'll be steady on my feet, warm in my long johns, sweet as chocolate, and wearing a little hog. The crew is over the moon about the fast-boat — you have no idea how much your donations mean to us all.

I pause, unsure what to say next. I, too, want to scream out to the heavens. "Take me back! I still love you!" — that's what I want to say. And I want the winds to carry the words around the world and blow them into his heart. But though his letter is full of his regrets over the past, there's no mention of a future for us.

And yet, it says he loves me "always." And haven't I been wondering about how things could have been different if I'd spoken up and put up more of a fight? I decide to write that down.

> *I also have regrets. I'm not sorry I came out here, but I am sorry I ran away — does that make sense? I wish I'd fought harder for us. Because despite what happened, I don't regret us — it's still the happiest I've ever been.*

This time, I sign it

Love, always,

Romy

And I hit Send before I can second-guess myself.

CHAPTER 42

FOUL

Outside, the pale Antarctic sun shimmers through the ghostly veil of mist shrouding the starkly beautiful sea, the pristine ice, the bleak and hostile endlessness. I'm in the common room waiting for my turn on the Net, and I'm trying to ignore the bitter cold and the unearthly noises rumbling through the ship as we crush through the thick polar pack-ice in our relentless, dogged pursuit of the *Koshitsu*. Captain Murphy says it's just ahead, hidden by the mist, trying to evade us even as we stalk it.

The *Syrenka* creaks and groans. The ice growls and cracks as it grinds along our sides. At any moment, a sharp edge on a chunk of ice the size of a house could punch a hole through our hull.

Once we've hobbled the whalers — and we're all determined to do it — we'll be heading back to Cape Town. I've decided that I won't sign up for another mission. Although this is what I'm meant to be doing — fighting the good fight — it isn't *where* I'm meant to be doing it. Truth be told, I'm a feeble sailor. I'm clumsy on deck, sick in a storm, not muscly enough to lob bombs or steer craft, and despite Libby's best efforts, I can't even cook very well. I miss high, green trees and long grass. I want to surf with my friends and lie on soft sand afterwards. And I *crave* the warmth of real sunshine on my skin.

I want to continue fighting for endangered species, great and small, beautiful and ugly, but on shore and in a warmer corner of the planet. I've already thought of ways in which the administrative and support sides of ecological organisations like the one behind the *Syrenka* can be improved. Maybe I'll work for the *Syrenka* in Australia, or maybe I'll sign up with Green Peace in London. Maybe I'll study, and maybe I won't.

Suddenly my future seems wide open. Was that really me a few months ago, thinking I had to choose between Dad's world or Mom's? Between being a gofer in the faux royal world of movies, or being a drudge in suburbia? Neither of those worlds was mine. For the first time in my life, I feel like I can create my own world, or at least my own way in the world. And I know that I need love. I need to love what I'm doing, why I'm doing it, and the people I'm doing it with.

As I sit down at the computer, the boat shudders, and there's a terrible crunching of ice against the hull — no wonder they call them growlers.

I log on, and before checking my email, I do a news search on Logan Rush. What comes up first is a string of reviews from the opening of his play last week.

Gold Rush! (Review)

10 out of 10 stars to this latest Broadway revival of Peter Shaffer's Equus! *Sir Nicholas Dwyer is exemplary as the questioning, cynical psychiatrist, but it is Logan Rush who stuns with his performance, delivering a virtuoso incarnation of the tortured, anguished, disturbed young man. Thirty seconds in and the audience forget Rush was ever the* Beast, *and see only the haunted victim in pain. A triumph!*

A Rush of Blood (Review)

When did Logan Rush stop being a beast and become an actor? Before last night's premiere performance of Equus *at Broadway's Paladium Theater, sceptical theatre-goers may have believed that they would struggle to buy the teen heartthrob as a twisted young soul in violent torment. On the contrary, having seen Rush's raw and powerful performance, it will now be difficult to buy him as the good-hearted but gormless hero of the* Beast *saga when the newest movie in the franchise is released later this year.*

There are a dozen other reviews, and all of them sing Logan's praises:

"Logan Rush brings a fresh and disturbing interpretation …"

"… a subtle and powerful portrayal of madness. In this sure-fire contender for a Tony award, Rush's raw and elemental performance dazzles and disturbs …"

"Rush is naked to the audience, even before he takes his clothes off …"

My gaze snags on one news item a little different from the rest.

Beauty's Beasts!

Britney Vaux, the star of the Beast saga who was previously rumoured to have been involved with Logan Rush, is rumoured to be dating her new co-star, the sizzlingly hot Macon Michonne. The two are due to star in Beast: Mars, in which the species-saving lead characters take their mission into outer space.

The movie will be worth watching just for the couple's chemistry, say set insiders. Beast *director, Cilla Swytch, would neither confirm nor deny rumours that Vaux was romantically involved with Michonne in real life.*

I've got to admire the way that cat always lands on her feet. I do a search for news from the last twenty-four hours.

Rushing to Save

Still riding the crest of his triumphantly received Broadway debut, Logan Rush today announced his latest plans, saying they have more to do with "getting real" than with acting.

*At a press conference in New York, Rush said he was proud to announce the launch of the **Rush to Save Foundation** — a non-profit organization that will raise awareness and much-needed funds for earth's most endangered creatures.*

"We are finalizing our board and management structures, and will soon be choosing those worthy causes and environmental organizations who most need our help. And we'll be asking my friends and colleagues in the industry to open their checkbooks."

To laughs from the assembled press and public, Rush added, "Personally, I have a soft spot for sharks," alluding to his latest role in Beast: Stars.

"Yes!" I punch the air in excited delight, and carry on reading.

When asked what had sparked his desire to champion the cause of conservation, Rush replied: "Last year I met an extraordinary individual who saved my life, twice — once from drowning, and once from terminal stupidity. She taught me a lot about our planet, and its creatures, and helped me see that I could use my position and money to do something which leaves a positive legacy for our planet. She inspired me by showing me it's possible to make radical changes. It's easy, in Hollywood, to be so wrapped in fame and the trappings of celebrity that you stop seeing the bigger issues. I can confirm that a good kick up the butt cures that kind of myopia."

Wow. Just wow.

I need to check my email — tell him how awesome he is. Plus, surely there'll be a reply to my last email from him?

At that moment, our siren blasts out — the signal for all hands on deck. I scramble upstairs and run with the others to the rail at the prow.

A ship has passed through the ice field before us, widening a passage in the pack-ice. We sail silently on through the channel — through the thinning mist, and also through the red and brown horror of water stained with blood and crested with floating whale entrails. Nobody says anything. We all understand what must have happened. While we were out of action, the *Koshitsu* caught a whale — at least one, but maybe more — slaughtered it, and illegally dumped the unprofitable bits and pieces back into the ocean.

Without a word, Captain Murphy returns to the bridge, and within minutes I hear the protest of the ship's engines as they are pushed to the limits of their power. We strain ahead for long minutes, then suddenly, we pass out of the channel in the pack-ice and into a section of open sea. As if anchored to the ice field behind us, the mist peels back, and ahead of us we see the *Koshitsu* in all its ugly deadliness. The captain maintains full speed as we close the distance, and I'm sure that in his wrath he'll ram us right into the whaler. But he brings us up parallel with the ship, keeping pace with it, a few hundred metres away.

We're so near the whaler that I can see the work being done on the deck — the slicing and carving of the vast carcass, the hacking of blubber, the sluicing of blood into the sea. We're near enough to see their filthy, lying signs again.

Internal examination of research subject in progress
Weighing organs
Collecting tissue samples

The same female voice as before echoes over the *Koshitsu*'s PA system: "Warning! Warning! You are too close."

"And we're about to get a lot closer, mate," Libby says grimly, then erupts in a coughing fit which leaves her weak and wheezing. "Better suit up, mate," she tells me.

She's got a bad dose of bronchitis and has nominated me to take her place on the mission. My ribs are still tender, but not so bad that I feel the need to sit out this fight, so when the second mate issues a command to ready the inflatable fast-boat for deployment, I put on a set of protective gear and join Tiny, Pete, and three others in the inflatable, along with a small mound of slippery packages and stink-bombs. Things are happening fast — too fast for me to get nervous.

Manami (a forty-year-old lawyer from New York, who speaks Japanese fluently) heads to the bridge, preparing to address the whalers in their own language, and Captain Murphy wishes us luck. I tighten the fastenings on my helmet and goggles, and hold on with white knuckles to the swaying side of the *Romying Free* as we're lowered over the edge of the *Syrenka*. When we touch down on the water, the female voice shrilly demands that our fast-boat turn back and stay away.

"Warning! Warning! This is the *Koshitsu*. Stop your aggressive actions immediately."

Above us, Manami begins broadcasting loudly from our own PA system. I don't understand Japanese, but I assume she's demanding that the whaler cease its illegal slaughter.

Then a piercing siren — ear-splittingly loud — screams across to us from the whaler.

"They've fired up the LRAD," Mike shouts in my ear.

I nod. "They're trying to silence us."

I've been told about the Long Range Acoustic Devices that the whalers sometimes used as deterrents, but I never imagined how distracting and painful the deafening, pulsing noise could be.

Tiny fires up the powerful engines of the fast-boat, and then we're zooming off at full speed, directly at the whaler. We draw up alongside the *Koshitsu*, start hurling bombs, and are immediately battered by the powerful jets of the water cannons. One torrent blows my goggles right off, flattens me on the bottom of the boat, and pins me there with a pummelling stream of freezing water. My ribs scream a painful protest as the others cheer — one of Tiny's missiles has hit the deck right where a whale carcass is being butchered.

After only a few minutes of exchanging missiles for blasts of water, we peel away from the large ship, because tainting the deck is not the primary goal of today's exercise. We have a new game plan — to cripple the ship by prop-fouling it. That's what Logan's floating rope is for — to throw in front of the whaler's prow in the hope that they sail over it and get it tangled in their propeller.

Gasping for breath and holding my aching side, I clamber back into a seat. It's entirely likely I'll die soon — if not from drowning then from hypothermia.

Captain Murphy's commands crackle through the static of the walkie-talkie that connects him to the fast-boat. "*Romying Free*, you are free to deploy. Good luck!"

"Copy that," Tiny replies.

We pull ahead of the *Koshitsu*, and along with the others, I stand up, bracing myself against the lurches and jolts of the bouncing craft. We each grab a section of the blue rope. As we fly over the waves cresting ahead of the whaler, Tiny shouts out, "On three, two, one … *Go!*" We fling the rope out onto the ocean, across the path of the ship.

"Rope deployed!" Tiny yells into the walkie-talkie.

We did it! I hear cheers from the *Syrenka* sounding out across the water. But then Pete curses and I see that the *Koshitsu* is still ploughing on at full speed, veering away from the red buoys of the floating rope bobbing and swaying in its wake. We all groan in disappointment.

"Operation unsuccessful. Repeat, operation unsuccessful. Over." Tiny's voice is flat with dejection.

"Copy that," Captain Murphy replies.

There's a moment of blissful quiet when the alarms and screeching voices and walkie-talkies all stay silent. I sigh. We tried so hard! We're fighting the good fight. Couldn't the universe be on our side for a change?

We rock on the waves, staring at our feet, nodding when Manami's voice, soft and consoling, tells us, "Never mind guys. You win some, you lose some."

But then Captain Murphy's voice growls out, "True, but I'm not losing this one. Again!"

"Again?" Tiny asks.

"Yes, try again! What do you think this is? A *game*?" Captain Murphy roars. "We don't give up after one failure. This is worth fighting for. Again, I say!"

"Go, Tiny!" I scream, squirming in my seat.

Tiny turns our craft and we retrace out course, retrieving the rope from the water and coiling it back, ready to be deployed. Then we start our top-speed pursuit of the *Koshitsu*, closing the distance between us with every passing minute until we draw ahead of its prow.

"At your command, Captain," Tiny shouts.

"Go! Go, go, go!" Murphy commands.

The inflatable kicks up an arc of water as it maxes out its

engines, curving across the water towards our mammoth prey. We streak directly at the speeding juggernaut, hurtling into the white water right under the prow.

My heart hammers. If I could get a breath, I'd scream, because we're too close. We'll be crushed!

But a fraction of a second later, Tiny swerves our boat. We cross right beneath the path of the ship, hurling out the rope, and then we're on the other side, with the floating red buoys trailing out behind us.

"Rope deployed. They're going over it! It's gone under the ship!"

Too nervous to get our hopes up this time, we watch and wait in frozen trepidation. The *Koshitsu* sails on, but no buoys bob up in her wake. Then a noise echoes across the water between us — a sound like the groaning, squealing cries of a dying animal. The *Koshitsu* slows. It sways on its keel, and with a last gnashing, mechanical bellow, it careens to a juddering halt.

And just like that, it's over.

We scream with joy, leap up and down, slap each other's backs, high-five our gloved hands, and wipe frosty tears from our eyes.

The *Koshitsu* is crippled. Below the water, Logan's rope is tangled around the blades and shafts of its propeller, seizing up the propulsion mechanism and disabling the engine. The harpoon vessels will no longer hunt if they have no mother ship on which to store their poached prey, so the floating abattoir will need to be towed all the way back to Tokyo, with its crew shamed and its cavernous holds almost empty. There will be no more whaling in the Antarctic this season.

We've won. And victory, I can confirm, tastes sweet — sweeter even than proper, non-vegan chocolate.

As Tiny steers us back to the *Syrenka*, the captain's words ring in my ears.

"Try again! What do you think this is — a game? We don't give up after one failure. This is worth fighting for. Again, I say! Go, go, go!"

CHAPTER 43
THE RIGHT VOICE

Cape Town has never looked as beautiful to me as it does on the day before Valentine's, when we sail through Table Bay towards the harbour, a month ahead of our original schedule. The rich, golden African sun bakes my skin and shimmers on the silver water. Cloud covers Table Mountain like a cloth, spilling over her sides and billowing down the steep ridges and stony bluffs of the Twelve Apostles.

Somewhere on that dockside, my parents — and Zeb, too, I'm sure — will be waiting for me. I've charged my phone and have it ready in my pocket because there's a call I want to make — a call I *have* to make — as soon as my feet touch the quay.

I have my own interception mission to initiate. It will be a more delicate snaring operation than fouling a prop, but much more vital to my personal happiness. Plus, there's a job I want in a brand-new environmental foundation, and I'm in a real rush to apply.

This time, when I step onto solid ground, I regain my balance quickly. The ground sways only once or twice beneath my feet, and then I find my land legs, and I'm standing steady. I'm ready to walk through the welcoming crowd and over to where Zeb holds up a banner saying: *Romy is a four-letter word for hero!* and Mom and Dad and Nana are craning their necks to catch sight of me.

Walking is easy, when you know where you're headed.

In minutes, I'm in their arms. Zeb's face is split with a wide smile. He looks as proud as if he gave birth to me himself, as if my adventure had been all his idea.

"I can see you've found your passion my dear sweet child!" Nana takes my face in her hands and squeezes my cheeks.

Mom dabs at her eyes with a crumpled tissue and says over and over how glad she is to see me safe and sound, and in one piece. Dad congratulates me, his voice breaking with emotion.

"I am so proud of you, Rosemary, so proud," he says, and pats my back as if I'm choking.

I'm not. My voice comes easily to me. "I love you guys, but give me a moment, okay?"

I slip out of their arms, and I'm then free and walking away. Walking towards. Because all this time my gaze has been stretching beyond them, and now it's fixed on a tall figure who stands on his own, apart from the crowd. He's wearing his best non-mullet disguise — a fraying grey baseball cap turned backwards on his head, oversized sunglasses, his old, worn jeans and sneakers. His T-shirt sports the outline of a wild hog, with a logo curved over it which reads *Rescue me!*

He's trying to blend into the crowd, to look like just another animal-loving *Syrenka* supporter. But I'd know him anywhere.

My feet stop a short distance away from him, and I stand and soak up the sight of him. He takes off his baseball cap, and rakes his long fingers through that thick, raven-black hair. Then he pulls off his glasses, and though he grins at me, I can see that his cobalt eyes are questioning — uncertain about how I'll respond.

But I'm ready. I'm sure.

"I have a gift for you," he says.

"Another one?"

"I think you'll like it." He fishes something small and shiny out of his back pocket and tosses it to me.

I catch it in one hand and look down. It's a metal nametag, engraved with six words: *Romy Morgan, Rush to Save Foundation.*

"Yeah?" he asks.

"Oh yeah. Definitely."

"I thought you'd like it." He gives me his best, lazy, sexy grin.

A smile is curving over my own lips. It grows and grows, blossoming from the depths of me. I can't move — the heat of his electric gaze welds me to the ground — but I don't need to. He closes the distance between us in two slow strides and folds me into his arms. They're the right arms.

And he murmurs, "Romy, my Romy," against my ear.

My fingers are knotted in his hair, the right hair. And his lips, when they close over mine, are the right lips. And even as they draw my breath from me, they drive my soul back into me.

"Come with me, Romy, and we'll change the world," he murmurs when we come up for breath. And his words are the right words. "Say you'll be mine."

"Logan," I say, and my voice is the right voice — strong and sure and my very own. "I already am."

~ The End ~

GLOSSARY OF SOUTH AFRICAN TERMS

Arum lily: a beautiful flower indigenous to southern Africa, more commonly known in the US as calla lilies.

Biltong: strips of delicious dried, cured meat made from beef, game, or ostrich strongly flavoured with salt, pepper and coriander seeds.

Bobotie: a Cape Malay dish of curried minced meat cooked with dried apricots, raisins and almonds, and topped with a savoury baked custard.

Boot of a car: the trunk

Braai: a South African social event where fish, chicken or meat is barbecued over hot coals.

Bunny-chow: a local delicacy consisting of a hollowed-out half-loaf of bread filled with a spicy curry made from meat, beans or vegetables. It originated in the city of Durban and may have originally been the way nineteenth-century migrant Indian labourers brought their lunch to the sugar cane fields, in much the same way as English miners carried theirs in the form of Cornish pasties. Some say it started later as a quick take-out lunch for workers who, in those days of racial segregation, were not welcome to sit down in whites-only restaurants. There are many theories as to the origins of its odd name. One says that the snack was originally served in a Durban restaurant run by *Banias* (an Indian merchant caste). Whatever its history, today the bunny-chow is a popular snack across the length and breadth of South Africa. If you're over here, be sure to try it — it's delicious, and no rabbits are harmed in its production!

Fynbos: natural shrubs and herbaceous heathland vegetation indigenous to the Western Cape.

Gogga: an insect.

Hooter: the horn of a car; to "hoot" is to honk the horn.

Matric: the final year of high school, or a student in the final year. Equivalent to the US "senior." In South Africa, school and university academic years run from January to the beginning of December. The longest vacation is over December and part of January — our summer.

Milktart: a baked tart consisting of a pastry crust with a sweet custard filling, topped with a sprinkle of cinnamon.

Slap chips: hot, fried chips, usually cut thicker than a French fry and cooked to be soft and floppy rather than crisp. (The word *slap* is Afrikaans for limp or soft.) Slap chips are traditionally served with a good dousing of vinegar, rather than ketchup.

Tokoloshe: in Zulu mythology, a short, mischievous water sprite who can be summoned to cause harm to others and has a special penchant for biting off the toes of its victims!

Veld: wild grasslands.

Dear Reader,

I hope you enjoyed reading Romy and Logan's story as much as I enjoyed writing it!

If you loved this book, I'd really appreciate it if you'd leave a review, no matter how short, on your favorite online site. Every review is valuable in helping other readers discover the book.

Would you like to be notified of my new releases and special offers? My newsletter goes out twice a month (at most) and is also a great way to get book recommendations, a behind-the-scenes peek at my writing and publishing processes, as well as advance notice of giveaways and free review copies. I won't clutter your inbox or spam you, and I will never share your email address with anyone. Pinkie promise! Visit my website, www.joanne.macgregor.com, to join.

I'd love to hear from you! Come say hi on Facebook (@JoanneMacg), Twitter (@JoanneMacg) or reach out to me via my website (www.joannemacgregor.com) and I'll do my best to get back to you.

- Joanne Macgregor

ACKNOWLEDGEMENTS

My thanks to my editor, Chase Night, who helped me improve this book enormously, and to my fabulous beta-readers, Edyth Bulbring, Nicola Long, Sarina Hateley and Emily Macgregor for their invaluable feedback. I deeply appreciate each one of you!

OTHER YOUNG ADULT BOOKS BY JOANNE MACGREGOR

The Law of Tall Girls

On impulse, Seventeen-year-old Peyton Lane accepts a bet to prove very tall girls can be as attractive and desirable as other girls. Now she just needs to go on four dates (including the prom) with one of the guys on her very short list of very tall boys. But when you really stand out, can you ever fit in?

Scarred

Life leaves you scarred. Love can make you beautiful … She's scarred, he's angry, and life keeps bringing them together. Scarred is an intense, beautiful romance with a twist of dark humor.

Recoil (The Recoil Trilogy, Book 1)

When a skilled gamer gets recruited as a sniper in the war against a terrorist-produced pandemic, she discovers there's more than one enemy and more than one war. The Game is real, and love is in the crosshairs.

Refuse (The Recoil Trilogy, Book 2)

Everyone wants Jinxy, except the one she loves. In a near-future USA decimated by an incurable plague and tightly controlled by a repressive government, teenagers with special skills are recruited and trained to fight in the war against terror. Now a rebellion is brewing.

Rebel (The Recoil Trilogy, Book 3)

Can you win a war without losing yourself? Sixteen-year-old online gamer Jinxy James has been trained as an expert sniper in the war against a terrorist-spread plague which has decimated the USA. Now she's a wanted fugitive, on the run with a rebel splinter group, risking everything to save and protect her loved ones.

www.ingramcontent.com/pod-product-compliance
Lightning Source LLC
Chambersburg PA
CBHW021059110726
47900CB00007B/1939